# THE LOST TREASURE OF CORTÉS

Raymond F. Cavanagh

Raymond F. Cavanagh

# The Lost Treasure of Cortés

© 2021, Raymond F. Cavanagh

# Table of Contents

The Lost Treasure of Cortés

Raymond F. Cavanagh

# For Charlie

The Lost Treasure of Cortés

Raymond F. Cavanagh

# Chapter One

## *Manhattan*

## *April 6, 1914*

Gideon Riot bolted awake and popped his eyes wide open as he emerged from sleep in the pitch dark of a tunnel. The train he was riding jostled its passengers as it hit a bad patch of track on its approach into New York's Grand Central Terminal.

He grabbed his carpetbag off the shelf above his seat and prepared himself for the insanity he had heard was New York City.

Gideon had left Tucson nearly a week before and arrived at his final destination aboard the 20th Century Limited, which he had taken from Chicago. The 20th Century was an exorbitant luxury for Gideon. He had decided to pay for the luxury because he was in a hurry. Traveling East to West in America had become increasingly easy due to expansion of the railroads and the desire for seamless transcontinental passage. But journeying latitudinally was still a challenge and Gideon had to use several means of transportation to get from Tucson to Chicago. He had limited funds but also limited time. He had to get to New York for the information he required and get back to Tucson to his wife, Carmelita. Although she had a job and many friends who had also migrated from her native México, she was still fearful of the status she held in the United States. Arizona had become a State only two years earlier, further blurring the lines between the laws of the United States and traditional cultural acceptance which occurred at the border towns.

Traditionally, people crossed back and forth between the two countries without worry. She and her husband Gideon had been married the same year Arizona became a State. Although she had married an American citizen, she was still consumed by the fear that she could be deported. Between the revolution in México, and impending war in Europe, she felt increasingly vulnerable to the whims of the U.S. government. Having lived in México her entire life, prior to marrying Gideon, she harbored a blatant distrust of the governments' assurances.

Gideon had made the long and arduous journey on horseback, stage, and local train lines to get to Chicago. From there, the luxury of the 20th Century was a blessing. Known for such amenities as a barbershop and secretarial services, it made the trip from Chicago in just 18 hours.

As he got off the train and stepped onto the platform, he reached into his waistcoat and pulled out a pocket watch. This was a replica and not the gold heirloom that his father had given to him after years of working at the railroad in Johnson City, Tennessee.

His father's watch was a beautiful 17 jewel, 18 size, railroad standard watch made by the American Watch Company. His father had prized this valued possession and was rarely seen without it. He wore it proudly in his vest pocket and would often use it as a prop. Whenever he was angry, hungry, or just bored, he would flip out this watch, study it for several seconds, and, with an exaggerated flourish, replace it back in his pocket. Gideon and his family were never really sure why, but whatever it was that caused his father to go through this ritual, they would recognize it and adjust their behaviors accordingly.

The one Gideon now wore was a less expensive replica he had bought from the Sears and Roebuck catalog a few years before. Still, it was accurate and railway approved.

He would have loved to wear his father's watch, but it was becoming frail and too valuable to use every day. For years now, he kept it at home, hidden away in a hand carved wooden box wrapped in satin.

Just as his father always did, Gideon instinctively checked the time to see how close they had come to their scheduled arrival.

His father had worked for a line called the East Tennessee & Western North Carolina Railroad. The ET&WNC ran from his hometown of Johnson City, Tennessee to Cranberry, NC, a distance of only 42 miles. The railroad had been built to carry rich iron ore deposits from North Carolina to Johnson City to be used in the foundries there, stamping out all types of metal goods. Due to the winding route through the Appalachians, the train was designed as a narrow gauge to navigate the twisted and winding mountain paths. The track was only three feet wide, nearly two feet narrower than a standard gauge railroad.

Its nickname, Tweetsie, was ironic given Gideon's propensity to speaking with excessive sibilance. The train was nicknamed in part due to its unique shrill whistle, which echoed as it wound its way through the mountains.

The train which had taken Gideon from Chicago to New York had been very close to on-time, only 3 minutes over, which he considered to be exemplary given the distance traveled and complexity of the Gordian knot of arrival tracks.

As he stepped into Grand Central terminal for the first time, he was awed by the sheer size of the building. Chicago had been big, but this was massive. As he walked up the ramp into the main terminal building, he was jostled and turned around as people ran past him on their way to better things. The terminal building had been open less than a year, so it felt new and vibrant. The excessive activity and hurried gait of everyone around him made it seem like a madhouse to Gideon. He stopped short, dropped his carpetbag, and simply stared out at a sea of humanity bustling around like ants on a mission to have the colony completed by sundown.

The first thing he noticed was a beautiful gold clock atop an information booth at the center of the terminal building. Instinctively, he took out his pocket watch, studied it for a minute, compared the time to the clock in the terminal and replaced his watch with a flourish. He noticed a porter walking by.

"Excuse, me sir."

He whistled these words out in his unique manner in which he always seemed to choose words that accented the whistle he produced when saying words with "s" in them.

"Is the time on that clock accurate?"

"Why, yes sir. That there clock is the one we all go by to gauge train time. It's got to be accurate."

"Thank you, sir. Can you tell me if the station masters office is …..?"

Gideon never finished his question. As he pointed in the direction of his query, a young boy ran past him and in one swift motion, swept up Gideon's carpetbag and ran towards the exit at the far end of the terminal building.

Gideon immediately took off after him, running as only a country boy who has had to run from Indians to save his own life can. Just as he passed the clock in the main terminal, he caught up to the boy, reached out and grabbed him by the back of his shirt, grinding them both to a sudden halt.

The boy couldn't have been more than ten years old and looked like he hadn't had a decent meal in weeks. His clothes were dark and dirty, his knees exposed and scraped, his hair a tangle of curls that looked like they hadn't seen soap and water since he was in diapers.

"Is this what your mother taught you? To steal from strangers just off the train?" Gideon whistled out in a huff.

The child rapidly shrugged his shoulders, tugging to get away from Gideon's strong hands.

"I ain't got no mother. If I did, she prob'ly help me."

The boy looked at Gideon with cold, flat eyes that belied his youth. His speech was not like anything Gideon had ever heard before. It was English, but with a thick accent of indeterminate origin.

"Stanislav. Get over here."

A thin, almost emaciated woman yelled out from 20 feet away. She had on a long dress that could have been used to mop the floor, it was so grey and worn. She had long, stringy, mousy brown hair and a sharp, pointed nose with dirt caked on her cheeks.

"Stach, now!"

She certainly could bellow for such a small and frail woman. Gideon looked down into the dark brown eyes of the boy and took pity on him.

He let the boy go, and he ran straight to his mother's side, wrapped his arms around her, and leaned his head on her hip. She looked at the stranger with cool detachment and simply nodded her head, as though in collusion.

Gideon set down his carpetbag and extracted a worn brown leather pouch with a zipper closure, which was an uncommon clasp and had only recently begun to gain in popularity. He unzipped the top and took out a shiny new gold Indian head quarter he had gotten in Chicago, where he had traded some of his paper money to coins.

As he lifted the coin out of its pouch, the boys' eyes lit up and turned as large and wide as saucers. The light reflected off the coin and cast facets of light around the expansive area throughout the entire terminal building.

Gideon had always been distrustful of paper currency. Now that he was out of the western territories, where bartering was as common as currency for payment, he wanted to make sure that he had hard cash rather than paper money to get what he needed.

His distrust of paper stemmed from his roots back home in Tennessee. His parents had moved him to Arizona from Johnson City when he was very young, to get away from the increasingly dangerous family business of selling moonshine.

Although his father worked for the railroad and was not involved in the illicit trade, the revenuers had been breathing down the necks of all the relatives of the Riot clan. Theirs was a cash business and Gideon had learned from an early age that "cash is king."

His mother had died from exposure during the long journey out west leaving Gideon and his father to start a new life without her. Although the railroads were expanding rapidly and jobs were plentiful out west, his father choose instead to establish a stagecoach run, which proved very successful. He had wanted to stay close to home to raise his son.

The lucrative run started in their new home town of Naco, a border town which shared its name and straddled the land between the Arizona territory and México. From there the route would be a short ride, no more than 10 miles to Bisbee, Arizona where there was a large mining operation. If there was enough interest, or he could bring more profitable commercial goods, he would continue on through hostile land to Tombstone. His father's tragic death at the hands of the Apache during a routine run forced Gideon to take over the family stagecoach business at age eighteen.

Gideon held out the coin to the child's mother, as the boy followed the gold with wide eyes and a slack-jawed expression.

"It's wrong to have the child steal from strangers' ma'am. I don't know where y'all come from, but I'm sure you feel the same way. I figure you're just down on your luck. Maybe this here gold piece will help you get on your feet."

The woman looked at Gideon without comprehension. She hesitated and motioned to the coin, then pointed at her son as if to say, "for him?"

Gideon approached the boy and knelt down. He handed the coin to him and the child grabbed it and clutched it to his chest. He looked up at his mother and spoke in a language unlike any Gideon had heard before.

"Máma, můžu si to vzít? Please?"

Gideon looked at the mother. It was obvious the boy was just beginning to learn English. She translated in hesitating and broken speech.

"He asks if he can have it."

"Please tell him it's for both of you, but you must promise not to allow him to steal anymore."

She nodded her head in assent and looked down at the boy and murmured in her native Czech.

"Stach – it's alright."

To Gideon she said, "Thank you for your help and kindness. We come from Bohemia two years ago and my husband died of consumption. We have done what we have to, to stay alive."

Gideon took pity on her, but there was not much more he could do.

"What's your name, Ma'am?"

"I am Anna, Anna Valášek and this is my son, Stanislav. I call him Stach."

"Well, Anna, my name is Gideon. Gideon Riot. I'm here in New York for only a short time to learn the taxicab business. Perhaps our paths will cross again. Best of luck."

Gideon picked up his carpetbag and turned back to the information booth located at the center of the terminal under the beautiful clock he noticed when he first entered.

"Riot – wait."

Gideon turned back to see Anna walking towards him with the coin clenched in both her hands.

"I have cousin who works at cab stand in Yorkville. Maybe he can help you. He knows everything about taxi business. Not all of it legal."

Gideon chewed on that for a minute, looking into her eyes for any hint of deception, but saw no sign of it.

"So, where is Yorkville? How do I get there?"

"On east side. Near 84th. Go by El."

Gideon had heard of the elevated railways, and could hardly believe that trains could run elevated far above the streets. He was eager to ride one.

"Sure, I'll speak to him."

Anna hesitated a second, looking sideways at Gideon and his funny way of speaking. She almost asked him to speak her sons' name, Stach Valášek, thinking it might be funny to hear him say it. But this was no time for humor. She wanted to get Stach out of the terminal to a safe area near her own people, especially with the gold treasure that she now possessed.

"Stach and I will take you to El. But you must not tell my cousin anything about where you met us or what happened here. Please – promise me."

Gideon could not understand why someone who was obviously homeless would not want a relative who was working to know about their whereabouts, but he reluctantly agreed.

"OK."

She quickly gathered up her dress, took Stach by the hand, and headed east toward Third Avenue and the elevated railway.

After they arrived and Gideon procured his ticket, Anna turned to him.

"Thank you, Riot. Godspeed."

As Gideon was about to board the train, Stach ran up to him, wrapped his arms around Gideon's waist, and squeezed him as tight as his small arms could. Gideon looked down and tousled the young boys' hair.

"Good luck, Stach. Perhaps we'll meet again. I wish you all the best."

The young boy looked up with uncomprehending eyes as the train doors shut on Gideon's face.

As the train accelerated, he went to his vest pocket to remove his watch and check the time of departure. As he swung the chain out, it came up fast and empty. He looked down, and saw his chain dangling, but the watch was not on the end where it belonged. He looked up, incredulous, as the train pulled away from the platform and saw little Stach winding the crown of his watch.

"Son of a bitch!"

---

Gideon had only planned to be in New York for two to three days at most. His primary objective was to learn what he could about the taxi industry. Cars were plentiful in New York, as they were in many of the larger cities in the east, but still rare in Tucson. He had just moved north to Tucson two years earlier from Greene Valley, after he and Carmelita were married. Gideon had sold two of his horses and rigs to buy an automobile to start a taxi service. As the business began to grow, he knew he had to learn more about the business and how he could expand. Moving into Tucson made sense because that's where the bulk of the business was, but also because Carmelita had a chance to sing at a new café that had opened there.

Gideon had known for years that his days as a stagecoach driver were numbered, and immediately started shuttling people in the new automobile he had bought with the proceeds from the sale of his stagecoach and horses.

The skills required to drive an auto were very different from driving a stage. He had practiced in the desert until he felt he had sufficient command of the electric beast. Navigating the town was a challenge, with the increasing mix of autos and horses. The horses became skittish when an auto approached, and Gideon believed that soon the autos would take over completely. Horses were expensive to maintain and the filth they caused on the roads was becoming unmanageable.

Gideon had used all his earnings from the sale of his rigs but still had to finance his purchase. He had to find a way to make a living in this new and rapidly expanding industry if he and Carmelita were to start a family.

His secondary objective, although in his mind perhaps just as important, was to learn more about a gold cross that figured prominently in his history with his wife, Carmelita.

*The Amulet of Cananea*, as it had become known, was now hanging above the altar at their church, *San Xavier del Bac,* in Tucson.

The golden, bejeweled cross was believed to have been brought to the region by *Cortés* nearly 200 years prior to Father Kino's founding of the church.

There was a deep mystery about the Amulet, and all Gideon really knew of it was that a man called Colonel Bill Greene had received it from a priest at St. Peter's in New York. He intended to go speak to the priest, if he was still alive, to find out more about the cross and its origins.

As the elevated train pulled into the platform at 84th and 3rd, Gideon grabbed his carpetbag, exited the rail car, and headed down the stairs to search for the cabbie who was related to Anna and Stach. She had told Gideon he was called Pauli and that all of the drivers would know him. She told him to mention, as he asked around, that his cousin Anna had sent him.

Cabbies in general were a close bunch and not open to strangers asking questions about one of their own.

Gideon approached the cab stand and went around to the driver's side window of the first taxi in line. The cabbie looked bored and had a cigarette fixed to the corner of his mouth, the smoke rising up to his eyes causing him to squint. He was a middle aged man with gray sprinkled through his brown hair and crow's feet deeply creasing his face around dark brown eyes. He had a swarthy complexion, and could have been from anywhere.

"Excuse me, sir," Gideon whistled out. "I have been sent to find Pauli, who drives a cab here, by his cousin Anna Valášek. Any idea where I can find him?"

The cabbie looked up at Gideon and squinted even more. He just stared for what seemed like an eternity, and finally removed the cigarette from between his lips.

It was apparent from Gideon's drawl and the way he dressed that he was from out of town.

"Who's looking for him?"

The driver had a strong accent but Gideon had no idea of its origin.

"Oh, I'm sorry, the name's Gideon. Gideon Riot."

Gideon held out his hand to shake, but the cabbie just looked at him and put the cigarette back in his mouth.

Gideon had never acquired the habit of smoking and could not imagine how this man could keep that smelly stick in his mouth while he talked.

"What do you want with Pauli?"

"I met his cousin Anna today when I arrived from Arizona. I'm here to learn about the taxi business. I was running a stagecoach in Arizona and bought a car to start my own taxi service, but I wanted to learn more about how things are done, and the types of vehicles you use. I heard about the new taxi meter that's in use and wanted to see if I could learn more about the business. Anna told me that Pauli can teach me everything he knows and how to make the most I can in the shortest amount of time. She said he'll know all the tricks to being successful."

"Ha! What is Anna up to now? Is her son with her?"

"Do you know Anna? Can you tell me where I can find Pauli?"

"I am Pavel, Anna's cousin. She likes to call me Pauli. She thinks it sounds more American."

"Well, Pavel. I'm happy to buy you a drink if you'd be willing to talk to me more about the taxi business."

Pavel wondered what kind of scam Anna was up to now. He loved his cousin, and loved her little boy even more. Anna was the wife of his only brother who was killed violently just after arriving in America.

"Come on, I'm done for the day. I already put in 10 hours and need to stretch my legs. We'll go have a drink and I'll tell you what I can."

Gideon climbed into the cab and Pauli pulled into a taxi yard where he paid a small fee to park each evening. Gideon walked with Pauli down 84th to 2nd Ave. and turned right to head to a local bar called the *New Bohemian*. On the way, Pauli explained that he was an independent.

"There are companies who hire cab drivers, but many, like me, are independents. We make our own hours and find a way to pay for the cabs and the rent. I will share some of my secrets with you, but you must promise to tell me what you know about my cousin and her son."

Gideon agreed, keeping in mind his promise to Anna, and they walked in silence until they came to the pub.

The taxi industry was in a state of flux, it was an extension of the horse-drawn hansom cab business, and not yet mature enough to have much regulation. Independents were common, if they could find a way to finance the automobile. There were multiple unions and all it took to get a license was a small licensing fee and letters of recommendation. No special training was required and there was virtually no regulation.

Gideon proceeded Pauli into the small, dark pub, and as he entered, all talk came to an end. The smell of stale beer and cigarette smoke filled his nostrils. His eyes adjusted to the dark and he saw a room filled with men in dark heavy clothes and peaked caps. The man nearest him had a swarthy complexion and a cigarette butt hanging out of his mouth. He scowled at Gideon as the door began to close behind him. It wasn't immediately apparent, but he soon realized there was not a single woman among the throng. He heard the sound of thick half full beer mugs as they were set down on worn, heavy wooden tables. He turned around to see Pavel enter and as he clapped him on the shoulder the noise resumed and things returned to normal.

"Teodor, set my new friend here up with a pint of your special homemade brew."

Gideon smiled as a frosty mug brimming with foam was set in front of him on the bar. Its content was so dark, he couldn't see through the liquid. This was far different than the pale brew he was used to in Arizona.

"That'll clog your pencil," one of Pavel's cabbie friends commented.

In a small, dark corner of the bar two men were having a heated discussion in their native tongue. As Gideon took his first sip of the strong brew, he asked his new friend what the commotion was all about.

"The fellow on the left, Tomas, is arguing that our native land, Bohemia, should secede from the Austria-Hungary Empire which is controlled by the Hapsburg Monarchy. Do you know what's been going on in Europe?"

"Not really." Gideon replied guiltily. He had limited knowledge of the conflicts that seemed to be escalating overseas, but started to hear more about it since he got to New York. Arizona was quite remote to Europe and most of the people there were more concerned about what was happening in México.

His mind wandered and he began thinking about the Méxican revolution and its impact on the U.S., particularly the border near his home in Tucson.

The situation in México was chaotic and dangerous. The revolutionaries were fighting the government and each other. Pancho Villa was attacking on U.S. soil, and yet he was also being paid by Hollywood producers to film his exploits. Often, they were re-staging the fights exclusively for the cameras.

Just a year before, the government ruled by President Francisco Madero had been displaced by a coup spearheaded by General Victoriano Huerta.

At the time of the coup, the U.S. Ambassador to México was a man called Henry Lane Wilson, who had been appointed by then-President Taft. Taft was hands off to the affairs in México, despite the ambassador sending frequent, urgent messages that the country was in chaos and something had to be done.

Ambassador Wilson had sanctioned Huerta's coup against Madero much to the surprise and chagrin of President Taft, who was much more concerned with the crisis in Europe. In addition, Taft was a lame duck President when the coup occurred, as Woodrow Wilson (no relation to the ambassador) was readying to take over the office.

President Wilson would prove to be much more hands-on and aware of the continuing crisis in México. The incumbent President would have his hands full trying to keep America out of the war in Europe, but he was well aware of the issues in México, and knew that attacks were spilling across the border.

He took office the month following the coup and summoned Henry Lane Wilson to Washington where he was summarily fired.

Now, a year later, the revolutionaries had banded together to fight the new Huerta government, and succeeded in forcing Huerta from power after the events culminating in a *La Decena Trágica* (The Ten Tragic Days.)

Pavel interrupted Gideon's thoughts. "Our brothers in Bohemia and other states ruled by the Hapsburgs in Austria-Hungary, desperately want to secede and establish their own countries. You may not know this, Gideon, but the lands in central Europe had been under siege for centuries and were ruled by various factions. The Hapsburg Monarchy has been the ruling dynasty now for almost four hundred years. Big changes are in store for our homeland. Those two are simply arguing the fine points of how the revolution should be handled and what will become of our beloved Bohemia when it is all done."

"I did hear there were serious problems in Europe, but I thought President Wilson vowed to keep America out of the war, so I haven't paid close attention," Gideon replied.

"That's true for now, my friend. But mark my words, your country will not be able to stay out of this forever. Drink up, Gideon. We have much to discuss."

"Thanks, Pavel."

"Call me Pauli," he said with a wink.

# **Chapter Two**

## *Arizona Territorial Prison at Florence*

The cell door slammed shut loudly causing a jangling hollow echo that reverberated with a resounding clang through the damp, dank hallway on cell block 6. A lone figure slowly shuffled down the corridor followed closely by a guard who poked him incessantly with his nightstick.

"Kiss my arse, ya rotten garda." Declan Cassidy mouthed the words to himself silently, not willing to stir up any trouble at this delicate juncture.

The prisoner was walking slightly bent at the waist. He moved slowly, due in part to injuries suffered at the hands of a scorned woman from El Paso. It was a testament to the justice of the scorned woman's act that the sheriff had taken no action on his attacker when he was summoned to the scene.

Although Cassidy was bent, he was forbidden to use the cane he needed to help him walk. It was removed after he had used it to repeatedly strike the sheriff during his prosecution. He had suffered severe injuries to his internal organs from the stabbing, which explained his stooped condition.

The cane he owned was quite unusual. Custom made of walnut with a knob of bone at the crown, it made an exceptionally lethal weapon.

Cassidy had emigrated from Ireland several years before, but never lost his penchant for Irish slang, particularly when it came to challenging authority. A small and slight man, he had a shock of red hair and a thin, wiry build that made his hands, feet, and facial features look large in comparison.

His ears stood out from his head making it seem even larger in relation to the rest of his body. Despite his mean streak, he had the Irish gift of gab and a smile that hid his true intent. He was often underestimated by friends and foes alike. Cassidy had the devil in his heart and his mind, and committing felonies seemed to be his only true talent.

Although he appeared to be infirmed now, he was still quick as a cat and could move his lower body very well if he needed to. His shuffling was primarily an act to lull the guards into a false sense of power over him.

It was true that he could not completely straighten up, and this served to make him appear weaker than he actually was, but he had worked long and hard to strengthen his body for the mission he was about to accomplish.

Only his hands had been cuffed. Most of the inmates when being transported were shackled hands and feet. But Cassidy's injuries were such that the prison officials did not believe he was capable of much mobility. The guards mistakenly believed that Cassidy was not a flight threat because of his affliction.

Declan Cassidy, aka Thom MacMurrough, had been imprisoned at the State facility for three years. He was waiting for his death sentence to be carried out at the hands of the Arizona Correctional facility, the date of which was expected to be handed down any day.

Cassidy had been convicted of murdering a Méxican worker at the Cananea Consolidated Copper Company, commonly called the "Four C's". He had served at the mines for several years as overseer. His methods for managing the workers were brutal, yet effective. His ability to drive increased production was accomplished through merciless means. It was this approach that led to an altercation with one of his workers. The argument ended when he stabbed one of the workers with a

Bowie knife which he had nicknamed "The Peacemaker." Ironically, it was the weapon that caused him his own injuries at the hands of a woman from El Paso, when she confronted him after tracking him down in Bisbee, Arizona.

Cassidy was incarcerated after he had initially been arrested on charges of theft under his assumed name of Thom MacMurrough. He was accused of stealing a precious, antique golden cross from a church in Tucson, *San Xavier del Bac,* also known as the *"White Dove of the Desert."* After his arrest, the authorities uncovered the warrant for murder and charged him accordingly.

As he slowly shuffled back from the prison yard after his dinner and isolated hour of outdoor activity, he appeared to trip, suddenly stumbled, and fell towards the cell door of a fellow inmate. Quince Thibodeaux was a noted horse thief from the Louisiana bayou who was convicted of four counts of murder and was scheduled to be executed later that same month.

The guard instinctively tried to grab Cassidy to break his fall, and just as he did, realized his mistake. Thibodeaux reached his large, gnarled hands out from between the bars, grabbed the guards' shirt, and pulled him with ferocious force, smashing his head against the steel bars.

The guards' skull clunked with the hollow sound of a ripe pumpkin being smashed with a ball-peen hammer. He crumpled into a ball and fell to the ground, permanently disabled.

Cassidy leapt to his feet, although still horribly bent at the waist, and checked the guards' belt for the keys to the cell. He found them just as the low moans of the other inmates, who could smell impending escape, began to gather steam. Quince glared at Cassidy who seemed to hesitate before opening the cell door.

"Hurra, Cass'dy." He yelled in his lilting Cajun English. "We only hab a minute before dem guars lock us don."

Cassidy slipped the key into the door, but before he turned it in the lock he glared at Thibodeaux with a poison stare and said, "I want to trust you, Quince, but I can't. I need your help to get me out of here, but I'll kill you before you make a move if I have any sense you're screwing me."

Quince nodded once. Two killers, neither one trusting the other. The only thing that kept them on task was the fact that Cassidy needed Quince for his strength and unique way with horses during the escape. For his part, Quince needed Cassidy for the golden stash he claimed would make them both rich. Cassidy was still infirmed, but he was quick and could move with speed in spite of the fact that his infirmity left him with limited upper body strength.

Quince was an imposing figure, much taller and heavier than most men. He was solidly built with thick strong legs and biceps that looked like hams.

He was unchallenged at the prison and the acknowledged alpha male of the inmates. Even the guards respected him and kept their distance, for it was rumored he had once killed three armed men with his bare hands in a bar fight.

His father had come west to Louisiana from the Virginia tobacco fields and met up with a petite Cajun woman whose ancestors had immigrated to Louisiana from Acadia in the mid 1700's.

Quince never knew his father. He had died in a boating accident when he slipped off his pirogue – a small flat-bottomed boat ideal for the swamps in the bayou. He was viciously attacked by a gator who chewed his body nearly in half. He died a gruesome death after a prolonged fight to survive.

His mother never remarried, and reverted to her maiden name of Thibodeaux, which she shared with her son. She affected what she thought of as a French accent and reveled in playing the part of the grieving widow. Ironically, she came to consider herself and her son a class above what she considered to be the tainted blood of the Cajuns.

With one last withering glance, Cassidy unlocked the cell door. Immediately, he hustled as best could down the dark corridor towards the back of the prison with Thibodeaux following close behind.

Cassidy was clever. He felt certain he knew what the guards' reaction would be. He had been in the facility long enough to understand the mentality of the prison guards. He assumed, correctly, that the call would go out before he put his plan into full effect. He also knew that the majority of the guards were inept and would wait for orders before figuring out how to proceed. That would afford Cassidy and Quince just enough time to complete their mission.

The prison itself was fairly new, having been completed only six years before, in 1908. All of the work to build the new facility was done by the inmates of the former territorial prison in Yuma, which itself had also been built by inmates thirty-three years prior. Overcrowding had forced relocation to the new facility in Florence.

The fact that the prisoners built the facility afforded no advantage to the escapees. The prison was solid and the floor plan was well thought out.

The facility still housed horses in a corral at the back of the prison. Although motor cars were rapidly replacing horses, this was still remote western territory and horses were irreplaceable. The prison had retained an old, traditional horse corral and Cassidy intended to use this to his advantage.

Although the exit to reach the corral was locked and guarded, once outside the horses could easily jump the wooden fence which contained the herd.

Cassidy had a plan, and needed Thibodeaux's strength and talent to execute it.

Despite Thibodeaux's background and the charge of horse thievery, or maybe because of it, he had worked at the prison stalls before he was moved to death row.

He was good with the animals and seemed to have the ability to bend them to his will. Perhaps it was his size and the lilting way he spoke to them, but time and again he was the only one who could soothe the beasts if there was a problem in the barn.

Cassidy and Thibodeaux's cells were on the first level of a two story cell block. The horses were housed in a large barn, separate and located at the back of the new building. The barn had been held over from the old facility and kept as it had been before the rest of the prison was rebuilt. To get to the barn, they had to get to the end of the corridor, past a solitary guard station, and down a long hallway to the left. The last door was locked, but for a man of Cassidy's talent, this posed no problem.

Cassidy's plan was simple and diabolical. He had gone through each step in the plan carefully and repeatedly with Thibodeaux, patiently waiting until the horse thief could recite it even in his sleep.

The prison was like any other in at least one way – when a break was about to occur, everyone could feel it. Whether it was the murmurs of the other inmates, as if they could almost smell the escape, or the guards as they felt a shift in the balance of energy, somehow the entire facility changed and people mobilized. The prisoners who would be left behind began to make noise, whether to cover what was happening or to distract the guards away from the escape was unclear.

Cassidy and Thibodeaux hustled down the corridor and reached the guard stand just as the guard was rising in his chair. Thibodeaux passed Cassidy quickly and with one continuous motion sent the guard flying though he air with one swift swing of his ham-like fist.

The guards' back hit the stone wall at its apex, as he had been knocked clear off his feet, and he dropped back to the ground in an unconscious heap. Cassidy got up and took the keys off a hook under the desk where the guard was stationed. He was about to follow Quince back down the corridor, when he spied his faithful and dangerous bone-handled cane leaning against the guard's desk. He stopped long enough to pick it up, which was invaluable in helping him move more quickly. The two of them hustled as fast as possible down the corridor towards the barn door.

Thibodeaux opened the doors of all the stalls but two and let the horses run free. He steered them all back towards the interior of the prison where they stampeded haphazardly, down the corridors towards the front of the prison looking for escape.

Thibodeaux then quickly threw a blanket and saddle on the two remaining horses and opened the barn doors to the back of the prison. Here the yard opened into a corral where the horses were given exercise and trained for hostile encounters with native or Méxican forces. The yard was secured by a standard three rail split wooden fence. Thibodeaux whipped his mount to a gallop and easily jumped the fence with Cassidy following close behind.

As they rode out of the yard, into the night and on to freedom, they could hear the sounds of the guards in a state of chaos trying to control the horses. Their attempt to turn them around in the narrow confines of the halls in the prison was a nearly impossible task.

Their efforts to dress and mount their steeds were almost laughable. Cassidy was laughing now, just thinking of the confusion as they tried in vain to mount a search.

Cassidy's plan had worked perfectly. It was exactly the reaction he had expected as he and Thibodeaux galloped down the hard packed dirt road toward freedom. The first to escape from the new prison at Florence.

# Chapter Three

## *Risk*

Carmelita finished a late breakfast and had just sat down to read the paper giving herself some rare alone time. Her shift ended late the night before and she just wanted to sit quietly and enjoy her coffee. Two years prior, she had landed a job as a waitress at the Iguana Café, a restaurant and bar where she worked as a waitress and occasionally sang.

A friend of hers from Cananea had moved his establishment to Tucson when the revolution in México proved to be too much and he could no longer make money. Like Carmelita and many others from Cananea, he was able to move across the border and establish residency among the turmoil and confusion of the Méxican revolution. That, and the fact that Arizona had only been admitted to the Union two years before, created a window of opportunity for enterprising Méxicans to establish residency before border crossing became much more difficult.

The owner had given Carmelita a chance to sing for the patrons of the bar, and she proved to be quite popular. She had dreamed of performing since she was a girl growing up in the harsh climate of the copper mines in pre-revolutionary México.

Her voice was always lovely and she would sing as often as possible. In her school at the mines, she would often entertain friends and relatives with her sweet renditions of familiar *corridos*, the narrative songs of the revolution.

The locals shortened the name from Iguana Café and simply called it Iggy's. The patrons who frequented the place were not the highest caliber of customer, and Carmelita was required to wear a low cut peasant blouse and traditional Spanish *mantilla* on her hair. She didn't love the look, but knew that it appealed to the Americans and increased the tips she received. It was more of an issue for her husband Gideon because Carmelita was always being approached by clientele as the night wore on and the booze began to flow. But the tips she received were often generous and worth the aggravation to her.

Carmelita had been raised a devout Catholic, conservative in dress and attitude. But being religious didn't stop her from being a staunch supporter of the revolution and women's rights.

Living in Tucson now with her husband, she felt that all her childhood dreams had come true. Even though she was not yet a naturalized American citizen, she was happy working in the small, but clean cantina, singing and cleaning tables. She was just far enough away from the border skirmishes, which had become commonplace along the border of México and the U.S., to feel safe and secure. She had left many sad memories behind in Cananea, and all she wanted now was to live a quiet life, singing in the cantina.

Eventually she wanted to raise a family, but they needed to save some money and she needed some time with her new husband first.

She had spent the majority of her youth raising her younger twin brother and sister, while her parents worked for low wages in the mining community. At twenty-four years old, she felt she could afford to take a little time before she and Gideon had children. Besides, he was in his own transition. Gideon had gone to New York to learn how to operate a taxi business. The days of the horse drawn carriages, and the stagecoach business he inherited when his father died, were rapidly fading and Gideon recognized the signs.

Even here in Tucson, every day she saw more and more automobiles, as horse-drawn transportation was rapidly disappearing from the landscape. The filth caused by the animals on the streets was becoming uncontrollable as the population grew and transportation became more important to a country that stretched the breadth of a continent.

She loved the romantic notion of lone cowboys riding the range as much as anyone, and she became a reader of all the stories of "cowboys" like Buffalo Bill and Kit Carson, which were written mostly by newspaper writers from back east who used the fantasies to sell their newspapers. Eventually these stories were published in short novels which captured the pioneer spirit, but not the harsh reality of the west.

Carmelita took another sip of her coffee and unfolded her copy of the *Tucson Sun*. She thought about Gideon and wondered how he was faring in New York City. Gideon was a strong and resourceful man, and she loved him with all her heart, but he did not know much about cities, and New York was known to take people in, chew them up, and spit them out. Gideon fought outlaws and Indians while settling in Arizona after moving with his family from Tennessee, but she wasn't sure about how he would handle the melting pot of New York. He did promise to be gone only a week or two, but he'd been gone six days now and she still hadn't heard from him and began to worry.

She read about the impending war in Europe on the front page, and the ongoing revolution in México with only half-hearted interest. She perked up and laughed when she read that Francisco "Pancho" Villa was starring in another movie about himself to fund his efforts. Villa was a true revolutionary, but a womanizer and a villain. He had been highly romanticized and was taking advantage of Hollywood's thirst for drama. She had heard that he had even solicited producers to film some of the border battles for a fee. Already the battles of *Ciudad Juárez* were watched by citizens from across the *Río Grande* in El Paso, safely ensconced in makeshift grandstands.

The river was better known in the area by the name used in México, *Río Bravo del Norte*. People would line up on tops of buildings to see Villa and his troops march on *Juárez* in their bid to revolt against the self-proclaimed provisional President of México, Victoriano Huerta. Carmelita could not understand why anyone would want to view the horrific reality that unjust wars caused. The people dying during battle were real, not like the movies.

She thought to herself "Maybe it's good that Villa is re-staging some of the battles for Hollywood. Better to have women and children see it in the theatres than in reality."

She read that they were filming a movie called "The Life of General Pancho Villa" produced by D.W. Griffith. To Carmelita it was both funny and sad, but she hoped in her heart that the carnage of the revolution would soon stop. Her people needed peace and prosperity. She loved México, but it never seemed stable. For a country that was once so rich and full of natural resources, she could not understand why they could not come together as a people and solve the problems that had arisen. But now she had her own life to think about and how the revolution to the south and the possibility of the U.S engaging in war in Europe might affect her future.

Carmelita reflected upon her youth in Cananea and the hardships she and her family had faced. They had it much better than most, but still it was a difficult life with many challenges.

She still had many friends and relatives back in México, and living less than one hundred miles from the border, she often thought of how lucky she was to have moved to America. The revolution had started as a people's revolt, but seemed to have deteriorated into multiple skirmishes with many different factions with differing principles. It was called a revolution, but in many ways it was really a civil war. The rich landowners against the underpaid working class.

Politics only made it worse since the assassination of Porfirio Díaz' successor, Francisco Madero. Madero was an advocate for social equality and democracy. He was instrumental in fostering the revolution. He was responsible for overcoming the *Porfiriato,* the thirty-five year oppressive rule of Díaz. A military coup spearheaded by General Victoriano Huerta removed Madero from power and he was assassinated a short time later. This sparked the *la Decena Trágica,* the ten tragic days which was a series of events that ignited the revolution for the next ten years.

Between the turmoil created by Villa in the north and Zapata in the south, the warring factions hardly seemed to make sense to her.

For Carmelita, Europe was too far away to even think about. It seemed like a fairy tale land anchored in the past. Since she had escaped México, she didn't even want to think about all that was going on there, and to her way of thinking events in Europe seemed as remote as the moon. She felt isolated from both fronts and her only desire was to sing, work, save money, and build a family. She couldn't fathom that any of the current world events could ever disrupt her idyllic life.

Carmelita got up to pour another cup of coffee and sat down again to flip through the pages of the local news. She read about an upcoming vote on prohibiting alcohol that was being considered by many States, but was imminent in Arizona. Arizona had won statehood in 1912, just two years prior, and she was aware that there were many amendments currently being considered.

Women's suffrage, which she strongly supported, was one of them. It was closely tied in the minds of the voters to the temperance movement which called for the prohibition of alcohol, another idea she did not support.

If that came into effect. It would have a seriously negative impact on her job at Iggy's.

She also read about the upcoming football season and expectations for the Arizona Wildcats. None of this was of particular interest to her.

As she turned the pages, her best friend and neighbor, María Elena Rodríguez, knocked loudly on the front door screen and called out urgently.

"Holá, Carmelita. Are you home?"

"In the kitchen, Lena."

Carmelita and María Elena had been friends back in Cananea where their parents were all employed by Colonel Greene's copper mines. Once Carmelita had settled with her husband Gideon, she had encouraged Lena, as everyone called her as long as she could remember, to migrate north and settle in Tucson. The border was tightening day by day, but in 1912, Mexicans to find a way into America and establish residence. Carmelita was already married to Gideon, so there was little risk of her having to leave, even though her border crossing was illegal at the time and she constantly worried about it.

Even now, in 1914, although the border crossings were becoming increasingly difficult, it was still relatively easy, once you crossed, to establish residence.

She heard the door slam as Lena entered and heard fast, heavy steps coming through her house to the kitchen.

Just then, a small article caught Carmelita's eye on page two. Under the heading "Inmates Escape from Florence," she saw a name that caused her to catch her breath and her blood to run cold. It appeared to her as if the letters on the page jumped out at her and increased in size to capture the entire page of the paper.

As she began to read the article, Lena ran to the doorway of the kitchen. Carmelita clutched the newspaper in both hands, dropped the paper to the table, and looked up at her. As they locked eyes, they both said, simultaneously, "*El Diablo* has escaped," and Lena solely finished the thought "from prison."

Lena came into the kitchen and poured herself a cup of coffee from the percolator that always seemed to be brewing on the stove. She went to her friend and hugged her as she sat. The two just stared at each other with uncomprehending looks in their eyes. Lena knew the story of *El Diablo* well.

Carmelita had kept her darkest secrets bottled up inside her for years. Although she and Lena had been friends since they could walk, Lena had never known all of the events that had occurred in her friends' life until Carmelita spent hours one day convincing her to move north and away from the madness that was México after the start of the revolution.

Border crossings had become increasingly difficult, particularly since the start of the revolution, but it was not too difficult for Lena to find a way across the border. There were thousands of miles of border and the crossings at Nogales, Naco, and Douglas were all designed to stop vehicles, mostly carriages and wagons, from entering the U.S.

Cananea was well south of Tucson across the Méxican border, about halfway between Nogales and Naco. Although it was a day's ride, it was common for natives to cross back and forth between the two countries. When Lena would come to visit relatives who had been separated by the border after the Gadsden Purchase had arbitrarily split families apart, she and Carmelita would meet at the church and talk for hours. Carmelita would talk about her new life in America, and Lena would regale her with talk of the revolution.

To Lena, the revolution, which had started out as a people's war against the political regime, had deteriorated into factions of power struggles. In her opinion the revolutionary leaders were no better than the politicians they were railing against. Although *Pancho Villa* was hailed as a revolutionary and hero of the people, she thought he was an opportunist serving his own purposes. His method of raising money by staging battles for Hollywood movies was both ridiculous and destructive.

Unlike Carmelita, who had distinct European looks with her tall, thin physique and mesmerizing grey/green eyes which contained flecks of gold, Lena was a product of her tribal heritage. She was several inches shorter than Carmelita and somewhat stout. She had dark, almost black eyes and raven hair which she wore long to the bottom of her spine. Although she did not have classical beauty, she was nevertheless striking and had a lovely face with a wide smile and a short, straight nose. Her teeth seemed to gleam in her mouth, offset by the darkness of her complexion.

Carmelita had finally told Lena all about Thom MacMurrough *né* Declan Cassidy who changed his name when he emigrated to the United States after the killing of a policeman in Ireland. He used the adopted name MacMurrough until he was banished from México by Colonel Greene's head of security at the mines, Francisco de Torres. He went back to using his given name, Declan Cassidy after that, and it was the name he was using when he was apprehended in Phoenix. Prior to Gideon's marriage to Carmelita, he had shot Cassidy who was subsequently arrested for the theft of the Amulet of Cananea. He was trying to broker the jewels and gold separately to avoid detection.

"Lena, I have to get word to Gideon in New York. I'm not worried about me. I can't imagine *El Diablo* would dare come anywhere near me, but I am certain he will once again try to steal the Amulet."

"How can you get in touch with Gideon in New York?"

Even though telephone lines were sprouting up everywhere, which is part of the reason the copper mines in Carmelita's hometown of Cananea were so lucrative, intercontinental phone calls were rare and would be outrageously expensive. Besides, Carmelita didn't have a place to call Gideon in any event.

"Lena, will you come with me to the Western Union office? When Gideon left for New York, he told me that in the event of an emergency, to send a telegram to him care of St. Peter's Church near Wall Street. It's the place where Colonel Greene originally acquired the Amulet and Gideon had planned to go there to learn more about the origin of the artifact. I know I can get a message to him there."

Lena nodded her acquiescence and poured the rest of her coffee into the sink.

"Carmelita, should we ride down to the mission and alert them as well?"

"I don't think so, Lena, I don't want to take a chance of running into Cassidy, if he's dumb enough to go there. But I think we should go to the sheriff and alert him. I'm sure the sheriff will want to be on the lookout for that thieving rat *El Diablo*."

Carmelita and Lena prepared the buckboard and left to talk to the sheriff. Carmelita was eager to get to the Sheriff's office, but she had to drive slowly and carefully. The advent of automobiles and electric cable cars over the past few years had left the downtown area with haphazard traffic patterns and a cacophony of sounds. Horses were still spooked by the errant and erratic movement of the automobiles that sometimes seemed to move of their own volition.

As Carmelita navigated the congestion, she thought about Thom MacMurrough, who her mother had always referred to as *El Diablo*. She thought about her last confrontation with him and the claims he made about her mother. She still didn't know for certain if he was her biological father, but she prayed every single day that this was not the case.

She reflected on her father, Manuel, who was gunned down and died in the street during an altercation between the workers and the strike breakers at the Cananea Copper Mines. She loved her father, who was a fair and gentle soul and who gave her so much love and instilled in her hope for the future.

Management at the mines had brought in Rangers from her adopted State of Arizona to stop a pay dispute and they had gunned down several of the strikers. Her father hadn't been there to strike, but rather to stop the confrontation, and was cut down in the prime of his life fighting to keep the peace.

An automobile suddenly swerved towards her from oncoming traffic and spooked her horse. He reared up suddenly, came down heavily, and stopped dead in his tracks.

Carmelita had let her memories distract her and she quickly came alert as if from a dream and spurred the horse on towards the far side of the road.

"Carmelita, are you all right? Lena asked.

"*Sí,* Lena. I was thinking about my mother and father and how the Amulet has changed everything. I want the sheriff to find this *gilipollas* and put him out of our lives once and for all. I really need Gideon to come home."

She cracked the reins on her horse and cried out, "¡*vámonos!*"

# **Chapter Four**

## *Truth*

Gideon awoke on a couch in Pavel's small flat in Yorkville, fuzzy from the effects of the alcohol they consumed during the hours they spent talking about the taxicab business. As he sat up and held his head in his hands, Pavel, called out in too loud a voice, "Dobrý den! Gideon. How did you sleep?"

Gideon raked his hand over his hair and got up groggily.

"Pavel, what was that brew we were drinking last night? I feel like I'm in a fog."

Pavel laughed out loud.

"Teodor's homemade brew. It's delicious when you drink it and goes down smooth and easy, but it does pack a wallop. You didn't seem to mind much last night."

"Well, I mind today."

"Did you see that large building under construction down at 90$^{th}$ & 3$^{rd}$? That's Jake Ruppert's brewery. He is making a fortune brewing his beer, which is light and easy to drink, but nothing like the dark, strong brew that Teodor makes. Maybe someday he will be rich from brewing his beer, too."

"Well, your friends at the bar were sure vocal last night. I haven't been following events in Europe – all of us in Arizona are more concerned with the revolution which drags on in México. It's hard for me to believe that President Wilson would send troops to Veracruz to fight with Huerta after what I heard about the turmoil in Europe."

"You're right Gideon. News seems to travel slowly and we only focus on what we know. The U.S. has vowed to remain neutral on the conflicts in Europe, but since the murder of

Ferdinand, the Archduke of Austria, I'm not sure that's possible. These events will have a huge impact on our families back home in Bohemia. Our people have been fighting for our independence for centuries and we want to be self-governed. Located where we are, surrounded by Germany, Austria, and Poland, we are always in defense of our land. I am hopeful we will win our independence. That is what the men in the bar were arguing about last night – self-government."

Gideon was still fully dressed and his hand went automatically to his watch pocket, only to find nothing there. He reminded himself he had to pick up a new watch while he was in New York. He felt naked without his trusty watch on its fob.

"What time is it , Pavel?"

"Nearly 10 o'clock. I need to get going to my shift. You can lock the door on your way out."

Gideon jumped off the couch. He had planned to be at St. Peter's first thing in the morning. At this rate, he wouldn't get there till almost noon.

"Thanks for everything, Pavel. I'm supposed to leave tomorrow, so I'll be staying downtown tonight. If I ever get back to New York, I'll look you up. And if you ever find yourself in Tucson, come and see me. Verde Transportation."

The two shook hands and Gideon took his leave and headed for the El.

When Gideon left Tucson, he had told Carmelita he was going to New York specifically to learn more about the taxi trade. But he was somewhat disingenuous. He did want to learn more about the trade, and what better place than New York City, but he had a more important agenda in his mind. He was going to St. Peter's Church down near Wall Street to speak to the Pastor about what was now commonly known as *The Amulet of Cananea*. He was sure she knew this, but they hadn't discussed it.

The amulet was a golden cross with jewels placed at the points where Jesus' hands and feet were nailed during his crucifixion. It was believed to have been handed down from *Cortés* to a priest who bequeathed it to St. Peter's through his descendants. It was further understood that *Cortés* had captured this item from Moctezuma II, commonly called Montezuma in America, during the capture of the Aztec capital of *Tenochtitlan*.

Gideon had a strong desire to learn the truth about this artifact. Since the cross had come into their lives, it had been nothing but a curse.

Now, as he rode the $3^{rd}$ Avenue El heading downtown, he reflected on the turn of events since he arrived in New York a little more than 24 hours ago.

He had hardly been able to grasp the expanse of the city and how fast paced it was compared to his youth in Tennessee or his life in Arizona. The number of people, the size of the buildings, and the hustle and bustle were more than he could have ever imagined.

His time with Pavel had been well spent. He learned how taxis had evolved from electric cars to gas powered vehicles only six years earlier, although the taxi he had in Tucson was electric. Now there were hundreds of cabs in New York.

He learned that they now charged by the mile instead of a flat fee. Gideon was still using the stagecoach pricing of a flat fee for his cab, which Pavel explained had also been the case in New York with the horse-drawn coaches and the earlier electric vehicles. A man named Harry N. Allen had changed all that, after becoming incensed by price gouging and rude and sullen behavior on the part of taxi cab drivers. He imported a fleet of gas powered vehicles from France in 1907, outfitted the drivers in military style uniforms and instructed them to treat passengers with courtesy. It changed the face of taxis in New York and elsewhere forever.

Pavel explained to him the art of the "scenic route," a clever way to add unnecessary miles to a trip. He also used other ruses to increase fares, such as claiming a street was closed or a sporting event was creating a diversion.

Pavel proved to be a shrewd and avaricious businessman. He had plans to start his own cab company and he saved all the money from his extra miles to buy another taxi.

Gideon did not have the same personality as Pavel, and believed that the clientele in Tucson would not stand for such antics anyway. Besides, the city there was too open and transparent to use some of the techniques that Pavel used in the congestion that was New York.

Still, he felt he learned a lot from him in a very short time, and he truly enjoyed Pavel and his friends and the time he had at the New Bohemian.

Gideon got off the El near Canal Street and turned southwest headed towards St. Peter's Church at Barclay and Church streets. He was ravenous, and after walking a few miles decided to stop for something to eat. A large country breakfast would be just the thing to set him straight after all the dark beer he drank with Pavel the night before.

He was enjoying the walk and it gave him time to absorb the sights, sounds, and smells of the city. It was a beautiful spring day, and the walk was very pleasant.

He had heard and read a lot about New York before his trip, but this was so much more than he expected in every way. The buildings were higher and spaced closer together and there were far more people than he imagined. They moved about at incredible speed without noticing one another. In his wildest imagination, he had not anticipated such a spectacle.

Gideon passed through an area of incredible squalor with men, women, and children dressed in rags similar to what Anna and Stach had worn. They were all lying on the porch stoops and the noise and smell was abhorrent. He passed through this neighborhood quickly, and after he passed through an intersection of four converging streets, the area showed marked improvement.

The number of taxis that Gideon saw as he walked along the streets was surprising to him. They all seemed to be trolling for fares, and instead of walking to a cab stand, people were simply standing curbside with their arms outstretched in an effort to hail one of the passing cabs. He knew this would never be the case in Tucson, but it made him wonder if there were another way to attract riders than simply sitting at a cab stand hour after hour waiting for a customer. He would have to figure something out to increase his ridership.

Every few blocks seemed to bring different smells of food cooking and strange languages he had never heard spoken before. As he passed one establishment, the fragrance of freshly cooked food with an aroma reminiscent of home drew his attention. His salivary glands responded and his mouth watered at the thought of sitting down to eat the delicious, aromatic food. He looked at the menu, which was written in a foreign language, and he did recognize a few items. He couldn't resist the temptation and entered through the darkened doorway.

Once his eyes adjusted to the light, he found himself in a small room, mostly empty, with few tables and fewer people. He had the same feeling he had when he walked into the New Bohemian with Pavel.

Once again, all talking stopped and everyone turned to look at him. He knew that his blond hair and blue eyes marked him as different. He realized he needed to buy new clothes to blend in better. He still had the western wear he had on when he left Tucson and it seemed everyone in this city wore black, head to toe.

Gideon ignored the stares and sat at a thick wooden table near the door. A woman approached him and spoke to him in English with a very thick accent. He could hardly make out her words, but she had a kindly demeanor.

"Howdy, Ma'am."

She looked at him and smiled. He took a printed menu from her and pointed to a dish with at least one familiar word, "Spaghetti alla Bolognese."

He asked for a glass of water and waited in uncomfortable silence until his meal arrived. As he sat, he ignored the looks of the clientele, who couldn't seem to ignore him.

He thought about his mission today and his motivation to find out more about an item that clearly had created nothing but trouble for his wife and her family. Still he felt it was important for him to better understand the genesis of the Amulet of Cananea and why Colonel Greene had come into its possession in the first place. He heard from Carmelita a story of using the cross as collateral for a loan to buy the copper mines. According to his wife, once the mines began to produce successfully, he bought the cross from the parish at an obscene amount of money. It was a romantic story, but Gideon felt there had to be more to it than that and he was determined to find out.

His food arrived hot and steaming with a plate of fresh, crusty bread and a mountain of shredded cheese on top. The plate of food was huge. He dug right in, swirled the spaghetti, and crammed a huge forkful of it into his mouth. It was incredibly delicious, but also too hot and the skin on the roof of his mouth burned. The woman who served the dish was still standing there and just stared at him with her mouth hanging open. Apparently she had never seen anyone in such a hurry to eat. He took a sip of his water, which didn't seem to help at all, and smiled at her. She shrugged and walked away.

He finished his meal and paid his bill. He simply held out his hand with what he thought was enough coin, and the woman scooped a few of them out of his palm, smiled, and went back to her kitchen.

After he finished what he would later describe as one of the most memorable meals of his life, he continued to walk the streets of New York. Completely full, he was eager to both walk off the food, and also get to his destination on Barclay and Church. He missed his home and his wife and wanted to finish what he had to do and get back home to the familiar sights and sounds of Tucson.

Gideon approached St. Peter's and was struck by how vastly different this church was from their mission church back home in Tucson. Although Gideon didn't know anything at all about architecture, he could clearly see the difference between the two buildings. The White Dove of the Desert had been built in a Spanish Colonial style while St. Peter's displayed Greek revival architecture.

The two churches were almost a continent apart, and their exteriors were prime examples of their architectural inspiration. Each had undergone many renovations to keep the integrity of the primary façades intact.

Gideon traversed St. Peter's steps and as he entered the vestibule, the first thing he noticed was a brilliant painting above the altar. He walked directly towards it with hardly a glance at the rest of the church. He came to the communion rail and gazed up at the beautifully painted rendering of Jesus' crucifixion. Gideon had not experienced much art in his lifetime, but he felt the artist had powerfully conveyed the pain and sacrifice that the son of God felt in his last dying breaths.

It made him think of the reason he came to St. Peter's in the first place, to seek out the truth about the Amulet of Cananea. He recalled the beautiful gold cross and the rubies that were placed at the points where Jesus' hands and feet were nailed. It occurred to him that he had come full circle, for this was the place where Colonel Greene had first come into possession of the Amulet.

"It's a beautiful painting, isn't it my son?"

Gideon whirled around to see a priest dressed in cassock and collar with an ornate book in his hands.

"Oh, hello Father. Yes, it's very powerful."

"It is appropriately titled *The Crucifixion* and was commissioned to be done by the famous Méxican artist José Vallejo, and bequeathed to the church by the Archbishop Nuñez de Haro of México City, just after the cornerstone was laid in 1789."

Seconds passed as they gazed at the painting, both lost in their own private thoughts. Gideon was amazed that he had come all the way to New York, and still influences from México surrounded him.

"Father, I wonder if you can help me. My name is Gideon, Gideon Riot. I've come here from Tucson to see Father Esperanza. That is, if he's still here with the parish. I sent a letter weeks ago to let him know I was coming to visit."

The priest extended his hand and they shook.

"Ah, yes. Nice to meet you Gideon Riot. I'm Father Beaudry. Well, I'm sorry to say that Father Esperanza has disappeared. Years ago. I understand he was a good man, but apparently he decided to relocate to the southwest without sanction of the church. I heard he had gone to México to preach the gospel to some of the native tribes still without the faith. I did receive your letter, though. I found it very interesting. How can I be of service?"

"Well, as I tried to explain in the letter, my wife had come into possession of a very valuable golden cross with rubies placed where Jesus hands and feet were nailed. It is now hanging at San Xavier del Bac in Tucson."

"Ah, yes. I know of the White Dove of the Desert. We are all aware of Father Kino's great work spreading the word of God. I am also aware that the cross resided here at St. Peter's for many years, although not on public display, before its ownership was transferred."

"That's the reason I'm here. I need to learn more about the cross and its history. I would like to know as much as you can tell me about its legacy, where it came from, how it got to St. Peter's – anything at all to help me understand its past."

"Tell me, my son. What is your interest in this?"

"The story that I've been told is that William Cornell Greene, known to all as "Colonel" Greene, worked nearby on Wall Street. Apparently, he had approached Father Esperanza about using the Amulet as collateral for a copper mine he wanted to purchase in Cananea, México. If his mine became successful, he would purchase the cross for an amount far greater than it's worth to be used to help fund church programs. If he was not successful, he would return to New York, repay the loan over time, and return the item to the church. From the stories I have been told, this was approved by the Bishop as well. Times were different then, I guess, and Father Esperanza must have had great faith in Colonel Greene."

"Yes, well, all that is true. It would never happen today. I think Colonel Greene was a very persuasive man, but I also think there may have been other factors involved. The fact that Father Esperanza left the country and went to México a short time afterward cast some suspicion on the entire affair. But no matter. What's done is done. Why is this so important to you?"

"Father, my wife's family were cursed by this cross. It has become legendary in its own right in Tucson and Cananea. I feel there must be something more to the story and I want to know what it is."

"You are aware that this cross had been handed down to the first born son from generation to generation since the days of Cortés?" the priest asked Gideon.

"Yes, I had heard that. I assume that's one of the reasons Father Esperanza was willing to accept Colonel Greene's offer. As a priest, he would not have a son to entrust it to, correct?"

"That would be true, but it wasn't even really passed down to Father Esperanza. In fact, the cross was the property of the Church at the time, not Father Esperanza. The true story, or true as far as we can ascertain, is that the cross came to this continent by way of a priest who came from Spain to spread the word of God. His mission was in your area of the country, in Sonora. The cross had belonged to the priest's uncle originally, but the uncle had no sons, so he gave it to his brother, who gave it to his son, Father Pachero. They all knew that was the end of the succession, but felt the priest would be the best person to find the proper use of the cross. It is true that the cross was given to Pachero's descendants, but where it was originally from is anyone's guess. Certainly, based on what we know now, the ability to craft such a magnificent piece did not exist at the time in the Aztec community. It has been suggested that the piece was originally brought to the New World from Spain, and when it was gifted to the Pachero family in Sonora, its provenance was misunderstood. By all accounts, Father Pachero while on his deathbed, the last of the line in his family, gave the cross to the natives, the Papago, to build a church. It's a fascinating story, if it's all true."

"So, let me understand. You think the cross was originally from Spain, came here with a priest who, on his deathbed, gave it to the Papago for a church to be built in Sonora. Is that right?"

"Yes, that is what we believe to be the truth."

"But still, it was a gift to the family from Cortés?"

"Yes, we believe that part is true as well," the priest replied.

"Someday I will have to tell you what has become of it since it was given to Colonel Greene. But tell me, Father, how did the cross get to New York?"

"Ah, I left out a key part of the story. Legend has it – and we also believe this to be true, that a Franciscan priest, Padre Velderrain, sold the cross to an anonymous benefactor to get the necessary funds to rebuild his church. That benefactor then donated it to his local church, St. Peter's in New York. It's odd when you think how it has all come full circle. Perhaps if Colonel Greene's timing had been different, he could have saved a few steps. But in the end it all worked out. The church in Sonora was rebuilt, St. Peter's received a valuable artifact, and Colonel Greene got the loan he needed to purchase his mines. And the most remarkable thing of all – do you know what church was rebuilt in Sonora?"

"Don't tell me, let me guess," Gideon said. "*San Xavier del Bac*. The White Dove of the Desert," he stated emphatically.

"That is absolutely correct, Gideon. Amazing, isn't it?"

Just then, another parish priest walked quickly up to Father Beaudry and anxiously stood by very close until he was acknowledged.

Father Beaudry turned towards him and raised one eyebrow slightly.

"Father, I have an urgent message here for you," he said as he handed him a single piece of yellow paper with typewritten words on it.

Father Beaudry unfolded the paper, read the contents, and frowned. He looked up at Gideon, handed him the paper, and softly said, "You have to read this."

# <u>Chapter Five</u>

## *Threat*

Cassidy and Thibodeaux rode south out of Florence towards Tucson. They rode at night and slept during the day. In the morning, well before dawn, they stole food and clothing from a local store that served the nearby ranches.

Cassidy was now outfitted like a ranch hand, although the clothes he wore hung loosely off his small frame. Thibodeaux, on the other hand, because of his size, was still outfitted in the thick black horizontal stripes of his prison outfit. The only clothes hanging on the lines that would fit him were the loose-fitting dresses that the women wore.

As he told Cassidy, "I ain't goan wer no dress."

"You have to Q. We have no choice"

Cassidy was wary of Thibodeaux. He was an ox of a man, with seemingly little intelligence. For the past twenty-four hours, Cassidy had tried to move surreptitiously towards Tucson and craft a plot with Thibodeaux on how to steal back the precious Amulet from the church. Cassidy liked to think of himself as clever, but he was planning the same theft he had attempted before, in the same manner. His plan to melt down the gold and sell the jewels off separately was uninspired and the exact same plan he had the last time he stole the cross and was caught.

His seemingly dim-witted fellow escapee was cloddish and coarse and Cassidy knew the liability of staying with him was too great. He had taken to calling him "Q". It was short for his first name Quince, which he thought too feminine, although he would never tell him that to his face for fear of retribution.

The second day of their escape, with Quince looking absolutely ridiculous in a floral printed woman's dress, they settled into a wooded area just 10 miles north of Tucson in the foothills of the Santa Catalina Mountains. They had covered much more ground than anticipated and expected to reach the church that night. The plan was to get a final day's sleep and traverse the final 10 miles into Tucson, head directly for the church, break in, and steal the Amulet under the cloak of darkness. Cassidy still needed Thibodeaux for his strength. He would never be able to handle the break-in by himself.

Sleeping during the day proved very difficult. The sun was high and hot, the horses were active, and since they were so close to Tucson, there was much more activity than there had been out on the trail. Finding a shaded, out of the way area with water nearby was extremely difficult. Fortunately, the route they had taken gave them cover and also access to water from mountain streams that secreted the run-off. This was still desert, so water was a scarcity. The horses had been ridden hard for the last several hours and had been overworked, but Cassidy expected they would soon be at their destination and could swap them out for fresh ones.

As Quince set up a lean-to for the days sleep, cursing at the restricted movements of the flowing dress, Cassidy walked the mounts towards a pool of water. He watched and listened as they drank, and heard a rumbling mechanical sound unlike any he had heard before. It was an hour past dawn now and although he was eager to complete the trip to Tucson, they still couldn't travel during the day. Especially with Quince in a dress, but his prison stripes would only be worse. He had to figure a way to lose him, and fast, once their mission was completed.

The rumbling sound increased in volume and seemed to be quite close. The horses got nervous and began to snort. Too loudly for Cassidy's liking. He was worried that the neighing sounds of the horses would draw unwanted attention. As he approached the thin copse of trees where they decided to build a lean-to, Quince walked up to him hurriedly.

"Cass'dy, we gots to leabe heah."

"What is it Q? What's that sound?"

"It be autmobeals. Dey mus be gwyn ta Tooson. Dey movin fas."

Cassidy turned toward the sound of the rumbling and walked fifty yards up a short, dry culvert, leaning hard on his cane as he went. At the top, he saw a dirt road and two automobiles driving south toward Tucson. The cars weren't going very fast, about the same as a cantering horse with rider, but they were loud and kicking up dust something fierce. Cassidy knew Quince was right – they had to get out of there and quick. Cassidy realized that his plan had a fatal flaw. He failed to take into account how dramatically the world had changed in the three years he had been in prison. He counted on things being the same, but automobiles had become much more common than he thought and his outmoded form of transportation, - the horse – was a visible liability. The two automobiles he saw were Ford Model T's, known as Tin Lizzie's. They had a cloth top which was retracted and hung over the rear wheels precariously. They were sleek looking to Cassidy, compared to the old horse and buggy, but terribly loud. There were two "dandies," as Cassidy called them, at the wheel. They seemed to be racing, although it was an awfully slow race.

"Must be the first time either of them rubes ever drove one of those things," Cassidy thought to himself.

"Q, change of plan. You settle in here and stay hidden. I'll head to Tucson now and see if I can get you something to wear. Your horse is a problem. I'll have to take it with me. It'll give away your location. Wait for me and I'll get back by nightfall."

Q crunched up his face and gave Cassidy the meanest scowl he had ever seen.

"Cass'dy, dat a bad plan. Leabe me heah with no hawse a food a nothin'. How I know I ken trus you?"

"Q, I promise. I'll be back. I need your help to get the cross. Besides, if it weren't for you, I would never have escaped. I owe you. Trust me, I'll be back by nightfall."

Thibodeaux was suspicious, but felt he had no choice but to trust Cassidy. He was virtually imprisoned in his outfit and his size made it nearly impossible to steal new clothing. He had to trust that Cassidy would come back for him.

They unsaddled Thibodeaux's horse, and Cassidy grabbed the reins and started the slow ride to Tucson. It would take longer with the extra horse tethered to him, but it was the only way.

"I'll be back, Q, I'll be back."

---

Carmelita and Lena arrived at the sheriff's office at just about the same time as Cassidy was leaving Quince behind.

"Lena, *por favor*, please let me do all the talking. I want to get in and out of here quickly."

Carmelita was taking a risk. Although she was married to Gideon, a third generation citizen of the United States, she was not yet a citizen herself. She had been intending to fill out the appropriate paperwork, and take whatever testing was required, but so far had not done so. The Arizona border at this time was still very lenient about immigration, although that was rapidly changing. Workers had been flocking north of the border to find work on the railroads for years, and the Americans needed the cheap labor so there was a mutual ignorance of the law. Besides, even though the two countries had agreed on the border demarcation, many of the people who lived there did not.

They had been residents for generations and the mere movement of a border couldn't magically change that in their minds. The politicians had ruined everything. Again.

Carmelita was worried when she entered the sheriff's office. With Gideon out of town, she took a risk talking to the sheriff. If he suspected her of illegally entering the country, he could send her back across the border or imprison her. She *had* entered illegally, but now she and Gideon were married, so although she was not a citizen she had a right to remain in the country. Still, she had not filled out the proper paperwork and it could become a nightmare for her.

Her light skin color and grey/green eyes, both a product of her mixed blood and old Spanish heritage, made it easier for her to pass. Still, she always worried.

Lena stayed outside with the horses as Carmelita entered. A deputy was sitting at the desk with his feet up and a mangled cigar sticking awkwardly out of his mouth. He was young, with a clean shaven face and clear blue eyes. A lock of sandy blonde hair peeked out from under his Stetson. He peered at her through a haze of blue smoke. His eyes widened when he saw this beautiful young lady with exquisite features. He swept his feet off the desk and sat up straight.

"Can I help you Ma'am?"

"Is the sheriff here?" Carmelita's voice crackled nervously.

"Sorry, Ma'am. He's out of town until the weekend. I'm in charge in the meantime. What can I do for you?"

Carmelita began to perspire and wondered if she had done the right thing. She fanned herself with a lace *abanico* which she carried everywhere. It was a complement to her traditional china poblano dress.

She wished that Gideon were home so he could handle this, but she knew the authorities had to be alerted right away.

Who knew what *El Diablo* was capable of and when he would appear?

"I have come to tell you of a man who escaped prison in Florence two days ago. I have reason to believe he will come to Tucson to steal a precious gold cross from *San Xavier del Bac*."

The deputy put down his cigar, stood up and came around the desk to face Carmelita. He sat on the corner of the desk and doffed his hat.

"And how did you come across this information, little lady?"

She ignored his condescending tone and continued.

"The man goes by the name Declan Cassidy. He raped my mother many years ago. He is a very bad hombre and he stole the cross once before. It is the reason he was captured in the first place. I just thought you should know, so perhaps you can be on the lookout for him. Talk to the priest at the mission. He can tell you."

The deputy gave Carmelita a slow look up and down. He came closer to her and she could smell the foul smelling tobacco on his breath.

"Tell you what, little lady. Why don't you and me go over to the saloon and you can tell me more about this escaped prisoner. Sure would be nice to look into your beautiful eyes over a whiskey."

Carmelita immediately turned and walked quickly out the door into the bright sunlight. Lena was standing on the wooden sidewalk patting the nose of one of the horses, trying to keep them calm amid the combustive sounds of the automobiles. Noise seemed to be everywhere and she could hear the sounds of workmen building a new concrete sidewalk just down the street. The first one to be built in Tucson, it had many of the locals up in arms. They liked their raised boardwalks, particularly when the spring rains came and the streets flooded.

"Let's go, Lena," she said as she clambered up onto the seat of the buckboard and taking up the reins. "The deputy isn't taking me seriously and he needs to get over himself."

As Lena climbed up into her seat, the deputy came out through the doorway with the brim of his hat in both hands. Looking sheepish, he approached Carmelita.

"Listen Ma'am. I'm sorry. I didn't mean to upset you. We get so many false reports of escaped prisoners. I was just distracted by your beauty. You can't blame me for that, can you? Hold up, and tell me what you came here to say."

Carmelita was angry, but the deputy was very young and he did seem sincere. Maybe he wasn't used to being in charge while the sheriff was away.

Lena took note of the young man and gave him her biggest smile. He looked over at her and returned the attention.

Carmelita took in a deep breath and quickly blurted out the facts as she knew them in rapid, staccato fashion.

"O.K., Deputy. The man was born in Ireland with the name Declan Cassidy. It's said he killed a policeman there and that's why he came to the States. He changed his name to Thom MacMurrough and found his way to the Cananea Copper Mines in México, owned by an American, Colonel Greene. My mother worked in the kitchen at Greene's home. Cassidy, or MacMurrough as he was known then, raped my mother - brutally."

Carmelita coughed back a choking sound. She had only heard this story from her mother, and had not really thought about it or what it really meant to her before now. She fanned herself rapidly, gathered her thoughts, and pushed on.

"I may be the product of that rape, although it's unclear – she married my father a short while afterwards. My mother was furious after the rape and secretly stole a precious gold cross from Colonel Greene and hid it in MacMurrough's – sorry –

Cassidy's room. It was found under his bedding and he was banished from Cananea, and indeed all of México, by Greene and his chief of security, Francisco de Torres. Cassidy vowed vengeance. At this point, Cassidy was somewhere in the States, but he was never prosecuted for his crimes. The cross had been donated to the mission, and Cassidy found that out, went there, and stole it. Gideon Riot, who I would later marry and is now my husband, learned of Cassidy's whereabouts through friends in the O'odham tribe and set off after him. Gideon didn't know the whole story, but he knew that Cassidy was a bad hombre and had done great harm to my family. Cassidy was caught with the cross before he could melt it down. Gideon shot him and Cassidy was sent to the prison in Florence. I just read in the paper that he escaped two days ago. I'm sure he is coming back here to try and steal the cross from the mission again."

Carmelita paused and took a breath. She looked up at the deputy and realized she had tears streaming down her cheeks. Lena sat stock still with her mouth open. Carmelita had been staring out into the middle distance and hadn't even thought about what she was saying.

The deputy still had his hat in both hands, twirling the brim. His mouth was slightly open and it seemed to him as if not to have drawn a breath the entire time.

He breathed out loudly and said to her, "That is some story little lady. If you didn't have so many facts, I might doubt it was true. But it's easy enough to check out. Tell you what, when the sheriff gets back I'll go over to the mission and speak to the padre there. If everything checks out, we'll keep an eye out for this hombre. Thanks for the tip."

Carmelita looked at Lena, who was seated and ready to go. The deputy replaced his hat on his head and tipped it to Lena. She nodded, and they cantered back towards Carmelita's home, watching carefully for automobiles.

# Chapter Six

## *Realization*

Gideon and Father Beaudry sat in the vestry at St. Peter's and whispered in conspiratorial tones. Gideon folded the telegram the priest had handed him and stuck it in his shirt pocket.

"Father, I need to get back to Tucson right away. I'll send my wife a return telegram as soon as I leave here. But before I go, I need to know all you can tell me about the story of the cross that Colonel Greene received from the former pastor. There is more to it, isn't there?"

"Gideon, I'll instruct Father Carroll to send a reply to your wife's telegram that you're heading back to Tucson today. I know you are worried about this man escaping prison. Is that sufficient?"

"Thank you, Father. I appreciate your help."

"As to your request about Colonel Greene's cross, I was wondering when someone would ask. Have you ever heard of *La Noche Triste?*"

Gideon shook his head, feeling for the second time in the two days he was in New York that he still had an awful lot to learn.

"No, Father. I'm sorry. Should I know of it?" Gideon still had only a rudimentary knowledge of Spanish, even though he and Carmelita had been married for two years now. He translated in his head to "The Sad Night," but it still wasn't familiar to him.

"Only if you had studied the complete history of México," Father Beaudry said with a smile.

" '*The Night of Sorrows*' occurred several hundred years ago. In the early 1500's, in fact. It was the night that *Cortés* and his followers fought their way out of the Aztec capital of *Tenochtitlan* after the death of Montezuma. Do you know anything about *Cortés* or the Aztecs?"

"No, Father. I'm afraid the only history I learned was when I was young in Tennessee. I can tell you all about Jeff Davis and the confederacy, though."

Father Beaudry laughed and nodded. "I know how important that is in the southern states."

He went on, "*Cortés* had been the titular head of the land of New Spain since he had claimed it for his homeland. If you don't know much about it, Montezuma, as the ruler of the Aztec empire, had amassed all of the gold and jewels throughout the vast territory of what is now México. It was a huge empire with over fifteen million people, which at the time included much of the western U.S. from Texas to California and then some. The city of *Tenochtitlan* alone had over 2 million inhabitants and was larger than either London or Rome at the time."

"I've never heard of *Tenoch*... What's it called again?"

"You know of it now as México City. Like Paris and New York it was founded on an island and expanded far beyond its original border. The extent of the riches at that time, all located in one place, is beyond imagination. It is a large part of the reason that so many explorers came from Europe to explore the new world."

The priest paused for a second as if contemplating, nodded his head, and continued.

"I'll tell you what, you have to catch your train this evening. Let me go with you and we can stop at the new library on Fifth Avenue. It's only a few blocks from Grand Central Terminal where you have to get the train. We can visit with our church's historian. She's also the archivist at the library. It's really quite impressive."

Gideon agreed and on their way out, he and Father Beaudry walked to the sacristy. The priest spoke to Father Carrol. "Father, can you please send a return telegram to Gideon's wife, Carmelita? Let her know he's catching tonight's train to Chicago and will be back in Tucson as soon as possible. Let's go Gideon, we have lots to do before you leave."

They rapidly walked back through the city the way Gideon had come, towards mid-town. They were fortunate to hail a taxi to expedite their way. Although Gideon had spent an entire evening talking to Pavel about the business, how it worked, and how to make it profitable, he had not yet been in a New York City cab.

On the way to the new library, which had only opened three years prior, Gideon spoke to the driver about his cab and the company he worked for, the Connecticut Cab Co. He learned that the taxi industry in New York was quite sophisticated, but also expensive. As they drove on, the priest interrupted the cabbie on two separate occasions to ask about the drivers' choice of routes. The driver was clearly aggravated, but took the priests' suggestion and re-routed to get them to their destination more directly. Gideon knew this was one of the most common ways that drivers padded the fare, especially for out-of-towners. It was obvious, even to Gideon, that he sounded like a country boy in this town.

When they disembarked in front of the library on Fifth Avenue, Gideon stood at the curb with his mouth wide open. The library was unlike any he had ever seen. In fact, it was unlike any *building* he had ever seen. He was, however, familiar with the two massive lions that stood guard on either side of the steps. The lions were well known to folks from Gideon's hometown in Johnson City, Tennessee. They had been carved of pink

Tennessee marble and several of his relatives had worked those mines to cull the massive stones required to carve the beasts.

Father Beaudry led Gideon up the stone steps and into the library's main entrance. He went to the north side of the building and clambered down a set of stairs pushing past a sign that read "Employees Only – Do Not Enter." They went down two additional flights of stairs and walked down a long, dimly lit corridor. Gideon posed a question to the priest in a soft whisper which the library seemed to automatically require.

"Father, where are we going? It seems as if we're in a dungeon."

Father Beaudry replied in what seemed to be a very loud voice, but was in fact, simply normal conversational volume. "The library's archivist, Sofie Pollak, works down here in an area known as the stacks. Right now, we're not even under the library proper, we're actually under Bryant Park.

"Sofie catalogs all the items the library houses, which includes books, photos, articles, and many other items. The stock of the library is rotated regularly and each month there are several special events, which require her to bring items up from the archives for display. It is a monumental task and she is incredibly well versed in the history of New York and elsewhere. Sofie married a member of our parish, although she kept her maiden name and still practices her own faith, a Bohemian Christian sect known as Hussites. She works for St. Peter's on a part time basis to help us with our humble needs as well. Her specialty is ancient native tribes of North America. Not because that is what we would be interested in at the church, or indeed, here at the library. It is just the subject she feels the most affinity for and one she studies on her own time."

They came to an area with tens of thousands of books lined up in neat rows. A conveyor system that resembled a Chicago wheel, like the one George Ferris had built for the

World's Fair Columbian Expedition in 1893, routed books to the main level.

Standing at one of the racks was a short, slim woman with dark hair turning to grey, pinned up in a bun. She was dressed all in black in a loose fitting dress, which fell to her ankles. She wore *pince-nez* spectacles perched on her long, pointed nose, with a black satin band attached which looped around her neck. She wore thick heels on her shoes that clicked loudly when she walked.

She looked up to see the priest and Gideon approaching, and turned off the conveyor.

"Father Beaudry, how delightful to see you. To what do I owe the pleasure?" Sofie had a pronounced accent, which Gideon recognized from his conversations with Anna and Pavel as Bohemian.

"Sofie, let me introduce you to Gideon Riot. He comes to us from Tucson and is on a quest to find out more about our mysterious cross of *Cortés*. It is a bit of a long story, but his wife, who is originally from México, was given the cross by Colonel Greene. She donated it to their local church, *San Xavier del Bac.* Apparently there is an escaped prisoner who had stolen the cross once before and is believed to be on a mission to steal it again. Gideon here is trying to find out all he can about the cross. I think it's time we shared what we know."

Sofie inhaled deeply, took off her glasses and wiped them with a handkerchief, which she had tucked into the cuff of the long sleeves of her dress.

"A pleasure to meet you Mr. Riot," she said as she extended her hand, "what does your wife think of a woman's right to vote?"

Gideon was somewhat taken aback by this bold question from a woman he had only just met.

"It's Gideon, please ma'am. I'm not really sure. She's still not a citizen of the U.S. yet. I'll have to ask her when I get home. Right now, she's worried because I'm so far away and the convict that Father Beaudry mentioned is believed to be in the vicinity of our home. I have to head back as soon as we're done here."

Sofie looked at Gideon again and marveled at the funny way he whistled as he spoke, but she liked it and he seemed to be so genuine. The priest looked on and was tempted to explain that Sofie was a radical suffragette and working to help win the vote for women. She was a strong activist and involved in demonstrations for peace. With an impending war in Europe, she did not want to see her new country become involved in it in any way.

"I understand and I will try to be brief."

She turned to the priest as he explained to her what he had already told Gideon of the Aztecs, the treasure, and *Cortés* expedition. She came right to the point.

"Cortés was a brutish Conquistador who vanquished the land through intimidation. After conquering the people of Tabasco on the Gulf coast, he was awarded twenty girls as slaves. One of them, who distinguished herself from the others, was named Marina. She became *Cortés* concubine and together they had a son, Martin. She became known as *Doña Marina* or Lady Marina and today is known throughout México, often disparagingly, by her Aztec name *La Malinche*.

"*Doña Marina* was instrumental in helping *Cortés* with Montezuma. She would translate the language of the Aztecs into the Mayan dialect for *Cortés'* Spanish priest, Jerónimo de Aguilar.

"Aguilar had been shipwrecked off Cozumel for many years so he knew the Mayan dialect. He could then translate what Doña Marina told him in Mayan to Spanish for Cortés.

Eventually Doña Marina learned Spanish and the extra step was not necessary. The role that this woman played in the overall history of México is remarkable and incredibly important.

"It was probably due to Doña Marina's efforts that Montezuma received Cortés.

"Once he met with the Aztec leader, he was given great amounts of gold and jewelry. He intended to take it all back to Spain, but during a skirmish, Montezuma was killed. The Aztecs grew tired of Cortés barbaric rule and he was lucky to escape with his life.

"*Tenochtitlan* was located on an island in the middle of a large lake, surrounded by swamps in what is now the center of *México City*. All of the gold and jewels disappeared. The event is called 'The Night of Sorrows', or in Spanish *'La Noche Triste'* to reflect the sadness at the senseless deaths and the treasures they left behind.

"The majority of the vast treasure has never been found. *Cortés* tried to escape with all of the precious items, and some say that it was lost at the bottom of that body of water. But others say he escaped with at least a portion of it, and people have searched for it ever since. There are rumors he buried it in all kinds of places; Utah, New Mexico, and even Kansas are mentioned as possible sites. But no one really knows for sure."

"That's all fascinating, Sofie. May I call you Sofie?"

She nodded her acquiescence.

"Really it is. But what has this got to do with Colonel Greene's cross?"

"Why, Mr. Riot. It has long been widely believed that the cross is the only existing relic of that lost treasure, but it really proves that some of the treasure *was* moved out of Tenochtitlan. Do you realize the significance of that? If word got out, there would be a stampede to the cross and a pilgrimage to find its source."

"So Sofie, are you saying that the cross really is from the treasure that Cortés tried to steal from the Aztecs? Father, I thought you said it came from Spain?"

The priest replied. "That's correct. We do believe it was originally crafted in Spain. But there is a secret that very few people know about. I wasn't sure I should share it with you, but you have a vested interest in the safety of this artifact and I believe you have as good a chance at keeping it safe as anyone."

"What is it, Father? What's the secret?"

"You must promise me you will tell no one what I'm about to tell you. Not even your wife. Many believe that the cross is cursed. You know some of the history, but the stories going back to Cortés own death indicate it is a cursed talisman. I know that I'm not supposed to believe in such things, but we all know that the devil exists. Some believe it exists in this cross which has had a long and cursed history."

"Father, I'm not a Catholic, I'm a Baptist. But I certainly believe in the devil. There's a piece of my story I didn't mention as well, but perhaps I should. My wife, whose name is Carmelita, was born in Cananea, México at the copper mines there owned by Colonel Greene. While her mother was on her deathbed, she told Carmelita a story of being raped by one of the mining supervisors. His birth name is Declan Cassidy, although he has used many aliases, and had one while working in Cananea. Since that day, my wife has searched to find this nefarious scoundrel. That's part of the reason I'm here – to learn more about the past. But is that the secret you don't want me to share? That the amulet is a cursed talisman? I'm not sure that's much of a secret."

"Gideon, the amulet that is hanging in the White Dove of the Desert is not the only artifact to leave with *Cortés* men. It is true that much of the vast treasure that Montezuma had amassed has been lost, but before he was imprisoned by *Cortés*, he had given him a very large numbers of items; gold, jewels and sculptured pieces that had tremendous worth. It is also true that *Cortés* was a scoundrel and heavy-handed tyrannical leader. Many Aztecs died at his hand and those of his men, but he sent much of the original treasure that he received when Montezuma mistakenly took him as a god sent by the prophets, back to Spain.

"I can't believe I'm telling you all this, but we, meaning the church, have been sitting on this information for centuries. When the priest in México originally handed the cross to the native girl as legend has it, not only was it inscribed with a phrase, *"Vaya con Dios"* or "Go with God," it was also wrapped in a single piece of leather to preserve it during travel. But let Sofie tell the rest of the story. She's really the expert here and I learned much of this from her."

Sofie took up the story. "Mr. Riot, the leather was a soft chamois and after years of use it had turned dark and brittle and was extremely dirty, in spite of being kept separate from the cross and fairly well preserved. Father Beaudry came to me with it years ago and asked me to catalog it in the church archives. Although it was separate from the cross, it had long been believed that it was originally handed down with the cross from *Cortés*. I took it, worked for weeks to revitalize it, and examined it, as I would any of the books we have from ancient times with leather covers, and I noticed what I thought to be a scribed message. I cleaned it up and saw there was a legend embossed into the skin. At first I didn't recognize it, so I took it to our linguistic expert. It was embossed with a phrase in Náhuatl orthography, the glyphic language of the Aztecs, and the language that *Doña Marina* spoke. We felt certain, since the leather covering was a separate item from the cross and would eventually deteriorate if it wasn't lost, that the cross itself must also possess this same phrase."

Gideon could see Sofie was excited about all this history, but he was worried about catching his train.

"I don't mean to rush you ma'am, but I have to go very soon. What was the message?"

"Let me show you. Wait here. I'll be right back." She left and walked rapidly to one of the stacks and started the conveyor.

Gideon instinctively went to his waistcoat pocket to look at his watch, only to be frustrated again that there was nothing there.

"Father, I really have to get going if I'm to catch that train. Is this important? Can you tell me what this is about while we walk?"

"Patience, my son. Sofie is very good at what she does. She'll be back shortly and you will see that this is all worthwhile."

At that moment, the conveyor stopped. Seconds later, Sofie briskly walked towards them carrying something in her hands.

"Gideon, this is the original leather covering. Can you see the images?"

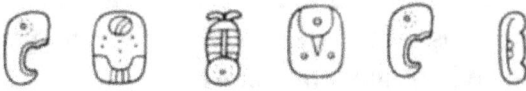

"Yes, but I can't make out what it says."

"It's a Náhuatl glyphic." She pulled out a separate piece of paper. "Here's what our linguistic expert interpreted it to mean."

On the page were the glyphics and a single word "*Atzlan.*"

Gideon looked at it, confused. "What does it mean?"

She smiled and said to him with confidence and bravado. "*Atzlan* is the legendary ancestral home of the Aztec people. We believe this is where *Cortés* hid the treasure. You must confirm that this same message is on the cross. Did you happen to notice if there was anything embossed on the top or sides of it?"

"Yes," he replied, "it's embossed all around the edges, but I thought it was just random designs."

"Take this paper with you. Don't lose it. Check to make sure the embossings match. If they do, we believe that when you get to *Atzlan*, you will find the lost treasure."

"So, where is this *Atzlan*?" he asked.

The priest smiled and replied. "Well, that's the trick Gideon. No one knows for sure. You'll have to find it. We believe the cross may offer some clues."

"Why didn't the church check the cross when they had it? Is this only coming to light now?"

Father Beaudry shrugged. "Sofie wasn't around then, and it seems no one knew the significance of the leather wrapping or the markings on the cross. If it had not been given to her for cataloging and she hadn't gone the extra mile and completed her extensive examination, we may never have known. Just as you did, it seems that the markings on the sides of the cross were taken as simply random markings. No one suspected it might contain a message."

Sofie added, "I cannot say for sure without examining the cross, but I strongly suspect that the glyphic will offer clues to the location of *Aztlán*. I would love to see it for myself."

"Why would *Cortés* put clues to where the treasure is hidden in the Aztec tongue? He was Spanish. Wouldn't he have it written in his own language?"

Again Sofie handled the response. "*Cortés* would not want anyone who had the cross to be able to decipher the meanings of the glyphics. He learned a lesson from Father de

Aguilar and Doña Marina. It is believed he would have ordered the markings in the Aztec language before returning it to Spain. Is there additional filigree on the surface of the cross?"

"Yes there is. Why?"

"The Aztec language, Náhuatl, used characters which did not directly represent the spoken word, as is the case in Western languages. They often provided clues that would not be easily understood by other cultures. When Father Beaudry came to me with the leather covering, I researched the Aztec, Montezuma, *Cortés*, Doña Marina, and the events of *La Noche Triste*. Gideon, I believe that the cross was given to Padre Javier Pachero's ancestor by *Cortés* to bring back to Spain specifically to alert them to the location of the treasure. The Amulet of Cananea is the key to its location."

Gideon bent down to pick up his carpetbag and stood up slowly with a faraway look in his eyes. He reached out his hand to the priest and slowly broke into a smile.

"You know, Father, Carmelita believes if she looks into Cassidy's eyes, she'll know for certain if he is her biological father. I need to help her learn the truth about her father, and *I* am going to learn the truth about the lost treasure of *Cortés*."

# Chapter Seven

## *Confrontation*

Cassidy arrived in Tucson and was struck by all the changes since the last time he was free. The town's population had grown dramatically. The streets were filled with a combination of horses, carriages, and automobiles, and many of the streets were now paved.

He knew he had to get back to Thibodeaux with some clothes, but he had been imprisoned for a long time and had an urgent need he had to take care of first. Prohibition may soon be coming to Arizona, he thought, but prostitution was still legal and not even on the upcoming ballots.

Cassidy's first order of business was to sell both horses. He did that at a ranch just outside town and asked the owner to give him a ride into town. The rancher was happy for the excuse. He had a classic Wood's Phaeton, an electric car which he loved to drive. It was essentially a horse and buggy body, but with an electric engine that could achieve a top speed of 14 miles per hour with a range of 18 miles. He was willing to give Cassidy a ride to town, where he would then would have to pay a local garage to charge his vehicle for the return trip.

The ranch owner loved this, because it gave him an excuse to spend some time playing cards in a saloon that he liked to frequent across town called Iggy's.

Cassidy had asked the rancher to drop him off on Meyer Street, near Gay Alley, an area frequented by prostitutes which offered all types of vice for a price. The area was populated primarily by illegal immigrants from all points of the world and was a perfect place for Cassidy to hide out for a while, spend a few dollars, and find a willing young woman to take care of his needs.

He hadn't made enough money off the two horses to purchase a car. He had to sell them cheap since they had obviously been stolen. Cassidy and Q had done their best to obliterate the Pima County markings, but it was still apparent to any horseman that the animals weren't his. He figured he would either steal a car or purchase a used horse and buggy. He thought to himself that a horse and buggy made more sense, because he didn't think he could figure out how to drive the automotive contraptions without taking more time than he wanted. He had already seen a few of them crash into the raised sidewalks that were rapidly becoming extinct.

They would only need the transportation for a brief time at any rate, only until they could fence the cross, their ultimate goal. Then they would have some real money and could afford train tickets and new clothes.

Somewhere along the line he would lose Thibodeaux, and his plan was to head out to southern California. He wanted to see movie stars and thought he might be able to talk his way into a job at one of the studios.

Cassidy had a mad crush on Mabel Normand, a Hollywood actress who starred in one-reel comedies. She was very young when he saw her in one of her first short films, "Mabel's Stormy Love Affair." He planned to go to the studio and meet her to see for himself if she was as sexy and exciting in person as she was on the screen. Just thinking of her gave him an erection. He needed to find a young girl to satisfy his needs right away.

As the midday sun passed, Cassidy knew he had to get back to Quince before nightfall, for he feared Q would try to strike out on his own in the dress he had on his back. He couldn't afford for Q to get caught and spoil Cassidy's plans. He made his way towards the many bordellos dotting the street and picked one that struck his fancy. It was called "The Gilded Cage."

Cassidy was familiar with a picture of that name painted by a fellow Irishman that depicted a women lying half naked bound by chains tied to a marble column. The thought of it aroused him to distraction. It reminded him of a popular song from several years past, "The Bird in a Gilded Cage."

Women loved that song, but to Cassidy it was an ode to women bought with money. He hummed to himself a snippet of the song;

> …. *her beauty was sold,*
> *For an old man's gold,*
> *She's a bird in a gilded cage.*

He stepped into the parlor which was adorned with scarlet velvet flocked wallpaper and dim lighting. A woman of some years was leaning on the bar, and moved off it, approaching him with a feather fan in her hand and a very low cut sweeping long dress highlighting her ample bosom and cleavage.

Cassidy was repelled by this, although he thought there may be some who would be excited. He had a taste for the very young, and the older he became, the younger his taste seemed to lean.

"Evening, sir." She said as she leaned close and he could smell both the perfume she wore and the musk of her own scent. "What is your passion?"

Cassidy was eager. He had no time for teasing and flirtatious behaviors. He was there for one reason and one reason only. He had a lot to do and needed to get back to the business of stealing the cross and getting his money and revenge.

"How much?" he asked coarsely.

The madam was somewhat amused by his gruffness, but not completely surprised. She had assessed his ill-fitting clothing and crude appearance with the practiced eye of a woman with years of experience with this type of man.

"Honey, it's too much for you. Down the street there's an establishment called Sadie's. Inside they have a small bar and on the upper floors there are cribs. You'll find the type of woman you need there, and the price will be right. Good luck."

She turned her back and walked away. Cassidy had a flash of anger, and grabbed the middle of his walking stick ready to strike her on the back of the head while her back was to him. But he quickly decided it could come to no good and ruin all his plans. He wisely took a breath and quelled his anger. He wanted a girl and he wanted her now. Cassidy had a long history of violently defiling women, but he knew he had to stay on his best behavior to avoid trouble. His main goal was to get the cross and hide away for the rest of his life. After all the trouble and physical suffering he had endured, his mission now was to release his inner tensions and move on. He walked out the door, went down the street, and took the Madam's advice.

---

Quince Thibodeaux could not sleep. The April day had risen sunny and warm, and it was too beautiful for him to stay under the makeshift lean-to, just waiting for Cassidy to return. He tossed and turned trying to get some rest. He cursed himself for trusting Cassidy and should never have let him take his horse. He refused to go out on the road dressed as he was, and he knew he couldn't put his prison stripes back on. But once sundown came, he was determined to strike out on foot and get as close to Tucson as he dared. Maybe he would find some clothes along the way and then find Cassidy. If he couldn't find clothes, he would wrap a blanket around himself. Then, once he did find Cassidy, he would kill him with his bare hands and go to the church himself for the cross. He spent the entire day tossing and cursing Cassidy.

As the sun began to sink low in the western sky, Quince had worked himself up into a frenzy believing Cassidy had abandoned him. He was trying to formulate a plan of attack in his mind, but he couldn't figure out the best way to accomplish this without some help. He couldn't go out in the daylight, and he had no transportation, little money, and no food.

It had taken all his persistence to figure out where they were headed, but he finally prevailed upon Cassidy, just before he left, that he had to know in the event Cassidy was caught. They agreed if anything happened to either one of them, that the other would find a way to steal the cross and bust the other out of whatever trouble they got into.

All day long he had heard horses, carriages, and automobiles traveling close by. He knew there must be a road that led to town. As he crept out of his lean-to to take a look in the waning minutes of sunlight, he heard a horse whinny behind him. He turned around quickly and was hit in the face with a bundled up package. Standing above him was Cassidy.

"What did you think you were going to do Q? Walk to Tucson in a woman's dress?"

Q looked at the package and was surprised to find himself happy to see Cassidy. Two minutes earlier he was ready to kill him.

"Put those on quickly. Here's a few tamales and some water. Sun will be down in a few minutes. We have a lot to do."

# **Chapter Eight**

## *Discovery*

Gideon arrived back in Tucson late in the evening. His return trip was quicker due to additional rail lines that had become available. Trains were going up throughout the United States at an incredible pace and he was fortunate to catch connections to make the return much faster.

His head was spinning with all that he learned from Father Beaudry and the church's historian, Sofie Pollak. He had promised to send a telegram or call if he could, and tell her what he found on the cross.

He left the station and paid the driver of a horse and buggy to take him to his home quickly, hoping to find Carmelita waiting there safe and sound. As they left the station, he saw an automobile pull up to the platform with a sign offering local transportation.

He thought to himself, "I'm only gone a short time and already we have competition."

He thought about Pavel and his methods, and knew he had his work cut out for him.

He had no idea what might have occurred since he left. He had only received one telegram from Carmelita so the threat of Cassidy on the loose was a great concern.

As he rode through town he grew increasingly apprehensive. He thought about all he had learned and what he had to do to both protect the cross, ensure its' future safety, and learn what he could about its past. Now, he also had to worry about competition from other taxi companies.

He dismounted from the buggy's bench seat, paid the driver, ran up the front porch, and burst through the door.

"Carmelita – where are you? I'm home."

He ran to the kitchen and sitting there was his wife, talking animatedly with Lena and sipping a cool drink.

She must not have heard him come through the door, because she got up quickly, startled, went to his arms, and held him tight.

"I have missed you so much. I'm so glad you're home safe with me," she whispered in his ear.

"Me, too, sweetheart. We have a lot to talk about." He noticed Lena standing there awkwardly.

"Hi, Lena," he nodded and smiled.

They brought each other up to date on what had transpired since he left. Gideon only told Carmelita about a portion of his trip, primarily that which dealt with the cross and its role as a key to the treasure. She, in turn, told him what she knew of Cassidy's escape, which wasn't much. There were follow up articles in the paper on the sheriff's efforts to track down the escapees, but nothing in the past few days.

They decided to ride out to the White Dove as soon as possible and talk to the pastor there about Cassidy's escape and also about the possibility of the cross being a key to the location of the treasure of *Cortés* and Montezuma. She hadn't wanted to go alone with Lena, but felt safe now that Gideon was home.

Gideon absentmindedly reached for his pocket watch only to be frustrated once more that it was missing.

Carmelita noticed.

"Gideon, where's your watch?"

"It's a long story. I'll tell you on the way, but I'll have to order a new one today. I can't stand to be without it."

Lena interrupted "Would you like me to go with you?"

"No, I don't think so Lena," Carmelita replied. "Why don't you stay here in town in case the deputy has any additional information. We should be back shortly."

At the mention of the deputy, Lena reddened slightly. She inclined her head and responded, "Sí, I would be happy to."

---

Cassidy and Quince had spent the time since their arrival in Tucson in a one room, walk-up hovel plotting the theft of the cross and enjoying the pleasures of Gay Alley, a three-block area encompassing Meyer and Sabine streets. Neither one of them could go to the church to scout out the situation. Cassidy was smart enough to know that after the first theft, they must have taken additional precautions for the cross. He only hoped it was still being displayed and not tucked away somewhere in a vault. But they had one major obstacle – money. They had none. Cassidy had robbed a small dry goods store on the outskirts of town on the way back to Tucson. Between the little money he made selling the horses, and the take from the robbery, which was pitiful, they rented the room and only had enough left for a couple of days' worth of food.

Quince ate a lot, and Cassidy wanted to spend more time with the ladies, so they needed to find a way to get more money quickly. The best Cassidy could do on his trip to Tucson was to steal a single horse for their transportation which aggravated him to no end since he had sold two better ones for next to nothing. They rode double until they hit the edge of town and then Q walked alongside.

Cassidy used his infirmity to his advantage whenever he could.

Prostitution was legal in Tucson, but that also meant it was regulated. The regulation made Cassidy furious. Gay Alley was a very busy place and was patrolled by the so-called "Mayor of Meyer Street," Jesus Camacho. Camacho collected the fees that the madams had to pay to the city. He was a tough policeman of Mexican-American heritage, but it was known that he would turn a blind eye if the price was right. He was very tough on illegal behavior, however, if it threatened the girls or his livelihood.

Cassidy had to be very careful in Gay Alley and avoided Camacho like the plague. The policeman would often spontaneously patrol the streets, day and night, either on his horse "Bebe", or on foot with the horse following close behind.

Quince was a convicted horse thief and Cassidy's conviction was for murder, although he had committed several other crimes, but neither one of them knew much about hold-ups. They didn't know how to plan the type of theft that would get them the funds they desperately needed without getting caught.

Cassidy came up with a solution, but not one either of them liked. They would have to find a new partner. One who could scout San Xavier del Bac and help them get some real money, and fast.

Quince objected but Cassidy persuaded him with a little help from the bone handle on his cane.

He left Quince and went to Meyer Street to Sadie's. This time not for a woman, but to find a partner who could help them with their problem.

Sadie's was a dump, but given the clientele who inhabited the establishment, it was just the kind of place where he could find the type of disreputable person he needed. Cassidy was smart, but he was blind to many of his own shortcomings, so didn't seem to realize that since this was his favorite place, it also put him in that category.

He had only been to Sadie's twice, but already he knew the madam well. She was familiar with his taste for young women, the less experienced the better. The name of the place was Sadie's but the madam was named Rosie. When he asked why it was called Sadie's, she told Cassidy that she didn't want to use her own name, although Rosie wasn't her real name either. Strange how people think, he mused.

He took Rosie somewhat into his confidence and told her he needed to find someone who could help with a "situation" and that it might entail certain abilities. He didn't go into much detail, just enough to give her the idea.

She responded immediately, "I know just the person you need. Go to room six and knock on the door. Say the words 'fool's gold' and go on in. That's so you don't get shot when you open the door."

Cassidy gave her a funny look, but did what she said. When he opened the door, he saw a young woman, maybe 18, but not much more than that. She was quite attractive, and looked very young, much younger than her years. Her skin was smooth and had a creamy complexion with tiny freckles loosely scattered across her nose. Her eyes were sparkling green, and she wore her natural strawberry blonde hair shoulder length. She was sitting, but looked to be quite tall, with long legs and small pointed breasts. He was baffled, thinking Sadie must have misunderstood his request, and realized he was staring at the girl with his mouth hanging open.

She was sitting by a desk on a chair turned around towards the door, dressed in standard western fare - boots, jeans, denim shirt, with a small Stetson hat tilted up on the back of her head. On her right hip was a hand tooled leather holster with a pearl handled .45 colt revolver. It looked to be a short barrel, the kind typically used for gunfights, because it was easy to draw, but a little heavy for a girl, he thought. It weighed at least half a pound unloaded. And no one carried an empty gun, he noted to himself. She stood up, looked at him, and said, "What's the job?"

Cassidy, Rosie, and the young woman, Mollie, sat at a table in the bar against the far wall speaking quietly.

"Rosie, I'm telling you, I need someone who can handle a very dangerous mission. This is no place for a girl, even if she is your niece."

Before Rosie could open her mouth to reply, Mollie jumped in, "Listen, pal, you have a problem with women? We can step outside right now and I'll cut your balls off and cram 'em down your throat."

"Calm down, Mollie," her aunt said. "Cassidy, Mollie here is what you might call a liberated woman. A strong supporter of women's rights and staunch suffragette. She's young, but she can hold her own with any man in a gunfight. Hand to hand could be a problem, but she's fast and mean. What's the job, anyway?"

"No offense, Rosie, but the less you know the better."

He turned to Mollie. "Let's me and you go for a walk and talk. We'll see if this makes sense or not."

Cassidy and Mollie left the brothel and wandered back in the direction of a more respectable area of town. He explained, in brief outline, what the job entailed. He told her about his partner and the challenge they both faced trying to scout a location without being noticed.

"Q is Cajun, six foot five and 305 pounds. I have an obvious limp, use a cane, and have red hair. Neither one of us can do what needs to be done without being noticed and remembered. But this could be dangerous. There's no telling what we might face. You're kind of young, have you ever been involved with something like this before?"

Mollie spit and turned an eye towards him. "Cassidy, I been in and out of trouble since I was 12 years old and shot and killed my own stepfather. He was a drunk and a wife beater. He tried to come at me once and I didn't think twice, I took his own gun from the holster hanging on the kitchen chair and shot him with all 5 shots. This here is the gun."

Cassidy glanced down and saw the six shooter in her holster. He knew the chamber would have been left empty, which meant she had to cock the gun before the first shot. He was impressed.

"I've been practicing with it ever since. I can shoot the eye out of an owl at 50 yards. As far as hand-to-hand, most men won't even try to hit me because of my age and the way I look. But if they do, I can outrun most any man."

Cassidy liked her grit. He turned to her and said. "You're hired."

Cassidy went back to get Q and the three of them met in the lobby of the Pueblo Hotel, a seedy little place where no one would pay them any attention. Q was smitten with "little Mollie" as he took to calling her, until he heard the mouth on the girl. She put him in his place in a hurry.

Cassidy realized what a good partner she could be. With her youth and innocent looks, it would be easy for her to not only scout the location of the cross, but she would be able to befriend the padre as well. He was starting to feel that this could be the beginning of a beautiful friendship. He was also strangely aware that he felt no sexual attraction to her. He almost felt like an uncle. He suspected that maybe she liked girls more than boys, but who was he to question a person's sexual orientation?

They talked late into the night and came up with what they all thought was a solid plan.

---

In spite of their intent to get to the church right away, Gideon and Carmelita couldn't go to the church the following day or the day after that, or even the day after that. Gideon had too much to address that required his attention after his long absence. When he had left for New York, he left the responsibility of handling day to day operations for his stagecoach and taxi business to his office manager, a spitfire of a woman named Maria Luisa Cardenas Castillon. She was known as Luisa to everyone except her family, who combined the first two letters of her first and second name and called her Malu as a term of affection. Even though Carmelita and Gideon were very close to her, she was Luisa, not Malu to them, and they were nearly as close as any family member.

Luisa was of Mexican heritage, but her family chose U.S. citizenship when the border was split after the Treaty of Guadalupe Hidalgo, when much of what had been Mexican land became U.S. soil. She was not alone. Well over ninety percent of those who found themselves on the U.S. side of the border did the same.

Luisa handled all aspects of the business for Gideon and was an invaluable employee. She acted as bookkeeper, dispatcher, and maintenance supervisor; virtually everything but driving, and on occasion she was pressed into duty to do that too.

Luisa commanded the respect of the other drivers that Gideon employed, but none of them could drive the new taxi. That was left only to Gideon. He wasn't even sure he'd be able to teach the stage drivers how to handle the auto. So Gideon found that although he went to New York to learn more about the taxicab business and how to transition his business to automobiles, he now found himself weeks behind in capturing the market. He had too much to do before worrying about the cross, which was not theirs anymore and not really their worry in any case.

Normally, Carmelita would be jealous of Gideon being in the company of a woman as attractive as Luisa, but had long been aware that she preferred women to men and felt safe with their relationship, although Gideon was completely oblivious to her sexual orientation and often flirted with her.

Carmelita hadn't known Luisa when she arrived from México. She had been referred by Jorge, Carmelita's boss at the Iguana Café. When Gideon was looking for an office manager, Jorge had recommend Luisa saying she was smart, competent, and tough. Jorge was a decent man, but he had a larcenous side to him, which was a trait Carmelita had seen in all the bar owners she had known.

Gideon spent all his time over the next few days teaching Luisa to drive the taxicab so she could hopefully train the other drivers. At night they worked on the books and the new method he had learned in New York of charging by the mile. His business was growing faster than he anticipated. Everyone wanted to ride in the new taxicabs, even if they didn't have a true destination in mind. He was rapidly phasing out the horse drawn coaches and planning new vehicle purchases.

Gideon and Carmelita finally arrived at the church in the middle of the day on Friday, and immediately found the pastor in the nave speaking to a pretty young woman dressed in cowboy gear. The pastor was always happy to see them and greeted them warmly. The young woman nodded at them and took a seat in a pew nearby. Carmelita thought the young woman looked familiar, but couldn't place the face. It nagged at her as Gideon spoke to the priest of his journey to New York and the reason for their visit. He noticed the cross was hanging above the altar, and it was fastened and secured in a metal shadow box frame. Apparently, even in the house of God, the lesson to be cautious had been learned.

Gideon informed the priest of Cassidy's escape, Carmelita's visit to the sheriff's office, and Gideon's trip to New York.

"Father Mendoza, I would like to ask if I may remove the cross," Gideon suggested. The priest looked at him with alarm.

"Gideon, with all we have been through, why on earth would you want to do that? We just had it firmly secured so it couldn't be removed easily."

"I know Father, I can see that. As you know, I just got back from New York, where I spoke to the historian at St. Peter's. She also happens to be an archivist at the main branch of the New York public library. We spoke at length about the history of the Amulet and she may be able to help us understand information which may be contained in glyphics on the edges of the cross. If I could remove the cross under your supervision and do a tin foil rubbing, I could send it back to her to translate the figures into Spanish and then convert that to English. She calls the technique 'frottage.' It's French, I think. She believes it may provide additional information on the location of the treasure that *Cortés* stole from the Aztecs. Carmelita also has friends who may still know some of the language as well, so we can look into it ourselves. And, although it's none of my business, I would suggest after that you remove the cross to a safer place until *El Diablo* is apprehended."

"Gideon, Carmelita, of course you may take rubbings of the cross. The church, indeed, the world, would not have its beauty if it weren't for you two. As to removing the cross. I believe that God will take good care of it as He has for the past hundreds of years. We'll take our chances against *El Diablo*. I don't really believe he will be a true threat."

Gideon and Carmelita turned and looked at each other, both thinking the same thing - that the priest was seriously underestimating Cassidy.

None of them noticed as the young woman slipped out of the pew and walked quickly towards the exit door.

# Chapter Nine

## *Interpretation*

Carmelita left the priest and Gideon to seek out a friend of hers from the days at the copper mines in Cananea. The caretaker at the mission offered to take her in the buckboard. The mission of the White Dove was in a somewhat remote part of the southern end of Tucson and nearby was a small enclave of the Papago tribe of the Tohono O'odham nation. The nation spoke a language that was related to the same linguistic branch that the Aztecs had spoken. She hoped there may be someone there who might have some knowledge of the Náhuatl glyphics.

She left Gideon and the pastor at the church to continue discussions of removal of the cross. Masses and a wedding were scheduled for Sunday, so they agreed to wait until Monday to remove the cross, execute the tinfoil rub, and send it off to New York. Gideon thanked the priest and left to find Carmelita and return home.

Carmelita arrived at the Papago site and was immediately directed to one of the oldest Papago tribal leaders. She told him of her request to interpret the glyphics on an ancient gold cross. He was very sympathetic and extremely interested in the item itself. He explained to her that they did have some very rudimentary knowledge of the spoken language, but that knowledge of the written glyphics were all but dead.

He did offer to take a look in the event he could identify some of the markings.

Gideon arrived and she rode back home with him, a little bit dejected. She was hopeful that they would be able to solve the riddle right away. Sending the frottage off to New York could take weeks.

As they were discussing the plans, Mollie arrived back at the rented room in Gay Alley. She explained to Cassidy and Q what she overheard at the church. Apparently, it never dawned on Gideon, Carmelita, or the priest, that anyone would care about what they were discussing in that holy and sacred place.

Cassidy was excited. "Are you saying that there may be a message to other treasures on the cross?"

"That's what I just said, you idiot," Mollie snarled.

Cassidy didn't like her brusque attitude, but he needed her. Mollie on the other hand thought Cassidy was a complete fool, sick bastard, and an insult to the human race. But for now they needed each other.

She continued, "My plan is to go back to the church and see if I can get a job there. I already spoke to the priest about the possibility, although he said they had no present need. If he won't give me a job, I'll offer to volunteer on an irregular basis to fit my schedule. That way, I can arrange to be there when they do the rubbings."

Cassidy looked at Q. He couldn't afford to have this young upstart think she had control and make her own plans. He knew she and Q liked each other although he couldn't fathom why.

"*I'll* decide how we proceed. In case you didn't notice, I'm in charge around here and you would be wise not to forget it. I know you can shoot, but you have to sleep sometime. Don't think I can't find another partner if I need to."

He looked at Mollie and then at Q to make sure they got the message. He wanted them to know he was in charge, but didn't want a mutiny, so he had to strike a balance.

"Now, your plan is a good one. I was about to suggest something along the same lines. But first, we need money. Me and Q can't stay here. What plan do you have to get us some dough?"

Mollie replied, "I hadn't really thought about that. I have a place to stay and I have a little money. I was counting on this job to get me more. Have *you* thought about it at all?"

"Of course. It's all I've thought about. Have you heard about all the robberies happening near the border? Villa's Méxicans have been crossing over and robbing U.S citizens at gunpoint. Most of it is happening right on the border towns, like Nogales.

"Tomorrow we'll head out to Green Valley. It's about 25 miles from where we are now. We'll take the stage there and scout the area at the border town. We'll need to steal two fast horses just before we make the hit. Once we get to Green Valley, we're going to dress like Méxicans with bandanas over our faces. We'll darken our skin and cover up real well.

"We're going to hit a Wells Fargo stage, so Mollie, you have to get the schedule and any information you can about which one might be moving money. We have to do this tomorrow, Saturday. It's when the most people travel and they transfer money for the following week. Once we're done, we'll head south on the horses, dismount at a prearranged location that has an empty barn or ranch house. We'll send the horses on their way with their saddlebags full of rocks to distract the law. Then we change into respectable clothes and the three of us take a wagon north. If anyone sees us, they won't think about two Méxican robbers. Especially with Mollie here."

"Dat a good plan," Q spoke up, "but two horses? What Mollie be doing?"

"Mollie will be with me. She and I are small like the Méxicans and the horses will ride a lot faster with us. You're too big and it will slow us down.

"Plus, Mollie is said to be very good with a gun, which may come in handy. Your job is to find a place to change and steal a wagon and horses. We need to hit the stage tomorrow, Saturday, then we'll lay low for a day and head back on Monday. We'll head directly for the mission church on the way back to Tucson. We can drop Mollie off there. Any questions?"

Q remained skeptical, because he inherently distrusted Cassidy, but they both shook their heads and all went off to do their part.

Three days later, the three were heading back to Tucson in a horse drawn wagon. The plan had gone off without a hitch. Q did an admirable job of finding an empty barn and an old but usable wagon.

Mollie had to draw her weapon, but no shots were fired. Cassidy did the talking using an affected Méxican accent. All this time at the Cananea copper mines managing Méxicans came in handy.

The take was three hundred and twenty dollars. Enough to get them housing and keep them in food and drink for several weeks if they were frugal. They were lucky to hit the right stage. There wasn't a bank deposit on it, but there were four wealthy ranchers heading to Tucson to gamble and have a good time.

Gamblers were drawn to Tucson, in part because of the sports programs at Arizona State University. The University that the town originally didn't want.

The ambition of the town fathers at the time they received a grant for the University, was to be named as the State Capitol. They had sent a man called C.C. Stevens to Prescott for the 13th Arizona Territorial Legislative Assembly of 1885, which became known as the "Thieving, Bloody Thirteenth Legislature." Depending on which version of the story you believe, either the Gila and Salt Rivers overflowed and he was waylaid, or he got drunk and lost a few days. Either way, the coveted bid to be named the State Capitol stayed in Prescott, which at the time was one of the top three cities in the State.

Phoenix came in second place and was granted $100,000 for hosting an insane asylum. By the time Stevens got to Prescott, all the plum government funds that had been allocated by the Morrill Land Grant Act, had been taken.

Stevens went back to Tucson with the consolation prize of building a State University and receiving just $25,000, a quarter of the funds Phoenix had received for its asylum. On top of that, the town was ordered to donate 40 acres of land, which no one wanted to do. The town was incensed and Stevens became the scapegoat.

Although initially widely denounced, the University at this time in 1914 was the pride of Tucson. It turned out that building the University was incredibly good for the city, and the money it brought to the town became a boon for Cassidy and his villainous colleagues as well.

As Quince counted his money, Cassidy thought about the gold cross, finally within his reach. He didn't know how long it would take to get ahold of the cross, but he expected to have it within a week. To Cassidy, all was right with the world.

They dropped Mollie off close to the mission church about mid-day on Monday, as Q and Cassidy went to find lodgings nearby. Cassidy went to work on the next phase of his plan.

As Mollie entered the church nave, she saw Gideon up on a ladder unscrewing the frame around the cross and the priest at the bottom holding the ladder. She approached the padre quietly.

"Good morning, Father. I've come to see if you can use any help here at the Church today. It looks like you have repairs to accomplish. You know, I'm an educated woman. I can also help with the little ones, if necessary."

"Good morning, Mollie. Oh, this? No, we're not doing repairs, we're just checking something out. As a matter of fact, we *can* use your help today. We're a little short staffed due to illness. Tell you what, grab hold of this ladder and keep it steady. I'll be right back. Gideon!" he called out, "meet Mollie. She's going to help us today. Mollie, say hello to Gideon."

Gideon called down in his extreme sibilance. "Pleased to make your acquaintance Mollie."

"Likewise, Gideon."

The priest left the two of them and headed out to the school to see about Mollie's offer to help.

Mollie held the ladder and looked up at the man trying to remove the cross. She was thinking about "accidentally" kicking it out from under his feet once he had the cross unhinged when the front door of the church opened.

"*Hola*, Gideon, we're here to help."

Carmelita and Lena came in and walked quickly towards the altar. Mollie looked at them, put on her best smile, and nodded politely. Carmelita nodded back, but Lena looked her up and down and pursed her lips. She thought Gideon and Mollie looked enough alike to be related.

He climbed down the ladder with the cross clutched tight to his chest. Just then, Father Mendoza came back through the sacristy.

"Well," he said as he looked at the four of them gathered at the base of the altar, "we quickly went from no help to plenty of help. Do you all know each other?"

Mollie immediately took advantage. She stuck her hand out to Carmelita and said, "Father Mendoza just introduced me to Gideon a few minutes ago, before he went to the sacristy. I'm Mollie. Mollie McGuire."

Her youthful appearance gave her an air of innocence, yet she had lived with Rosie long enough to learn how to manipulate people.

Carmelita tentatively shook her hand and Mollie repeated the greeting with Lena and finally, Gideon. She held his hand a little longer than the others and made a point of looking him in the eye and holding his gaze. Lena noted this and turned away mumbling.

"Well," Father Mendoza said, "Let's see about taking a rubbing of the glyphics on the cross so we can place it back where it belongs."

Mollie grinned to herself. Father Mendoza didn't know her at all, but referencing that he introduced her to Gideon made them all think that he did. It worked perfectly. She didn't understand the significance of interpreting the glyphics, but intuitively felt it could be important. More important than stealing the cross. She was now pleased that she had been interrupted before she took the ladder out from under Gideon.

"I have the tinfoil here and a pencil. Once we complete the frottage, we will need to carefully package it to prevent damage during shipment. Gideon, let's take a closer look at the cross before we start."

Just at that moment, a woman walked into the nave and up to the altar with loud clicking heels. She looked familiar to Gideon, but he wasn't sure he knew her until she got closer. He was shocked to see Sofie Pollak walking towards him lugging a very large suitcase and wearing the same type of black outfit she obviously favored, since it looked identical to the one she had on when he met her in New York.

Father Mendoza looked around him. Amusingly, he thought to himself that if he could command a turnout like this during confessions, he would be a very happy priest.

"Mr. Riot! What a magnificent, beautiful, and ornate structure this is. You did not do it justice when we spoke in New York. I had long heard of its beauty and incredible architecture, but the Moorish style and Spanish architecture is absolutely breathtaking. I am in awe."

Father Mendoza beamed and Gideon was struck speechless that Sofie was there.

Hers was the reaction of many who came to Tucson to view the magnificent structure of *San Xavier del Bac*. Although not a cathedral, it was indeed extremely ornate with multitudes of gold statues and colorful displays of religious paintings and murals. With high arching masonry vaults throughout the structure, the mission is a breathtaking mosaic of colors and symbols. Anyone approaching the altar would be dazzled.

Sofie noted Gideon's confusion and continued.

"After you left, I convinced both the Church of St. Peter's and the New York City Library to allow me to come here to examine the cross. It's historical and monetary value are just too important to the church and to posterity. They both agreed and collectively funded this trip. Now, may I take a look?"

Gideon was baffled, but pleased. It would take far less time, and be more accurate to have her here. He couldn't have been more pleased.

But in noting her outfit he thought she was lucky it wasn't August.

Gideon introduced her to his wife, Carmelita, her friend, Lena, Father Mendoza, and lastly, Mollie McGuire. Sofie noted Mollie's outfit and liked the look, thinking she might go back to New York with new clothes. They all went back to the sacristy to take a closer look at the cross.

Sofie opened her luggage, rummaged through and pulled out a pair of white cotton gloves and a black velvet cloth and laid the cross on it gingerly. She snapped on a strong focused light which had multiple right angle joints that allowed her to manipulate the light source over the cross. She took out a very powerful magnifying glass and held it close to the edges of the cross.

They all stood around her in a circle giving her enough distance to work, but closely watching her every move.

"Mr. Riot, can you please draw the curtains and turn off the lights?"

The darkened room had an eerie, mysterious glow. It almost seemed as if the cross was ethereal.

"The first thing you can see is that the markings on the outside, the words *"Vaya con Dios,"* are filigree. They were added after the embossing on the outer edges of the cross. If what we suspect is true, *Cortés* had this added before he sent the cross back to Spain."

She leaned in close and turned the cross onto its edges, examining all sides.

"You can see markings on the top of the cross and on both sides. The top is what we have already seen on the leather covering, the Náhuatl glyphics of the word *Aztlán*."

"What is *Aztlán*?" Mollie inquired. Lena stared at her, wondering what her role was in all this and reminding herself to ask Carmelita later.

Sofie explained. *"Atzlan* is the legendary, some say mythical, ancestral home of the Aztec people. I have postulated that this is where *Cortés* hid the remainder of his treasure. The treasure was accumulated by Montezuma over the period he ruled all of the Aztec nation. It is believed to be enormously valuable. When *Cortés* conquered the Aztecs, he was rumored to want to send it all back to Spain. Most of it didn't get there, and historians believe that a sizeable portion was removed and hidden by him only sending a portion to the king to appease him. This cross could be the key to where *Cortés* hid the rest of the treasure before going back to Spain the first time. The treasure has been lost for centuries and many, many people have tried to find it in a wide range of locations. I believe that if we can find *Aztlán*, then we can find the treasure."

They all looked one to the other. Gideon had heard much of this before, and perhaps the dark room, the expertise of Sofie, and the glowing markings on the cross brought it all home, but they all seemed to tingle with expectation of locating this lost and valuable treasure.

Sofie continued, "I don't want to bore you with too much history, but there is a precedent in a document called the Boturini Codex, known to the Spanish as "*Tira de la peregrinación*," or the pilgrimage strip. Essentially, it's a graphical depiction by an unknown Aztec author believed to have been done in the early to mid-1500's, just a couple of decades after they had been conquered by *Cortés*.

"The pictorial was transcribed on a long piece of fig bar known to the Aztecs as *amatl,* what the Spanish call *amate*. It was over twenty pages long, and was folded, accordion style, depicting the travels of the Aztec from *Aztlán* to the Valley of *México*, settling in what is now known as *México City*. It came into the possession of Lorenzo Boturini Bernaducci, an Italian born historian sometime in the 1700's. It's widely referenced by scholars looking into the true location of *Aztlán*."

Gideon asked, "Sofie, do the glyphics on the cross tell us of the location of *Aztlán*?"

"Well, Mr. Riot, not exactly. It does seem to indicate that the treasure is buried in what *Cortés* believed to be *Aztlán*. Remember, though, he was a Spaniard, not Aztec. His interpretation may be wrong, although I have to believe it was *Doña Marina* who had the cross updated with the glyphics. Still, she would have added the place *Cortés* asked her to, whether it was correct or not. If we can find what he *thought* was the location, we will be on the path to finding the hidden treasure."

She paused to look at each of them to make sure they were all following her explanation. She was satisfied that they were.

"See this group of markings on the left side of the cross? That seems to indicate direction. I have to verify with my translation dictionary, but I believe it's indicating northwest. We know that it would be northwest of *Tenochtitlan*, what is now called *México City*. The characters for *Aztlán* are at the top on the curved round head. The right side, and again I have to check my dictionary, seems to indicate specific location. It appears to suggest an island with a large tree surrounded by an outcropping of rocks. If I can verify this, we may have finally identified the true location of *Aztlán*, and the wealth of riches *Cortés* left behind."

Sofie turned on the room lights and caught them all staring into space with a look of wonder on their faces.

# <u>Chapter Ten</u>

## *Folklore*

"Where the hell is she?" Cassidy fumed. "She was supposed to be back yesterday. I don't think I can trust her."

Q sat on the bed counting their money for what seemed to be the twentieth time. Most of it was in gold coins, so he wanted to make sure the count was right. They decided to split it evenly between the three of them, and Q didn't trust Cassidy, so counted and re-counted to be sure he got the right amount.

"She be here, Cass'dy. Doan sweat it. She be here." Q went back to counting.

The plan was for Mollie to scout the cross at the church to see what it would take to lift it. Then they would go back late at night, steal the cross, and take a rubbing of their own to be interpreted when they found the right person to do so. Cassidy thought he knew someone at the University who could handle that.

They would still melt down the cross as soon as possible to take the cash. Cassidy's secret plan called for him to ditch his two companions before selling off the gold and jewels, and take the rubbing with him.

Q would never be able to find him. Mollie might be a bigger problem, but he wasn't above killing her, if necessary. He was sick of this whole thing and just wanted to get enough cash to go to an island someplace in the South Pacific and live the rest of his life in peace with a bevy of young girls whom he would pay well to take care of his every need.

"Cass'dy – I hear summon comin'."

The door opened and Mollie came in breathless and flushed.

"The cross is back on the wall. If you want to get it, go ahead. I'm out. I did what you asked. Give me my slice of the money and I'll leave you two alone."

Cassidy didn't trust this cowgirl. She was stubborn and pigheaded. "Maybe a bit too much like me," he thought to himself, "but what's she up to?"

Q was upset. He liked Mollie and felt she was a good distraction for him from Cassidy's cruel behavior.

"Why ya leavin', Miss Mollie?" he asked.

"Look. They got a woman from New York to come down and look at the cross first hand. She's smart. She really believes they'll be able to find the rest of the treasure if they follow the clues to *Aztlán*. There are four of them. Plus me. They're all smart and well connected. They don't have to sneak around to get things done. They have the financial support of the Church, the authorities, and the historical institutions. They think I'm one of them, which is what you wanted. So, I'm done with you, Cassidy. I'm going with them. You can have the cross and get what you can for it. I'm placing my bet on the big money."

"Wait a minute. What's Aztlán?"

Mollie realized too late she had said too much. She tried to toss it off casually.

"Oh, it's a mythical place that's supposed to be the Aztec birthplace."

Cassidy thought about this for a minute. He tucked the name away in his mind for future reference.

"OK, Mollie. Q, give her her share."

Q counted out some coins, got up off the bed and brought them to her. He looked sad as he dropped them in her hand.

"Don't come crawling back to me later asking for a piece of the pie. Q and me are going to get that cross and sell it right away. I already have buyers lined up for the gold and the jewels. We'll be on our way to an island within a week. Good riddance."

Cassidy said the words, but a big part of him wondered if she wasn't right. He could see no way he would be able to be part of their expedition without Mollie. Unless.....

Mollie gave Q a hug, nodded to Cassidy and backed away out the door. She kept her hand on her gun, just in case. Cassidy turned away and heard the door slam when she left.

"Q, that is one messed up bitch."

He turned the word Aztlán over and over in his mind. He had to do some research.

The following day, Mollie showed up early at the church. She had fresh clothes, a small carpetbag with several changes of underwear and shirts, and extra ammunition. She also had a box of tools. The next to arrive was Sofie Pollak, the librarian and historian. They went into the sacristy, as they had previously agreed to with Father Mendoza, but no one else was there yet.

Mollie instantly engaged Sofie in conversation.

"How was your trip, Sofie? Have you ever been out west before?"

"Since coming to America, I've never even been out of New York, Miss McGuire. The trip was long, but I enjoyed seeing so much of the country. All of my life has been spent with books."

"Well, welcome to Arizona. We may have been the last territory to become a State but we're one of the first to give women the vote. I assume you're in favor of women's right to vote?"

Sofie laughed, "Funny you say that. The first thing I asked Gideon when I met him was how his wife felt about it. He wears a wedding ring, but I didn't know at the time that his wife is Méxican. I'm not sure things are the same there as they are in the States."

"No, they're not. I don't really know Carmelita very well, but of what I've seen, she is definitely in favor of women's rights. She's quite outspoken and seems to be highly opinionated. You know, since you're so interested, I'd like to introduce you to one of my Aunt Rosie's good friends, Frances Munds. She goes by her nickname, Fannie. She's been a strong advocate of the women's suffrage movement and is planning to run for the state senate this year."

"It's amazing to me," Sofie replied, "that many of the states in the West and Midwest seem to be in the forefront in the battle of equal rights for women. It frustrates me that in the so-called "liberal" northeast we cannot make the strides you seem to have made here. I'm an active member of the movement. I marched in the New York parade in May last year, although I wish I could have been in Washington, D.C. the day before Wilson's inauguration and marched then. I heard that was an amazing event. Tell me, Mollie, how does your aunt know Fannie Munds?"

Fannie was well known in feminist circles and Sofie was well acquainted with her work.

"Oh, Aunt Rosie owns her own business. You'd be surprised at the people she knows. Thing is, many women here in Arizona who support suffrage also support the temperance movement. The two seem to be inextricably intertwined here. It's in Aunt Rosie's best interest to stay involved in anything that may impact her business, and prohibition is *not* something she wants to see happen. They're talking about putting it on the ballot in November, and Aunt Rosie is lobbying against it. Although she's strongly in favor of women's suffrage. She knows many important businessmen and politicians and knows how to get them to do her will. We'll see how all of this plays out. The woman's vote here in Arizona will definitely have an impact on the outcome of the nation."

Gideon walked through the back door of the sacristy alone.

"Where's your wife, Gideon?" Sofie asked. She was hoping to ask about her feelings on the suffrage movement.

"Carmelita and Lena are speaking to some friends of hers who migrated here to the States. This war in México is creating a mess in all of the border towns. She's actually trying to find someone who may have knowledge of the Aztecs and the *Cortés* treasure. No offense, Ms. Pollak, we realize you know a lot, but the natives here have a long tradition of handing down stories from the past strictly through the spoken word. Maybe we can get some help that we can't find in books."

"I'm all for that, Mr. Riot."

Father Mendoza came in last. "Sorry I'm late. The Bishop has agreed to help fund the expedition if we can offer him solid information to back up the claim of the existence of *Aztlán* and approximate location."

Sofie chimed in, "I received a telegram from the library in New York. They're also willing to contribute a limited amount. Apparently, St. Peter's is taking up a collection too. I have to tell you though, that the library does expect that they'll be able to display any items we uncover."

"That's fine with me," Father Mendoza agreed.

Just outside the door leading to the sacristy, a small man was bent over a mop wearing a long poncho and large sombrero. Father Mendoza had just hired him to clean up the church proper. He had begged the priest to allow him to clean up as a penance for past sins. Father Mendoza took pity on the man, who appeared to be slow of wit and possibly had a disability. The man never looked up while speaking and only conversed in an odd dialect of Spanish. The priest wouldn't allow him to work for free, however, and agreed to pay him for a day's work, sweeping and washing the floors.

The man pressed his ear against the door to the sacristy and leaned on his mop. A lock of red hair fell out from beneath his hat, and he quickly swept it back. Cassidy was taking a big chance being here. But Gideon had not seen him in several years and his appearance had changed quite a bit. Mollie continued to be a problem, however. She knew him pretty well now and he felt she would recognize him despite his disguise.

All he needed to do was find out what the plans were and where the treasure was thought to be located. He and Quince could then make a choice - attempt to get there first; shadow them on their journey; or wait until they returned with the treasure and hijack it.

Sofie was just then explaining what she had found after examining the tin rubbing and checking the figures of the cross to her Aztec dictionary.

"The markings are definitely pointing us to what *Cortés* believed to be *Aztlán*. I was up all night checking and re-checking. I have a map of the territory that includes all of the land that was New Spain at the time, and I think I know the location marked by *Cortés*."

"Well, don't keep us in suspense," Gideon exclaimed, "tell us where it is!"

"The word *Aztlán* translates into "The Place of Herons," so we know it must be on or near the water. When the Aztecs left they believed they would be told by their gods where to settle. We now know that was *Tenochtitlan*, now *México City*. It is believed that *Aztlán* was also located on an island in the middle of a lake. The markings clearly mention this. Again, keep in mind, that what we are looking for is not necessarily the true location of *Aztlán*, it is what *Cortés,* or perhaps more accurately, *Doña Marina believed* was the location."

At that moment, they all heard a loud crash. Cassidy had inadvertently kicked over a bucket filled with water. He had been listening at the sacristy door when the front door of the church opened, and Carmelita and a woman he did not recognize appeared. In his haste to disguise himself so he wouldn't be noticed, he knocked over the bucket. As Carmelita and Lena walked towards the altar, he fell to the floor and called out in a loud, heavily accented voice, "*Está bien,* I clean."

His years in México helped him to fake a very good accent as he quickly got down on the floor with his mop to clean the mess. The last thing he needed was to be discovered now, when he was so close to finally getting his hands on the cross. He cursed Mollie under his breath. This was going to be so much harder without her.

Carmelita marched past and paid him no mind as she advanced towards the altar.

"Good morning, Father. Sorry I'm late, everybody. I was out visiting the Tohono O'odham tribe again. I have some news. There is an elder there who can recite folklore about a lost treasure. He says there is a story told in song of a lost treasure. It mentions Moctezuma and may be of help to us in our search. I didn't ask him to sing it to me, but he is willing. Do you think this can help?"

They all turned to Sofie.

"Yes," she replied quickly. "The legend may help us to substantiate what we have here and could even help with pinpointing the location. Let's go talk to your elder."

Father Mendoza said, "It's getting a little late. Do you think we can head out first thing tomorrow morning?"

They all nodded their heads in agreement.

As they left the church, Cassidy was on the floor sponging up the last of the water. He thought to himself that he had to find a way to shadow this group of treasure hunters. He and Quince couldn't do it alone. A plan began to form in his mind.

# **Chapter Eleven**

## *Aztlán*

The next morning, Quince and Cassidy sat on the bed and decided that now was the time to make a play for the cross. They knew the others would be heading out first thing to meet with the Tohono O'odham to listen to the folklore in song, and then would spend far too much time waiting for Carmelita to translate it. They would be gone all day and no one would be at the church. There could be no better time.

"Q, saddle up. We'll have to ride double until we can find a buckboard we can steal. Then, we head for the church, take down the cross, and head for the border."

Q didn't disagree often, but he did this time. "Cass'dy, can't go cross de bordah. Méxican's fightin' everbody. Les go ta Lusianne."

Cassidy thought about that, and realized Quince was right. The Méxican border was a mess. Villa was actively attacking U.S. interests across the border, bringing federal troops into the mix. There was no money to be had down there anyway. They had to find a place that was remote, with lots of people and activity, and plenty of places to fence goods. New Orleans was perfect. There they would be able to catch a boat for the Caribbean. Plus, he had always wanted to go to New Orleans. He heard great things about the nightlife.

"Good idea, Q. Let's go."

---

As morning broke, Carmelita, Gideon, Sofie, and Mollie left the church and headed out to the Tohono O'odham settlement. Lena returned to Tucson, and Father Mendoza changed his mind about going and opted instead to stay at the church to keep an eye on things.

Carmelita brought Sofie up to date on the history of the cross and the involvement of Cassidy and Colonel Greene. Sofie in turn told them what she knew of the history of the cross, *Cortés*, and Montezuma.

None of them knew that the place they were headed was almost exactly the same spot where centuries before Father Pachero handed the cross to the natives for safekeeping and as a symbol for their new church.

When they arrived at the Tohono O'odham village, Carmelita took over and introduced her friends. Her fluency in the native tongue from her years in Cananea was invaluable. Although she was raised speaking Spanish, many of the workers at the mines were members of the local tribes and she knew the Tohono O'odham language well. Sofie had all she could do to contain herself. She had many questions to ask of the people, not all related to the treasure. Never having been out of New York, she was fascinated and curious about the dress, habits, foods, language – virtually all aspects of the tribe. From the little she had seen thus far in this part of the world, it was a far cry from the dime novels she had read of the "wild west."

The Papago elder took them into an adobe hut which was one small room with a dirt floor. He instructed them to sit, as one of the native tribesmen handed out cool drinks. They were arranged in semicircular fashion and incense was lit lending an ethereal quality to the close surroundings. It was hot outside, but the interior was pleasant and cool.

Carmelita once again explained their mission and what they were hoping to learn. The elder listened intently and asked a few questions.

He closed his eyes and took in several deep breaths. Soon, he began a slow chant in a deep baritone that boomed off the walls which offered a natural echo.

Carmelita listened intently and did not interrupt until the elder paused and nodded. The story he told would fascinate them all and Gideon found himself mesmerized by the entire affair. He began to wonder if the incense was just a fragrance or if there was something more in the smoke.

It took a full ten minutes for the elder to complete the chant. They fell into an almost hypnotic trance and each felt their whole being transcended into a sublime state.

Carmelita broke the reverie when she quietly explained a little bit about Aztec gods and their myths. She then went on to loosely translate the elders' words.

"The Aztecs had many gods and believed in human sacrifice, which they practiced religiously on festival days. There were many such festivals dedicated to different gods and rites, but the one we are interested in, the one that is the subject of the elder's chant, is the god who is known as the "left-handed hummingbird." His name in Náhuatl is quite difficult to pronounce.

"He was the national god of the *Méxicas,* of which the Aztecs were a part, and also a god of the sun. He was also the primary god of war for the tribes, and was fully credited for both the successes and failures which the Aztecs suffered.

"The Aztecs offered human sacrifices to the gods and this god of war incited particularly vicious and unspeakable sacrifices."

Sofie, as the historian in the group, couldn't hold her tongue and spoke up. "What type of behaviors if I might ask, Carmelita?"

"It is gruesome but if you must know, the person selected for sacrifice would be placed on a sacrificial stone. The priest would take a blade made of some hard substance like obsidian, and cut through the abdomen of the victim while he was still alive and awake. The heart would then be torn out of the victim's body and lifted to the sky in honor of the sun-god. It is said that the heart and perhaps other parts of the body would then be given to a powerful warrior for a cannibalistic ritual. The remains would be incinerated, and the smoke floating towards heaven, was a further symbol of sacrifice."

"That's barbaric!" blurted Gideon.

"*Sí*, Gideon. It is to us. But to the Aztecs and other México's it was commonplace. In fact, there are stories that warriors would fight for the right to be the one chosen for sacrifice."

"Carmelita, what does all this have to do with a search for the treasure?" Mollie asked. She had to ensure her involvement and was trying to find a way to be useful.

"It's not important to the location of the treasure, but I thought you wanted to know all about the chant. I'll skip the rest of the gruesome details."

"Thank goodness for that." Gideon whistled.

"Let me try to make it simple. As we know, *Cortés* massacred the Aztecs and took their precious gold and jewels. Many believe this happened on the "Night of Sorrows," *La Noche Triste.* Actually, the massacre of the Aztecs occurred a month before in an event that has come to be known as the Massacre in the Great Temple.

"According to the elder's chant, the massacre occurred during the Toxcatl fiesta, a festival dedicated to one of their main gods, Tezcatlipoca.

"That would be very difficult for me to pronounce." Gideon chimed in.

Mollie smirked, but Carmelita ignored him and continued. "The festival culminated in the sacrifice of a young man who had portrayed the deity for the year prior to the event.

"*Cortés* was away at the time on the coast battling a contingent of soldiers sent to remove him back to Spain. One of his soldiers, Capitán Pedro de Alvarado, carried out a slaughter of the elite during the fiesta in his absence. The Spanish claimed it was due to the barbaric sacrifice which they attempted to stop, but the Aztecs believe it was because of the lust for the gold and jewels worn by the elite.

"The fiesta had begun with much singing and dancing. The Aztec people were dressed in their finest regalia and were unarmed. As always during fiestas, there was much gold worn to celebrate and this may have provided an additional incentive for the attack. No one really knows why, but Capitán de Alvardo had the exits blocked and had his soldiers brutally slaughter the celebrants.

"An alarm was sounded from within the temple, and stirred the people to action outside in the main square. Warriors broke through the barriers and launched a counter attack using spears and arrows. The Spanish forces were driven back into the palace enclave where they found Montezuma and put him in shackles. The Spanish retaliated with gunfire in an attempt to repress the siege.

"*Cortés* was on his way back from his travels and received word of the insurrection. He amassed an army of warriors from a tribe of the Nahuas sect as reinforcements. When he arrived back in the city, he found his troops sequestered and cut off from food supplies. By this time, *Cortés* and Montezuma had established a strong relationship and he thought he could quell the conflict by having Montezuma implore his people to stop the fighting. Unfortunately, Montezuma had lost the confidence of his own people due to his close ties to *Cortés* and the barbarous Spaniards."

Mollie interjected again. "So, the Spanish thought the Aztecs were barbarians and the Aztecs thought the same of the Spanish. Neither trusted the other, and the Spanish simply wanted the precious gold and jewels that the Aztecs possessed. This was all about greed."

"*Sí*, it was all about greed to the Spanish, but it was about religion to the Aztecs. Remember, they had thought *Cortés* was a god sent to them based on their legends. He proved to be anything but."

"So, Carmelita," Gideon inquired, "how does this relate to where *Cortés* believed was *Aztlán*? Where is the gold that the Spanish took that evening of the massacre?"

"Sorry, I know you're all eager to find the treasure. I just thought it would be important to know the whole story. Just to close out the story of the Temple, Montezuma at this point had lost the respect and admiration of his people, most likely because he developed a close relationship with *Cortés* who was now viewed for what he was – an opportunistic, sadistic conqueror. When *Cortés* brought him out to the balcony of the temple in an attempt to quell the conflict, Montezuma was stoned to death. Some say by the residents of the city, *Tenochtitlan*, and some say by the Spaniards, but either way, Montezuma met a tragic death.

"It was after this event, weeks later that *Cortés* and his soldiers left the city during *La Noche Triste*.

"So, what happened to the gold, you want to know? *Cortés* interacted with many other tribes during his time in México As evidenced by the fact that he solicited help from the Nahuas sect. Because of this, he heard many stories of *Aztlán* and its rumored locations. Now, there are many guesses as to where *Aztlán* was located, and some even say it was a myth, but

*Cortés* believed in its existence. We also know that more than a dozen years after his escape from *Tenochtitlan,* after he spent time back in Spain, he returned to explore the land in New Spain, but this time, to Baja California, a place he himself had discovered and named.

"It is believed it was there that he sent his men with as much of the gold and jewels as they could carry. Although it has been widely believed that the treasure *Cortés* smuggled out was lost during the time between the beginning of the Massacre and the Night of Sorrows, it has also long been theorized that he hid the treasure until the conflict cleared, to be moved at a later date. This chant seems to confirm that theory."

Mollie again spoke up, "So, all of this was in the chant that the elder just sang?"

"*Sí,*" she replied. "And most importantly, the name of the place where *Cortés* was told *Aztlán* originated."

She stopped and watched the faces of her audience. She knew they were dying to find out the location, but couldn't help but stop to enjoy the moment.

"Sweetheart," Gideon blurted out, "Where is it?"

"It is an island called *Mexcaltitán*. It has long been believed by many that this is the true location of *Aztlán*, although there are as many theories to where it's located as there are birds in the sky."

Gideon spoke up. "How can we know if that's the right place? Do the markings on the cross say anything about this island?"

Sofie took that one. "Most interesting. No, it indicates *Aztlán*, but not the specific location. I'm sure that is *Cortés* being clever. *Mexcaltitán* has long been rumored as the possible site of *Aztlán*, along with many other places. It is very well known to historians of the Aztecs. It's a small, man-made island on the mainland, southeast of the Baja across the Gulf of California, and a few hours north of Puerto Vallarta. The island is northwest of *México City* located on an estuary of the Sea of *Cortés*. The island floods during the rainy season and the locals have to use canoes to navigate the waters and go about their daily business. And to add to the intrigue, the streets of *Mexcaltitán* are in the shape of a cruciform – a cross. My guess is that Carmelita's correct. That's the best place to start."

Gideon made a decision. "Carmelita, please thank the elder. I think it's time we made plans to go back to México."

"One more thing," Carmelita interrupted, "the last verse of the chant may have been the most important, although its meaning is a little cloudy. It says, and I quote, 'The cross unlocks the treasure.' I think the Amulet of Cananea is that cross."

# **Chapter Twelve**

## *Border Wars*

Pancho Villa watched his image on the movie screen again, surrounded by his followers, commonly called the "Villistas." He never tired of seeing himself and loved that fact that Hollywood money was funding the carnage of his revolution.

Many of his battle scenes had to be reshot to appease the sensibilities of the American audience, whose taste for westerns seemed insatiable. The real battles were often deemed too graphic and grisly to play to a wide audience. One scene from an actual battle had to be deleted after projectionists in the Hollywood editing room were found scrambling for the bathroom as nausea swept over them. They had been reviewing scenes of Pancho's men knocking the teeth out of the heads of corpses to retrieve the gold in their teeth.

For a bandit who had changed his name from José Doroteo Arango Arámbula to Francisco (Pancho) Villa, and was hated and hunted by both the U.S. and Méxican regimes, he had a strange penchant for publicity.

Villa had his hands full. He was battling the current Méxican administration of President Huerta; the United States government all along the border; and also other revolutionaries who were jealous of his prominence. México was a political mess. Factions were everywhere. Villa's purported goal was primarily to usurp the current regime. He was an agrarian who wanted to give the land back to the people.

The politics of the revolution and rapid changes in leadership led to his alliance with Emiliano Zapata. Villa patrolled and led the revolution in the northern sectors of México while Zapata controlled the south. Between the two revolutionaries and the infighting of the generals and politicians, México was an unsafe place to travel, particularly for Americans. Villa had even been known to cross the border and lead attacks on U.S. soil.

An incident highlighting the risks for Americans had recently occurred in México. U.S oil companies had a substantial presence throughout the State of Veracruz, on the coast of the Gulf of México. They had significant investments in the area and large settlements of Americans were living there. The Méxicans were extremely hostile to the Americans. The turmoil of the revolution and the class war that started it all, fed the fear and hatred of the wealthy American workers, just as had occurred at the Cananea mines eight years earlier.

To make matters worse, President Woodrow Wilson had never acknowledged the Presidency of Mexican General Victoriano Huerta. Relations between the two countries were strained to say the least.

The American ambassador to México when Wilson came into office was Henry Lane Wilson, who was no relation to the President. He had been suspected of conspiring with Huerta and the revolutionaries, resulting in the coup d'état and execution of Méxican President Madero and Vice President Suárez.

Huerta, for his part, could never forgive the slight of Woodrow Wilson. When eight U.S. sailors were arrested by Méxican forces in the coastal town of Tampico, it created an international incident that led to a breakdown of diplomatic relations between the two countries.

The sailors had been tasked with facilitating the purchase and pickup of much needed fuel from a dealer located near the defensive line of Huerta's troops. They were confronted by soldiers of the Constitutionalist government. Neither side could speak the others language, causing further tension, and the sailors were marched off under armed guard.

Fortunately the situation was quickly resolved. But the Commander of U.S. naval forces in the area, Rear Admiral Henry T. Mayo, demanded an apology and 21 gun salute from the Méxicans. President Huerta released the sailors within 24 hours and sent a written apology, but refused to raise the U.S. flag on Méxican soil or offer the requested 21 gun salute.

With President Wilson increasingly being pulled into the European conflict, he was strongly encouraged to forget México and concentrate on the impending war. But he could not ignore U.S. interests in México. Not only were there substantial investments in both money and people, but strategically it was an important outpost for the U.S. Navy.

Wilson asked for, and received, backing from Congress for an armed invasion of Veracruz. The Méxican troops held their ground but U.S. forces continued to pour into the region. Several weeks of fighting lead to losses on both sides of the skirmish. The U.S eventually captured virtually all of the city and the relationship between the two countries was irreparably damaged.

---

Gideon and Carmelita sat in their kitchen late in the day with Mollie and Sofie discussing what they had learned from the elder at the Tohono O'odham village. Carmelita drank pulque, a milky alcoholic beverage made from the fermented sap of the agave plant, with just a little bit of water, just as her mother used to drink. Gideon preferred Tennessee Whiskey, Jack Daniels Old No. 7, since he couldn't get his grandfather's private batch in Arizona. He was worried that soon he wouldn't be able to get any whiskey. Prohibition was rearing its' ugly head. Fortunately, he had stockpiled a case of Jack anticipating just such an event.

And if the war in México would end anytime soon, he could always go across the border to get some. That's what they had always done when they wanted tequila before the revolution.

Sofie didn't drink alcohol and stayed with water, but Mollie matched Gideon and helped him through his bottle of Jack.

Given the threat of the Villistas and the border wars between the U.S. & Méxican governments, they could see no easy way to get to the place they believed *Cortés* thought of as *Aztlán*.

"We have to find a way to get to *Mexcaltitán,"* Gideon proclaimed, "this secret may have been buried for centuries, but now that we've cracked the code, there's no way to prevent it from leaking out. Even if we all vow to keep it secret and stay together, these things find a life of their own. Someone will get to it if we don't first."

"I agree with Gideon," Mollie jumped in. "We know that Cassidy is going to keep looking until he knows what we know. Eventually I have no doubt he'll find out what we're doing. We have to find a way, and fast."

Mollie was once again being disingenuous. She really did not add any value to what the others offered, but she was accepted into the inner sanctum by default and wanted to make sure she kept her hand in. She may not have done much to this point, but she was pretty sure she was the most deft at larcenous behavior.

"Carmelita," she continued, "you lived in México for most of your life. Did you know anyone who was involved with the revolutionaries, or maybe someone who had a military background who may be able to help?"

Carmelita thought for a few moments, and just shook her head no.

Gideon looked at her. He nodded his head slightly and whistled softly "Sure you do."

She looked at him, uncertain.

He whistled the next words with such pronounced sibilance, albeit quietly, that he startled Sofie who had been lost in thought contemplating the treasure and *Mexcaltitán*.

"Francisco de Torres. Wasn't he involved with Kosterlitzky?"

At the name Kosterlitzky, Mollie looked up sharply. She had lived on the border of México her whole life and knew that name well and the harsh reputation he deserved. The "Méxican Cossack of Sonora" was a brutal and widely feared military leader who had emigrated from Russia, and became one of México's most feared generals. He had been a staunch supporter of Porfirio Díaz during his reign. He believed in Díaz' disciplined rule and his desire to improve the fortunes of México through foreign investment. The current strong relationship between Germany and México could be traced to the policies enacted through the *Porfiriato*.

Kosterlitzky admired Díaz and his politics and used brute force tactics to squelch the uprisings of the proletariat. He retired just after the Revolution began and Díaz was overthrown. But when Madero, who he considered to be an ineffectual and weak leader, asked him to return, he could not resist the call of duty.

Kosterlitzky didn't like Madero, but he actively loathed Huerta. His sense of honor and commitment could not be compromised, however, and he continued to serve.

After he was captured by General Obregon at the first Battle of Nogales, he decided he had had enough and retired to the U.S. where, incredibly, he became a spy for America. But his reputation and legacy as a fearless and vengeful fighter was well known, particularly to those on the border.

Nogales was one of several towns that had been split in two after the Gadsden Purchase. The U.S. had purchased territories from México to resolve lingering border issues after the Treaty of Guadalupe Hidalgo, which had ended the first Méxican American War. Anyone living along the Arizona border would be well acquainted with Kosterlitzky's reputation.

Mollie knew his reputation and found she had new admiration for Carmelita based on Gideon's comment.

"Carmelita, who is this Torres?" she asked.

"He was head of security for Colonel Greene who owned the Cananea Copper Mines where I grew up. He was tough but always looked out for me. He's the one who hid the cross we now know of as the *Amulet of Cananea,* for years. He's also the one who helped my brother, sister, and me escape México after my parents died the day of the uprising and fight with the Arizona Rangers."

Carmelita did not feel the need to tell Mollie the whole story of Cassidy and her mother's rape. She knew that it may all come out someday, but not this day.

"He may be one person who can help us to get to *Mexcaltitán* safely, but I haven't spoken to him in years. I don't even know if he's still in Cananea. After Colonel Greene died, so many of the people I knew there had left."

Gideon piped up. "Carmelita, let's send a telegram to the copper mine office offering a time to make a telephone call to speak with Torres. If he's there, I'm sure he'll take the call, and if not, well, at least we'll know. We can use the phone at the Western Union office."

Sofie spoke up. "Wait a minute. Before anyone runs off to *Mexcaltitán,* we have a problem to solve."

"What's that, Sofie?" Gideon asked.

"Carmelita told us that the elder chanted, and I quote, 'the cross unlocks the treasure' right?"

"Yeah, so?" Mollie commented petulantly.

"Well," Sofie continued, "we know that the cross holds a clue to the location. But we don't know if the reference to the cross unlocking the treasure is allegorical, symbolic, or physical."

"Meaning what, exactly?" Carmelita asked. She was beginning to worry that maybe they were all overthinking this.

"Well, if it's symbolic or allegorical, then we have to find out how it relates, but if it's physical, we will need the cross with us to unlock the treasure. That means we would have to take the cross with us over the border. As dangerous as the journey is to begin with, taking an item with such historical and religious significance - not to mention its monetary value - is insane. But to go without it makes no sense at all if we need it to unlock the treasure."

Sofie looked at each of them in turn and saw the realization in their eyes. They did indeed have a dilemma. The seconds turned to minutes as each of them puzzled this out in their minds.

Gideon took charge. "O.K. right now, we have several issues to contend with. One - how do we get across the border safely and get to *Mexcaltitán* in the midst of a revolution? Two – who should go and who should stay behind? Three - if we were to get to *Aztlán*, if such a place exists except in legend, how do we "unlock" the treasure? Four - even if we succeed and could uncover the treasure, how would we ever get it back to the U.S.? And lastly, who does the treasure really belong to? Do you think we can just take millions of dollars' worth of gold artifacts and precious gems and walk across the border with it all? How would we even turn it into cash without attracting serious attention?"

They all sat for some time, absorbing the dilemma and trying to think of what to do. Carmelita spoke up. "Sofie, you already have the rubbings from the cross. So we have any written information we may need, correct?"

"Yes, that's right."

"If the reference is symbolic or allegorical, we can use that to figure it out, right?"

"Well, I can't be sure, but yes, that seems true."

"So, we would need the cross only if it is a physical key to the treasure. Right again?"

"Yes, I suppose. But Carmelita, I don't see what you're getting at."

"Well, we took rubbings to translate the language. We don't need the original in hand for that. What if we made a cheap metal casting of the cross? We could use it as a surrogate for the key and it wouldn't be of enough value to steal. Do you think that could work?"

"That's a great idea, Carmelita," Mollie enthused, "I can help you get a cast done of the cross. I know a blacksmith who used to shoe horses, but now does fine finish work on cast iron railings. I'm sure he would be able to do the job. I'll introduce you to him."

Sofie issued a word of caution. "It could work, but it may not. It's a risk, but I guess a much smaller and less dangerous risk than bringing the cross itself. OK. I guess it's a solid plan."

Mollie nodded her agreement.

They finished their drinks and made arrangements for Carmelita, Sofie, and Mollie to go to the church in the morning to talk to Father Beaudry about casting the cross. Gideon would go to the Western Union office to send a telegraph to de Torres using Carmelita's name, and inquire about a phone call once they received his response.

Mollie smiled to herself. She was successful in assimilating herself and helping search for the treasure. The

larceny in her heart had her thinking of her own plans for the
future.

# Chapter Thirteen

## *Theft*

"Q, saddle up. Take whatever you need. We're not coming back."

"What the plan, Cass'dy?"

"Look Q, Mollie knows where we are. She's decided to leave us behind and go after the treasure in México. That's a big gamble. What if nothing's there? She could be turning us in right now. She might have already stolen the cross and blamed us. It's happened to me before. She'll leave us behind and take off to México to find the rest of the treasure. I know you have a soft spot for Mollie, but I don't trust that conniving bitch."

Cassidy didn't want to tell Quince too much, but still needed his help. "I know a Méxican who will do what I ask with no questions asked for the right price. We're going to set him up as a guide for our group of treasure hunters. Then we're heading for the church to get the cross. Worst case is, we get the cross and leave town. If we can get the Mex set up with our 'friends', then we'll also have a crack at the treasure. Let's go. I'll explain more on the way."

Cassidy couldn't know about Carmelita and Gideon's plans travel to México, but he did know they were thinking of trying to find the treasure. He had heard many stories of where the lost treasure of *Cortés* might have been stored, and his personal belief was that it was located somewhere north of the border in the U.S. At the time of *Cortés*, of course, that was still México aka New Spain. Cassidy believed that it was probably not far from where they were now, near Tucson. But either way he would try to get his friend set up as a guide for the Sonoran region and offer his services to Carmelita and her colleagues.

As they rode towards *San Xavier del Bac,* he offered a brief explanation of his plan to Quince.

Cassidy never had many friends while he was in Cananea, or really anywhere else for that matter. But for the brief time he lived in El Paso, he bonded with the closest thing to a friend he ever had. He got himself into a world of trouble there, and, in fact, it was there that he met the woman who would eventually lead to his arrest and imprisonment.

He explained to Quince that he knew of one man who came from there of Méxican descent who was a kindred spirit. His name was Desiderio Camino, known to all as Desi.

He met Desi at Madam Tillie Howard's Parlor Cantina. You couldn't call them friends, but they both had an appetite for young ladies. They ran across each other frequently in the bars and cathouses, and Cassidy and Desi had once teamed up to scam an out-of-towner of his hard earned wages, leaving him destitute and under arrest for vagrancy.

Cassidy told Q that Desi could be counted on to shadow the treasure hunters – for a fee of course, and that he was a personable hombre who could charm them and earn their trust.

"The good news is, Desi is here, in Tucson. He came this way after he ran out of friends in El Paso. I'm sure I can find where he hangs his hat. But we can't give him all the money up front. Otherwise, he'll be gone. We give him half in advance and the other half on completion of the mission. We'll also promise a bonus if the treasure is found. I can't completely trust him, but he'd rather take his chances with us than with them."

"Why, Cass'dy? How you know he not sell out to them for mo' money?"

"That's easy, Q. We'd give him up to the law if he crosses us. The others too. He has larceny in his heart, and as they say, there's honor among thieves. He can't take a chance of being found out by Carmelita and her crew. They're not in it for the money so much as for the glory. He'll take his chances with us. "

Q listened and nodded. Quince wasn't taken to saying much, but he would let Cassidy know if he disagreed. He knew that Cassidy thought of him as stupid and a muscle-bound oaf to do his bidding, but Quince had another side. He had graduated high school and was accepted to attend college at Louisiana State before he got into trouble with the neighborhood gang. He had a football scholarship due to his size and speed, and he also had a much sharper mind than he let on. Cassidy, like others from outside Louisiana, thought his accent inferred stupidity, but nothing could be further from the truth. Q was watching Cassidy closely and making his own plans.

"Q, you're from Louisiana. You figure out a place to hole up in New Orleans after we have the cross. I'm going to talk to Desi and see if I can get him set up with the priest at the church. He can take my place. I'll tell Father Mendoza that I have to leave due to family issues and recommend Desi for the job. Then Desi will find out what the plans are to find the treasure and, hopefully, act as guide. All of this hinges on the treasure search being done outside the area that Carmelita and Gideon already know, but I have a good feeling about this. This is going to work."

Quince nodded once again and thought about his own next steps.

# **Chapter Fourteen**

## *Ironworks*

Gideon entered the Western Union office on the south side of Tucson to send the telegram to the Cananea Copper mines. He was a little concerned about this part of the plan. Carmelita had left Cananea just after the workers strike. A shootout at the mines at the hands of the Arizona Rangers, who had crossed the border illegally, was widely considered the spark of the Méxican revolution. Her father was gunned down while trying to stop the battle, unarmed and unafraid.

Carmelita and Gideon had spent many late nights talking about her experiences in Cananea and the difficult times she and her family had there. He knew she trusted Francisco de Torres, and that she had revered Colonel Greene. But Greene had died two years earlier and the mines were now owned by a conglomerate. He doubted de Torres was even there anymore, and wasn't sure he wanted to alert anyone else at the mines to Carmelita's whereabouts.

He gave some thought to the idea of sending the message to de Torres in some type of code by referencing Carmelita without specifically mentioning her name. He wanted to protect her whereabouts since he didn't know who would receive it. With no idea if de Torres was even still working at the mines, he had good reason for concern.

Still, she had insisted that he send it in her words, and he was convinced he didn't have to worry about anyone crossing the border. The ongoing revolution saw to that.

As Gideon headed out of the Western Union office after sending the message, the sun rose high in the Arizona sky and the temperature soared. It was late spring as Gideon passed by the new *Tucson Citizen* newspaper building. The original building had burned down two years earlier and the replacement building had only recently been completed. Gideon walked down the new pavement walkway – the first one in Tucson. He crossed the street to drive back to his business in one of his electric cabs, a late model which he got at a good price. The newer gas models were still rare in Arizona and it was easier for him to charge the taxi with electricity than find a gas station.

As he slowly drove out of town, avoiding horses and the mess they left behind, he didn't notice the two men crossing the street in the other direction, a hundred yards down the road. Had he looked that way, he would have witnessed a sight straight out of one of the new Mack Sennett Keystone Kops movies – a small, pale man with a shock of red hair who was hunched over as if in constant pain, followed closely behind by a giant of a man of considerably darker skin. It had a comical effect – a small redheaded man with a cane followed by a dark skinned giant.

Had he witnessed this amusing spectacle, he would never have guessed at the events that would transpire in the coming weeks caused by these two seemingly hapless buffoons.

As Gideon drove home he noticed that the roads were filled with many more cars than was the case only a few weeks earlier. He also noticed that they were all gasoline powered which had become so much more popular than the electric models in the past couple of years.

Pavel had warned him of this. When Gideon decided to buy electric cabs, he sought out Pavel's counsel. He had sent Pavel a long letter. He really would have liked to go back to New York and spend more time with him but the journey was too long and he had a business to run. Luisa did a great job in the office, but it needed his guidance and knowledge to really make it successful. In his closing comments he did invite Pavel again to join him in Tucson. He thought Pavel would do well in the growing town.

A telephone call would have been a good alternative for reaching Pavel if it wasn't so expensive. Plus, few people in Tucson had telephones in their homes and he was sure Pavel didn't. He thought about sending a telegram, but they were not designed for long communications and could also be expensive.

Gideon was surprised when he received a letter back from Pavel a few weeks later. It was crudely written, and when he opened it he thought the writing looked like that of a woman. In fact, once he read through, he realized that Pavel's cousin, Anna, wrote the letter which Pavel must have dictated.

Gideon smiled at the thought of Anna and her son, Stach. He couldn't stay mad at the boy even though he had stolen his watch. He actually reminded Gideon of himself when he was young – full of piss and vinegar.

Pavel strongly cautioned Gideon not to purchase electric cabs. "They are quiet and easy to start and women can handle them. They don't have the smell or noise of gas models, and you don't need a hand crank to start them," he wrote, "but they don't go very fast, and the new gas models now come with an electric starter which makes it much easier."

Gideon was familiar with the trouble with hand cranks. It was a major reason he chose an electric cab instead of gas. Men would often suffer injuries from the onerous task of cranking the engine, sometimes even suffering broken arms.

Pavel's letter continued, "New cars also have drum-style brakes. The old lever brake was too dangerous."

Gideon knew he was referring to the fact that sometimes, drivers forgot to apply the lever brake when they cranked the starter. Too often, it would roll forward over the person cranking the engine.

The letter concluded with a personal note from Anna herself. "Gideon, we have you to thank for bringing my family together again. Pavel and Stach tell stories about you and your funny ways. Stach wants me to tell you he's sorry he took your watch. It was habit. He knows no other way. I hope we someday see you again."

While Gideon drove back to his office, he reflected on Pavel's recommendation and thought of his business and buying gas model taxis. He also wondered about the new fueling stations which he had read about beginning to take hold in the northeast. He heard that Gulf oil had built a drive-in gas station in Pittsburgh on Baum Avenue the previous year and it was very popular. So popular, in fact, that auto dealerships were growing up all around it, touting the fact that you could drive out of the lot with your new car and "fill 'er up" at the new drive through. The area became known as "automobile row."

Until that time, a driver bought gas in cans. They were sold in hardware stores, general stores, even pharmacies. It was expensive and only came in small containers.

As Gideon drove along thinking of all this in his cab, which hummed quietly along thanks to the electric engine, Cassidy and Quince were combing the saloons and cathouses on the South side of Tucson.

Cassidy, meanwhile, was thinking that the impending temperance movement and women's vote was going to have a serious impact on the businesses he and Quince were searching. He could envision it wouldn't be long before there were no more saloons and brothels in Arizona at all. He would soon find out how right he was.

For now, he knew that the places still in business would surely be on the list of things to do for Desiderio Camino. Desi was a creature of the shady side of life. He spend all day hustling and had both legitimate ventures as well as illegitimate ones. He always found a way to make money and the money he made during the day was all spent at night.

It didn't take long for Cassidy to find Desi. He and Quince had split up and Cassidy went directly to his favorite haunts in Gay Alley on Meyer Street.

He pushed through the double swinging doors of a place called The Lone Stallion, just across the street from The Gilded Cage, the bordello he had previously been asked to leave. As his eyes adjusted to the light, he noticed Desi sitting at a table with a bottle of cheap bourbon talking to a young girl who couldn't have been any older than 17. As Cassidy started across the room to the table, the young girl stood up quickly and slapped Desi across the face, hard. She threw what was left of her drink at him and stormed out of the room.

Desi stood up and seemed about to run after her when he saw Cassidy slowly approaching. He wiped his face, sat down, and poured himself a drink. Desi was average height, but even sitting down, he was face to face with Cassidy who stood behind the chair opposite him. Cassidy's infirmities seemed to have eaten away at him and he appeared much shorter than the last time Desi had seen him.

"Well, Desi, I see you still have your legendary charm." He sat down and poured himself a glass of the bourbon, using the same glass as the young girl.

"Cassidy." He said the word without any inflection at all. Just a blank statement. "What the hell are you doing here? I heard you broke out of Florence, but thought for sure you'd be out of the States by now. With the craziness of that so-called revolution in México, it should be easy to get across the border. Just head out to El Paso and get a job as an extra in one of the movies that madman Pancho Villa is making. You could slip back across at night with the rest of his crew. I swear the mess they have down there – what they call a "revolution" will drag on for another 10 years. It's total madness. Even the revolutionaries fight one another."

"Yeah, well, who cares? Let 'em all kill each other. Listen, Desi. I don't have much time, I have a proposition for you. The payback could be huge, but it'll take some time and there's risk. You interested in hearing more?"

"Cassidy, I have nothing but time. This state is about to pass prohibition, and prostitution won't be far behind if the damned suffragettes have anything to say about it. I'm getting out either way. What's your scheme?"

---

While Cassidy was explaining the plan to Desi, which took an entire afternoon and most of the bottle of bourbon, Mollie was on her own mission – finding a way to cast as near perfect a copy of the Amulet as possible without making it look valuable. Since all that was needed was a physical representation, she thought that the jewels were irrelevant, and the metal could be cheap casting iron. It would be heavy, but that only made it less interesting to anyone thinking of stealing it.

Tucked away in a side street just a few blocks from where Cassidy and Desi were conspiring, Mollie approached one of the last surviving blacksmith shops in Tucson. The remaining few rarely catered to farrier work which had long been a staple of their business. Shoeing horses and hammering out the shoes had always been only a small portion of what a skilled blacksmith could accomplish. Now, with the rapid increase in the use of automobiles and decline of the need for their traditional skill of molding, twisting, and manipulating metal objects, many of the blacksmiths had turned to automobile repair to make up for the decline in their conventional business.

While most had moved into working with automobiles, a few had continued on the tradition of forging and shaping metal into objects such as lattice fences, gates, and other types of decorative metalwork, including religious items. Such was the case with the man she was going to see.

Mollie's thoughts went back to her father, who had been a cattle rustler by trade, but called himself a "maverick rancher."

He inherited this trait from Mollie's grandfather Earl, who had done some jail time with Sam Maverick. Sam was an ornery man, who had always refused to brand his cattle. The owners of surrounding ranches always suspected Maverick held to that view so he could claim any unbranded cattle as his own, a technique Earl copied with limited success.

The story Mollie heard from her father years later, was that her grandfather Earl had fought the Méxicans side by side with Maverick when Santa Ana sent General Ráfael Vásquez in an attempt to reclaim Texas in 1842.

Mollie's grandfather was a major bullshitter and told stories most would never believe. She suspected this was just another in a long line of stories that he told to justify his family's illicit history. Her father inherited this trait and continued in the grand tradition of stealing horses. There were few unbranded cattle left when her father, Stoney, plied his trade.

His specialty was in brand changing, using a branding iron to add a symbol to an existing brand and claiming the horse as his own. Stoney was a drifter and he would drive his stolen cattle hundreds of miles to sell. He would then stay just long enough to rebrand cattle, steal fresh horses, and move on. He stopped when he was caught in Yuma and hanged for horse thievery. Mollie never really knew him and she was just four years old when he died. She had been raised by her mother and grandparents until her mother met and married the stepfather she would later shoot.

Her grandmother was a kindly soul, very self-sufficient and resourceful. Her grandfather came and went over the course of her early childhood, moving cattle all across the west. After the shooting, Mollie, her grandmother, and mother lived a comfortable life on the ranch with only two ranch hands. Mollie never knew where the money to live came from, always assuming raising horses yielded enough money to take care of their needs.

Her grandfather would leave for months at a time and only stay for a very short while when he returned. Her grandmother, whom she called "Nana," didn't seem to mind. She worked all day, cooking and cleaning, and after dark sat with a bottle on the covered porch until bedtime. She would just sit and rock in her chair, looking out at the landscape of mesquite and the hardscrabble land just waiting for Earl to come home.

The ranch hands took care of the horses and bought and sold them when Earl would inevitably show up again driving dozens of horses. She rarely saw her mother, even though they all lived in the same small ranch house. Her mother seemed to have had the life sucked out of her after Mollie killed her stepfather, and just never recovered. She died of natural causes a few years later and Mollie stayed with her grandparents until her grandmother passed on.

At 16, Mollie left and went to Tucson to stay with her Aunt Sadie. She had already lived a hard life and exposure to Sadie's lifestyle only made her that much tougher.

As Mollie entered the one-story blacksmith shop, where much work had been done for her father and then Nana when she ran the ranch, she called out for the owner.

"Vernon, its Mollie Maguire."

Mollie had been aware of the irony of her name for as long as she could remember. Her Nana had told her it had been her father's idea to name her Mollie. He liked the sound of it, but more than that, he liked the stories he heard about her namesake, the Irish secret society. The society had begun in Ireland to protest the poor working conditions in the fields. The rift between landowners and workers often turned violent and when the horrendous working conditions in Ireland became too much to bear, they left for America to start anew in the coal mines in Pennsylvania. They were greeted there by conditions as bad or worse than what they had left.

The workers rebelled yet again, and took up the Molly Maguire battle cry, instigating aggression and anarchy against atrocious and deplorable working conditions. The mine owners would employ children to work the mines, many of whom died from starvation, heat stroke, cave collapses, and other horrifying conditions. As a secret order operating under the aegis of the Ancient Order of Hibernians, their mission was to fight by any means possible for improved conditions in the mines. They were combative and controversial and effective in causing trouble, but ineffective in forcing change.

Mollie changed the spelling of her first name in large part to distance herself from the anarchistic group, but in her heart she held the same beliefs as her namesakes.

A short, stocky man with a day's growth of dark stubble stepped out from behind the forge wiping his hands on a cloth that must have once been white, but was now as black as coal. He wore a long leather forge apron with bits of scale attached, scattered like frozen bubbles of water. His boots were heavy and scarred with sores where the hot metal bit through the leather and exposed the metal toe.

His fine, dirty blonde hair was receding and he had the same perpetual smile on his face that Mollie remembered well.

"Mollie McGuire," he fairly yelled, "as I live and breathe."

He came quickly towards her and lifted her up in the air as if she were a small doll.

Mollie had known the man she called "Uncle Vern" her entire life. Although her father, and his father before him, were scoundrels and horse thieves, Vern never knew this about them. Her father, when he was still in the area, always paid well and took trouble not to expose any of his illegal affairs while in the Tucson area. Vern also did work for her grandmothers' ranch for years. Mollie would never know it, but Vern rarely charged her for anything more than the cost of materials.

Vern was a god-fearing, church-going man who loved the country his parents had adopted as home. His strong English and Irish roots gave him the gift of gab and of song, and he sang all the while as he would lean over the incredibly hot furnace he needed to ply his craft. He also had the Irish love of drink and was known to frequent the bars in town singing at the top of his lungs until the he was finally the last one to leave.

Vern's favorite song was George M. Cohan's "Yankee Doodle Boy" from his Broadway show "Little Johnny Jones" about an American who goes to England to ride in a derby and is accused of throwing the race. It had been a huge hit in New York a decade earlier, and songs from the show were often played by piano players in the saloons. Vern loved that it had elements of his parent's country of birth as well as his own.

He was an advocate for joining the impending war in Europe, a controversial subject which President Wilson had been avoiding since he was inaugurated in March. Vern was often heard saying "If I were a younger man, I would be back in England right now signing up to fight the Huns."

Mollie loved Vern and would trust him with her life. She knew he could be trusted to keep a secret.

"What brings you to see me, Mollie?"

Mollie explained the situation to Vern, who listened without interruption. When she mentioned she was working with Father Mendoza at the White Dove, he was immediately interested. He knew the church and the priest well and was more than happy to help.

"So, Mollie, let me understand. You need a replica of the cross in case it really is the key that unlocks this treasure?"

"Yes, Uncle Vern. That's what we believe. Although it might just be the glyphics on the cross that's needed. But we have those on paper so don't need the cross to be an exact replica."

"Well, since you don't know what you don't know, I think the safe thing would be for me to replicate the cross including the glyphics, don't you?"

"You can do that?"

"Sure. It'll take a little longer, but I can do it. I can add cheap replicas of the jewels as well. But a key would need to have all the same dimensions of the original, right?"

"Yes – why?"

"What about its weight?"

"I never really thought of that as being important. Is that a problem?"

"Well Mollie, I don't know. I'll have to see the cross and take dimensions including the weight. When can we go see it?"

"Now's good."

Vern laughed out loud.

"Mollie, I can't go now. Sunday would be best. I'll be there anyway. For Mass. Can you arrange it with Father Mendoza?"

"Thanks, Uncle Vern. I'll take care of it. See you Sunday."

As Mollie rode away on her quarter horse, Vern looked after her and shook his head.

"That girl is something else," he thought to himself.

Little did he know.

# Chapter Fifteen

## *Replication*

After Mass on Sunday, Gideon, Carmelita, Sofie, Mollie, and Vern met in the sacristy with Father Mendoza.

Vern turned the cross over in his hands and marveled at the intricate work and the weight of the gold. He could not believe this precious artifact had been displayed and exposed in the church's altar.

As he turned the cross over in his hands, he realized the difficulty of replicating the weight of this object. Gold is an extremely heavy and dense metal and there is really nothing like it, and certainly nothing inexpensive enough to be economically feasible.

"Well, you're right. This is solid gold. 24 carat, which is essentially one hundred percent gold. No other metals mixed in. I had hoped it may have been a lower grade, but this is definitely real. The problem is, there is no way to fake the weight of gold. At least not at a reasonable cost. The only thing that comes close is a relatively new substance called Tungsten. Also known as Wolfram, it is virtually the same weight, but it's still rare and expensive. It's being used by the Germans now for hardened steel in weaponry. Oddly enough, they won the rights to mine the Wolfram in England and ship it home for just that purpose. I suppose the Brits will rectify that soon with the increasing tensions in Europe. I just don't see how we can fake this weight."

They all looked to Sofie who seemed to be lost in thought. After what seemed like minutes, she looked up and realized they were all looking to her for direction.

"Well, since I'm the one who raised the question of the various ways the cross can be used as the key, I guess we have to make a decision. We can't fake the weight of the cross, so,

Vern, can you do the best you can to approximate it given what you know? We'll just have to take our chances."

Gideon spoke up. "Agreed. Now that we have that out of the way, let's plan our journey."

Vern left with his measurements and a roughly drafted sketch of the cross, including the location and types of stones used, as the others set about the task of planning the trip. He could calculate the weight based on the dimensions. He promised to have a fairly accurate replica within a week.

Gideon took charge. "Father Mendoza, thank you for your help and support in this effort. With all you have to do to tend to your duties here, I don't think it would be wise for you to accompany us to México. Rest assured, however, that we will ensure the Church is well represented and compensated if and when we find and retrieve the treasure."

The priest simply bowed his head slightly and began to take his leave.

"We do want you to help us with our planning. Please stay and contribute your ideas."

"Carmelita, you should stay behind also and take care of the business. I expect it'll be rough going and I don't want to take a chance of you getting hurt in México."

Carmelita nearly exploded. *"¡Estás demente! No es posible. ¡Me voy!"*

"Calm down, Carmelita, I can't understand you." Gideon tried to hug her as she continued her rant.

Carmelita took a breath and switched to English continuing in rapid fire.

"Gideon, I am the only Méxican here. I speak the language. I have seen both parents killed and witnessed the start of the Revolution. Without me, you wouldn't even have the amulet. There is no way any of you can get to where you need to go without me." She huffed and stamped her feet all the while, then slipped back into Spanish, marching around the room and yelling loudly.

"Carmelita's right, Gideon."

He turned and stared at Mollie as if he forgot the others were even there.

"She has to go," she said. "No one else knows all that she does about the Amulet, the country, the history, even the native tribes. Especially de Torres. She has to go, and I can help. I shoot better than anyone here. I'll be good support for you, too."

Gideon looked from Mollie to Carmelita, to Father Mendoza. They all seemed to be slightly shaking their heads in agreement.

"OK. I guess you're right. There's strength in numbers. What about you Sofie? Do you want to come along too?"

"I came all this way to do what I could to help. The library and St. Peter's are counting on me to help find the treasure. I think I'll be an asset when we find it. But don't expect me to do any fighting."

"OK. Then it's settled. But I'm not sure about three women and one man on an unauthorized mission through hostile territory smack in the middle of the revolution. Maybe we should talk to the tribes and see if they can help.

"Sofie and I can go talk to the Papago," Carmelita suggested. "They'll be interested to hear about what we're doing. But I want to be careful. With so much at stake, we can't have the whole world involved."

"OK. We have the beginnings of a plan. Let's meet up at my office tomorrow and we can go through the logistics. Think about it overnight and bring your ideas. See you tomorrow. I'm going to stop at the Western Union office on my way back to see if we have a reply from Torres yet."

---

Just as the group left the mission, Cassidy and Desi rode down the approach road in a buckboard on their way to speak with Father Mendoza. Cassidy was dressed in his peasant garb. He instructed Desi to speak in broken English, although he had been born in South Texas and spoke English much better than Spanish.

They entered the nave and Father Mendoza was there with the cross in his hands climbing a ladder.

"*Hola, Padre Mendoza,*" he called out.

Cassidy raised his hand in greeting and elbowed Desi. He whispered, "That's the cross I've been telling you about."

Father Mendoza approached the apex of the altar and affixed the cross in the metal shadow box which had been built especially for the display and then set the combination. The man who made the custom frame suggested that a combination lock would be more secure as no one could lose or steal the key.

The effect was not lost on Cassidy and he resolved to somehow get that combination.

Father Mendoza said to Cassidy, "You do understand English, correct amigo?"

Cassidy hung his head and nodded "*Un poco.*"

"Well, I'm glad you stopped by, but unfortunately I have to let you know that I will no longer need your services. I feel bad about this, but the Papago have offered to help with things at the church in exchange for me to help some of their little ones learn English. It has been a long time, but they finally see the value in learning the new language. You are welcome to join them."

Cassidy was crestfallen. His whole plan had been predicated on setting up Desi for the job so he could tail the others on their treasure hunt in México.

Father Mendoza could see the concern on his face.

"Tell you what. I'm sure we can find some work for you in town or maybe even at the reservation. Do you want me to see what I can do?"

Desi looked at Cassidy and then said to the priest, "Father, I am Desi Camino. I heard about the plan to go to México and use the cross as a key to the lost treasure of *Cortés*. Don't ask how I know this. Let's just say that it's a small town and word gets around. I asked my *compadre* here to introduce me. The reason is that I am extremely knowledgeable in the history of the lost treasure and know the country well. I believe I can help your friends locate the treasure and help protect them from harm. Would you do me the honor of introducing me to them? I am sure they will see the value in what I can offer."

Cassidy was taken completely by surprise at Desi's impromptu invitation, but saw the wisdom in what Desi proposed. Without some type of scheme they were out of luck. He held his tongue and put on his most sincere face.

Father Mendoza thought back to Gideon's comments about three women and one man, and Desi looked to be an able bodied man. He saw no harm in an introduction. Gideon was smart. He would know if it was the right thing to do. But Father Mendoza had been pastor of this parish for many years. He was cautious by nature.

"Well, Desi. Your request seems reasonable. Let me talk to the others and we'll get back to you. How can I reach you?"

"I don't have a place in town yet, Father. Let me stop by in a couple of days and see if you have had the chance to discuss with them. By then I will have a place to stay and we can work on the details."

With that, Cassidy and Desi bid the priest a good day and left quietly.

Father Mendoza stared after them and turned to the altar to say a prayer for his friends.

Cassidy was uncharacteristically quiet on the ride back to town. He had to catch up with Quince and fast.

When they got back to town, Desi dropped Cassidy off at this hotel and went to pack for his trip to México. When they split, they congratulated each other on the impromptu plan which seemed to have worked, and Desi promised to keep Cassidy informed.

"Pick me up first thing in the morning, Desi. I know better than to trust you. You don't want to double cross me and Quince."

Desi nodded. Cassidy may not be much of a threat, but Quince was another story.

Cassidy climbed the back stairs to his room and entered to find Quince oiling what looked like an older model Colt SSA (single action revolver.) Ironically known as "The Peacemaker," the same name Cassidy had given his Bowie knife, it had been in use by the Army for decades, but was also used by almost every gunslinger Cassidy had ever known.

"Cass'dy. How it go wid Desi?"

"I hate to say it Q, but you were right. Desi doesn't need us now, and he probably wouldn't have anyway, once I introduced him. The priest doesn't need my services any longer. The tribes are helping him in exchange for teaching English to their kids. They also promised to help protect the cross. Desi was quick enough and smart enough to offer his services as guide and the priest is going to talk to the rest of them to propose that. We're screwed. Where'd you get the gun?"

"T'ree card monte off greenhorn just got ta town. Taught he know'd eveythin."

Cassidy eyed Quince. He had more skills than he imagined.

"Listen, Cass'dy. We ben heah too long. Flo'ence prison not sebenty five miles from heah. I got to go. Cain't wait no longer."

Then it hit Cassidy. They were betting on a guess that treasure existed and was where they hoped, when they had a sure thing just waiting to be taken. The cross would give him enough to be happy for long time. Why be greedy?

"You're right, Q. Time to move on. This cross has been nothing but trouble for me. But we have to have money, the take from the stage is running low. Tell you what – let's leave tomorrow. We can get out of town before dawn. But maybe the best idea is what you said the other day – let's take the cross and fence it in New Orleans, we have enough to get us that far. Then we can catch a boat to South America. The priest just told me today that the tribe will be protecting the cross, but I don't think they'll start till tomorrow. Let's grab some shut eye. We can get to the church in the middle of the night, take the cross, and be out of the state before they know it's missing. This is our chance."

"Now ya talkin' Cass'dy."

Cassidy and Quince sat at the small table in the hotel room and mapped out their plans.

"Q, you go to the hardware store and buy the things we need to remove the cross. You'll need a hammer and screwdriver. Better get some rope too, just in case."

"Wud 'bout a ladder? Din't you say the cross is bove da altar?"

Cassidy looked at Quince again and stopped a moment. He really was brighter than he was giving him credit for.

"Good idea, Q. Get a small ladder. Get me a Bowie knife too. Nothing too expensive. I've been feeling naked without my knife and we need to have weapons. Now go – we need to get some shuteye. We're getting up early."

# <u>Chapter Sixteen</u>

## *Divine Intervention*

The town was dead quiet under a moonless sky. The only sound to be heard was a lone coyote howling at the luminous stars. Cassidy shook Quince's foot roughly. "Q," he whispered. "Time to go."

Quince rubbed the sleep out of his eyes and nodded. Once the decision had been made the night before, they planned the theft and packed their few belongings into a canvas rucksack. Everything in one for the sake of expediency. Except for the Bowie knife Quince had brought back for Cassidy. That was strapped to his right leg. It was a nice one too, not expensive, but it had a nice ten inch blade and the handle was solid. The cross guard was long, which was a style Cassidy preferred. Quince had hitched the horse to the buckboard before he went to sleep and left some hay and water so they would be all ready to go.

"You have the gun?" Cassidy whispered.

"Cos I hab de gun, Cass'dy. What kinda question dat?"

Quince was getting increasingly irritated with Cassidy. They hadn't known each other very well or for very long at the prison. Quince pretty much kept to himself. Cassidy had approached him only a few weeks before the break out, and Quince knew it was because of his size and his strength. He also knew that Cassidy thought he was dumb. Quince let him continue to believe that. He had his own plans and they didn't include Cassidy. He was shrewd enough to suspect Cassidy had a similar plan, but now that Quince knew the location of the cross, he didn't need Cassidy anymore. The only reason he was keeping up the pretense was to set Cassidy up for the theft. He was well aware that Cassidy needed Quince due to his infirmities, so he let him continue to believe he didn't have the smarts. Cassidy would find out soon enough.

The mission was several miles from where they had stayed in south Tucson and it would take the better part of an hour to get there. Located in an exposed area of the parse and barren land, it was tough to approach unseen. Cassidy had scouted the location and noted that there was a hill just to the east of the mission covered in scrub that was close enough to hide the horse and buckboard allowing them to approach on foot.

Thirty-five minutes later, they arrived. Much sooner than they expected, and that was a bonus. Pulling up behind the ridge to the east of the mission, Quince climbed down and looked up expectantly to Cassidy.

"Cass'dy. Ya comin?" he whispered.

"No, Q. I'll wait here. I'll only hold you back. It's just a small cross we're after. It won't take two of us to carry it. Besides, I can stay behind and act as lookout. Once you have the cross and I see you come out of the mission, I'll giddyap and pick you up. We'll get out of here, and fast."

Quince stared at Cassidy He was trying to see how this could be a trick, but if he had the cross, he couldn't see why it wasn't a good idea.

"K, Cass'dy. Makes sense."

"Give me the gun, Q. I'll need it, if we're found out. Plus, it might come in handy for rattlers."

Quince was more than suspicious, but could see the logic in what Cassidy was asking. He couldn't very well shoot him here in front of the mission. It would wake the padre and all the workers and bring the Tohono O'odham breathing down both their necks. Plus, he would have the cross.

He handed the gun to Cassidy, who checked it to make sure there was a bullet in the chamber.

140

"Now hurry, Q. Let's get this done once and for all. I can almost smell that jambalaya cookin' now."

Quince couldn't help but smile at the thought of having some good home cookin' back in New Orleans. He grabbed the hammer, screwdriver, rope, and ladder, and headed out to the mission. The moonless night helped cover his movements, but he also worried about the rattlers Cassidy mentioned. He got to the back door of the mission without incident, within minutes. He entered through the same door Cassidy had entered during the brief time he worked there. He had made a copy of his key for just this reason.

Quince realized then that Cassidy always intended to steal the cross whether they followed the rest of the group to México or not.

Quince was not the most nimble person, and he made much more noise than he intended. The ladder was the problem. It was awkward and he kept banging it on the ground as he walked along from the sacristy to the altar. Once he got there, he set it up and realized the cross was much higher than anticipated. Even with the ladder and his height, he had to stretch up to reach the brass covering that they had installed to protect it.

The interior of the mission is covered in a number of paintings, murals, frescoes, statues, and other crosses. It is dazzlingly colorful and a perfect example of Spanish baroque architecture. The high arches gave it a cavernous feeling but for the dizzying array of color which made the church feel warm.

Quince had anticipated an easier time of it. Cassidy had left before the new brass enclosure was in place, and they had both assumed it would be no more difficult than simply prying it loose.

Quince began to sweat as he reached as far over his head as he could to attack the covering. The cross had been secured with a type of brass security shadow box. There was no glass or see-through covering, it simply had the shadow box surrounding the cross with brass anchors securing each point. The anchors appeared to be screwed firmly into the thick limestone walls. Prying the anchors out was proving to be a difficult task. Quince realized he would have to remove the outer shadow box first, then attack each of the individual anchors on the cross points. He thought, if he could pry just one of them completely out, then he only had to loosen the remainder in order to free the cross.

Cassidy, meanwhile, wished he had a watch. It seemed to be taking Quince a very long to time to get the cross. The longer they were there, the greater the chance of being discovered. Without a moon in the sky, Cassidy couldn't get any sense of the time it had taken. He was tempted to go in after him, but knew he had to stay and keep watch.

They had arrived at about 3 am and the padre was a notoriously early riser. They had about an hour and a half, tops, to the get the job done. Cassidy figured he would give it a little bit longer and then he would have no choice but to go in after Q.

Quince's arms were aching from the effort of reaching up over his head. He couldn't get the leverage he needed to pry the screws loose, but as he worked, he could feel the screws beginning to slip. He thought it was lucky the walls were made of clay brick and lime mortar. Although very thick, the material was fairly soft and even though the anchors seemed to be sunk deep, he could move them with a little effort. But it was time consuming because of the awkward way he had to approach it from beneath.

He took the screwdriver and wedged it under a corner of the brass plate and used the hammer to knock it further under to try and pry it loose.

Sweat poured down into his eyes making it difficult to see. The sting of the salt caused his eyes to burn as his arms began to shake from the effort. He was moving them down to his sides more and more often and he was starting to think he would not be able to remove the cross at all.

As he reached up one more time, he thought he heard a noise and stopped dead, lowering his arms to his side. He stopped breathing and waited to see what it was. Hearing nothing more than the howling wind, he thought it must be his imagination. He decided to give it one last try and if he couldn't get one of the anchors to move, he was going to head back to the buckboard. He was pretty sure Cassidy would shoot him then, because without the cross, he could then claim to be a hero for saving it.

Meanwhile, Cassidy sat impatiently in the buckboard with only a limited view of the back of the mission where Q had entered. This was the workers entrance, the doorway where Cassidy and others who worked at the church usually entered. It occurred to him he should take a peek around to make sure there was no other activity, although at this hour of the morning, he couldn't imagine it.

He was perched beyond a hill which was part of a grouping of low hills that interrupted the barren landscape like bumps on a log and comprised a ridge along the river, which was usually dry. He secured the buckboard to a scrub of mesquite and got low to the ground to peek out to get a better view of the front of the church.

As he chanced a better look, he thought he heard a noise from within the church. Due to the cavernous interior, one would think noise would reverberate, but the thick walls and all the artwork covering them muted the sounds.

He didn't see anything unusual, so went back to the buckboard to wait out Q. He thought that he had to be done soon. If not, Cassidy may have to take a chance and go find him. The sky was just beginning to show a sliver of pink on the horizon and Padre Mendoza would be up soon.

Q made one last effort, giving it all he had left, and hit the hammer as hard as he could. The screwdriver suddenly entered the space behind the brass plate quickly and to the hilt. As he pried with all his might, the plate came loose and gave him an inch of space as he tumbled off the ladder and crashed to the floor.

The noise was loud to Quince's ears, but was actually dampened by the thick walls and artwork covering them. Quince replaced the ladder and took the same approach with the two other plates he could reach. The plate at the top of the cross was too high for him to get to. But the three were enough, and he finally pried the cross loose from its secure place and jumped off the ladder tucking it under his aching left arm.

"I'm rich," he thought to himself.

Outside, Cassidy was jumpy. He was trying to keep his horse quiet and it seemed as if Quince was taking forever to get the cross. He was just about to take another peek at the front of the church when he saw Q emerge from the workers entry. The gold of the cross was unmistakable and he felt a shiver in his bones. He slapped the reins hard and the horse bolted the buckboard forward with a start.

Quince was running flat out as Cassidy urged the horse to move the buckboard closer to meet Q.

Cassidy had his gun out, as Quince heard a shout come from behind. He saw Cassidy rein the horse to a halt and stand up on the wagon to take aim. He couldn't turn around to look, but had to believe the Padre had awoken and was chasing after him.

Although Quince was running hard, it seemed as if there was no sound but the wind blowing the tumbleweeds across the barren land. The sky was dawning a brilliant blue with dots of small, puffy white clouds and it seemed as if the birds stopped singing and everything else in the world ground to a halt.

Cassidy was only 50 yards ahead and seemed to be aiming the gun at Quince. He figured whoever was chasing him must be right on his heels and about to overtake him. But Quince was thinking that even Cassidy was not stupid or brazen enough to shoot a priest. He risked a glance behind and saw two O'odham on foot with bows drawn and arrows loaded, running towards him.

Quince suddenly dropped to the ground to give Cassidy better clearance, just as a shot rang out. It ricocheted and hit the ground right next to Quinces' head.

He realized it then.

"Cass'dy's tryin' ta kill me."

Cassidy stood as high as he could on the buckboard and took careful aim.

"Shit, Cass'dy. Don' do dis. Ya can hab de dam cross."

He buried his head on the ground covering the cross with his body, waiting for the bullet. He heard a loud cry and looked up with one dusty eye and saw Cassidy with an arrow embedded in his left leg.

Cassidy's face was wrenched in pain and tears were streaming down his face. Quince could only watch as he saw Cassidy reach down and snap the arrow just short of where it entered his leg. He placed the broken wood between his teeth, clenching down tight. He sat down hard on the bench of the buckboard and whipped the horse around, moving quickly behind the hill and south towards the border.

"Up, amigo."

Quince sat up as the native demanded.

The other native took the cross out of Quince's hands.

"No one steals from a church and no one can run from the O'odham for long."

Quince looked back to see a cloud of dust that rose from the wagon which Cassidy was driving as hard as he could, and wondered how long he would last with no allies in this barren land. The loathing he had for Cassidy was palpable. He wished he knew what his plan was so he could help the authorities find and catch him. He would love to meet up with him again in Florence.

Quince hung his head and the last thing he thought about before they tied his hands behind his back was the smell of jambalaya cooking on his mamas' stove.

# Chapter Seventeen

## *Heritage*

Mollie entered the office to Gideon's taxi company, Verde Transportation, for the first time. Luisa was already there and looked up from a pile of forms she was filling out for the State licensing board.

The two could not have been more different in appearance. Luisa had long, dark hair which she wore combed out. Her eyes were dark and smoky and she had a perennial hint of capriciousness on her face. She was short, measuring only five foot two in the sandals she always wore.

Mollie on the other hand, had strawberry blonde hair worn shoulder length, although almost always tied in a ponytail or up under her hat. She had startlingly sparkling green eyes, and long legs, standing nearly five foot seven, but seemed much taller in the boots she wore with a riding heel.

Mollie approached Luisa and reached out to shake her hand. As soon as they touched, it was as if sparks went off. Luisa looked up at Mollie and smiled. Mollie couldn't take her hand away.

"Howdy, ma'am," she fumbled for the words. "I'm here to meet with Gideon. Name's Mollie."

"*Buenos días, Mollie. Me llamo Luisa. Encantada de conocerte.*"

Mollie looked at Luisa strangely. She had been in Tucson her whole life, but never really learned much Spanish besides the usual greetings. And Mollie had never met a woman before who made her feel the way she did this time.

They held each other's gaze for what seemed to be a long time, when Carmelita entered the room, carrying a large, steaming pot filled with something that smelled delicious. She took notice of the two staring into each other's eyes and could feel the energy between them. Something was going on that she had never witnessed between two women before.

"Morning, Mollie. You're here early."

The two broke their trance and looked up.

"Mornin', Carmelita."

"*Buenos días, jefe.*"

Carmelita smiled at the reference to her as the boss.

"You two haven't met before, have you?"

"No, Ma'am. This is the first time I have been here."

"Well, welcome. Luisa, can you get cups for all of us for the coffee? *Gracias.*"

Gideon entered shortly after, followed a few minutes later by Sofie.

Carmelita had prepared a specialty of hers for breakfast. Menudo, a spicy stew which was usually reserved for special occasions as it took hours to cook properly. She had made it the day before since it always tasted a little bit better reheated the following day.

The ragtag crew took their steaming bowls of stew and prepared their coffee. They arranged themselves around a small round table that Gideon used for meetings with his drivers. There would be a meeting later that same morning to introduce Luisa as temporary head of operations while Gideon and Carmelita were in México chasing the treasure. He was a little worried about their extended absence, but he trusted Luisa and knew the drivers would respect her position. Mollie took a seat next to Luisa.

Gideon spoke up.

"Delicious stew, Lita." Lately, Gideon had taken to shortening Carmelita's name as his term of endearment.

"So, has anyone had a change of heart about the task we're about to undertake?" He waited a beat, but everyone was eating their stew or drinking their coffee and he didn't make eye contact with any of them. Not even his wife.

"Listen," he continued, once again choosing words that accented his sibilance, "this trip is dangerous. More than that, it may be for nothing. We have no proof that a treasure even exists, much less that we have divined the location. As you know, many have tried before, although not in *Mexcaltitán*. We are undertaking a huge risk and it will be very dangerous. México has been in a revolutionary state for four years now and it shows no signs of stopping.

"On top of that, it looks very much like the U.S. will be sucked into the war in Europe. This may not be the best time to go traipsing through a man-made island looking for treasure, no matter how exciting that may seem or how rich it could make us.

"It's going to take weeks to get there and who knows how long to get back. It will be dirty, hot, without a lot of food and not much water besides what we can carry. Think about it."

Gideon was trying his best to scare away anyone who was faint of heart. They could not afford a weak link on this journey. The stakes were high, and the risk was higher.

He walked over to the coffee and poured another cup. He slowly stirred in cream and took it back to his place at the table.

Mollie spoke up. "I know the risks and I'm willing to take 'em. Let's get to the business of planning so we can get there sooner rather than later."

Gideon smiled as Lita and Sofie nodded and mumbled their assent. Luisa looked at Mollie with admiration, but a part of her was very scared.

"OK. Here's what I have so far. We can take my old wagon to the border at Nogales. We'll cross as Americans under the cover of bringing food and supplies to the resistance fighters. Once we cross, we head southwest, towards the Gulf of California. I don't think there's much fighting near the west coast and that's the general direction we need to head anyway. Villa is fighting border wars with the U.S. and Zapata is mostly in the southeast fighting against the regime. Once we ..."

Gideon was interrupted with a loud banging on the office door, which caused Carmelita and Luisa to jump.

"Who's there?" Gideon called out.

"Gideon, it's Chico."

Chico was one of the drivers who had been with Gideon since he first started the company in Green Valley.

"Come in then." Gideon couldn't imagine why Chico would need to interrupt him. He was a seasoned driver who had been with him for a few years and had plenty of knowledge and experience in all aspects of the business.

"What's so urgent, Chico?"

"I thought you might want to know..."

"Know what?"

"I just came back from the mission. Someone tried to steal the Amulet of Cananea again."

Carmelita jumped up, "Who was it? Did they succeed?"

Gideon commented calmly, "Well, that's unfortunate but no real surprise, I suppose. I'll have to go see Father Mendoza though, to talk to him about better security for the cross."

"It's not just that, Gideon," Chico replied, "they've captured one of the *banditos*. He is one of the men who escaped from the prison in Florence."

Carmelita looked at Gideon in alarm.

"Gideon, could it be?"

"Chico, you said *one* of the banditos. How many were there?"

"I wasn't there, señor. I only heard. It seems there were two, just as had escaped from the prison. They didn't get away with the cross, though."

Carmelita's mind was reeling. She didn't notice the look of shock on Mollie's face. Mollie was worried that whoever had been captured would give her up to the authorities. In that case, her cover was blown.

"Do you know what this man looked like, Chico?"

"*Sí*, he was *gran hombre negro.*"

"A big, black man? What about the other one, the one that got away?"

"He was *un hombre blanco pelirrojo.*"

Carmelita shook as though a shiver had passed up her spine. A red haired white man? Somehow she knew, as soon as she heard, that it had to be Cassidy.

Gideon made a decision.

"I'm going to go speak to Father Mendoza and see what the authorities are saying. Cassidy has nine lives, although I think he's used most of them, but I'm not comfortable going to México while he's still on the loose. Let's get back together after we put this to rest. Sofie, do you have a place to go?"

"I'll be fine, Gideon. I'll send a note to the New York library with an update and let them know how long I plan to be away. In the meantime, there's a wonderful library here at the University. I'm going to go do more research and see what I can find."

Mollie spoke up. "I'm heading back to Tucson to talk to Aunt Rosie. It wouldn't surprise me at all if she had a line on Cassidy."

"Good idea, Mollie. Keep me posted on that," Gideon replied.

Mollie headed out the door, not sure if she would be back. It all depended on what Quince had to say and if Cassidy had stayed in the area or left for good. She planned to find out for certain.

# Chapter Eighteen

## *Justice*

Gideon left the office of Verde Transportation and headed straight to the mission. Carmelita wanted to go along, but he convinced her to stay at the office. There was no way Cassidy would show up anywhere near there now.

He spent time talking to Father Mendoza who recounted his conversation with the police. They had led Quince away and back to the prison in Florence.

Quince was to be brought before a judge who would impose further penalties, which seemed senseless, since he was already on death row for his past crimes. However, the police told the priest that the likelihood of Quince going to solitary was most likely.

When Gideon got back to the office later that day, Carmelita was there waiting for him.

"Have you been here the whole time?"

"If you had let me go with you, I would already know what I want to know. What did the police have to say?"

"Well, as it happens, the man they captured, Quince Thibodeaux, was the one who escaped with Cassidy from Florence."

"I could have told you that," she huffed in reply.

According to the police, Thibodeaux was quite eager to tell them everything.

"Thibodeaux was nearly twice the weight of the O'odham who stopped him and a good eight inches taller. Holding a cocked arrow in a bow to his head, they told the police they were scared to death once they had him."

It turned out that the Tohono O'odham used a technique for subduing the big man by using leather strips to tie his hands together. Once tied, they looped a long length of rope around his neck and secured it to the leather bands so his wrists were held up, near his neck. If he tried to move his hands in any way, the rope would pull taut and cut into his neck. It's a clever technique because the arms become fatigued, so typically people secured in that manner have to lie down otherwise their arms eventually want to drop to their sides, tightening the rope.

There was no way Thibodeaux could do anything but wait for the police. Even if he tried to run, the rope would cut into his neck causing pain or disabling his ability to breathe.

Gideon showed Carmelita by holding his hands near his neck as if tied and how any movement could be debilitating.

"It's a very effective way to incapacitate your captives."

She looked at him bug-eyed, understating how they handled the situation with such a monster.

"Too bad it wasn't Cassidy, the pig," she spat out with hatred.

"I know, Carmelita. Please put that out of your mind. He can't stay on the run forever. The Sherriff told Father Mendoza that Cassidy is not in very good shape, physically. He's getting older and the wounds he suffered in the past are taking a toll. Plus, he took an arrow to the leg and broke it off, so it's still in there. Now that he doesn't have a strong partner to help him, they don't believe he'll get far. They have bulletins out all over the State and now the O'odham are after him too. It won't be long until he's caught again."

Carmelita looked at Gideon with hooded eyes. She started to say something but thought better of it. Her look said it all.

"Carmelita, I'm going to head back out to the Western Union office to see if we've heard anything back from Francisco de Torres yet. We have to make a decision soon if we are going to go to *Mexcaltitán*. Do you want to come with me?"

She nodded her head and ran out the door.

As they rode to Western Union, they passed the sheriff's office and saw Lena standing on the boardwalk talking with the Deputy. Lena was laughing and the deputy had his hat off and a piece of straw was twirling in his mouth. She knew many cowboys did this to lessen the smell of smoke on their breath. The attraction between the two was so obvious, Carmelita couldn't help but smile. She waved to Lena as they drove by.

When they arrived, Gideon asked about his message to Torres at the Cananea mines.

"I was just about to send a messenger out to your place. A reply just arrived," the clerk told him, handing him the note.

Gideon shook open the yellow envelope and unfolded the message. He read it slowly and then read it again. He handed the message to Carmelita.

The reply said he had received Carmelita's message. He was still working at the mines in Cananea, but only part of the time. He is also fighting for Zapata and would be honored to escort her and her party. He was careful to point out, however, that he would only be able to escort them part way to their destination.

"Oh, Gideon." She was surprised and pleased. It didn't surprise Gideon at all. He knew the power Carmelita held over most men. Lena came in just as Carmelita was reading the note.

"Well, you're glowing, Lena. How is the sheriff's deputy?"

"Wonderful, Carmelita. He is really a very nice man. He's asked me to a movie this weekend."

Well, I'm glad you're happy, Lena."

"What news did you get? Good news, I hope?

"Yes, it's from Francisco."

Lena knew Francisco only by sight and reputation. Since her parents also worked at the mine, they, like everyone else there, knew of him. His reputation was as a stern disciplinarian, which would be expected of a man who had the overall responsibility for security of the entire mining community in Cananea. Plus, it was known he had fought with Kosterlitzky, the dangerous Russian.

"He says he'll be happy to help us in our quest for the treasure. He'll meet us at the border when we have finalized our plans. Oh, Gideon, there can be no one in México who would be a better guide and protector."

"Carmelita, I just heard from Earl that Kosterlitsky was released from prison and moved to Los Angeles with his family. It's said he's using his skills as a linguist, working as a translator for the U.S. Postal service," Lena chimed in.

It was widely known that Kosterlitsky was a polyglot who could speak English, Russian, Spanish, German, French, Italian, Polish, Danish, and Swedish. His skills for the postal service could prove invaluable if the U.S. were to enter the war.

"Earl?" Carmelita asked.

Lena's skin turned bright red from her face down her neck. She giggled.

"Earl is the deputy we met."

Carmelita smiled and took Lena's hand as they turned to leave.

"Carmelita," Gideon called, "what do you want to say to Francisco?"

She was so happy for her friend that she almost forgot why they were there. They decided to tell him they planned to leave the following Wednesday and would send a message when they were on the way. They both decided that taking the train from Tucson to Nogales would be much quicker and easier than the wagon, so changed their plan. They expected to be at the border by noon. They needed to move quickly, as April was soon coming to an end and the warmer weather would become a factor for the long distance they all had to travel.

"Lita, I'm going to go speak with the sheriff to see what he's learned from Thibodeaux about Cassidy. I'll feel much better leaving here once I know he's back in custody."

"Lena and I will go with you. I want to know as much as you do, and I'm sure Lena would like to tag along."

She winked at her friend and they left to seek out the sheriff.

---

Cassidy had ridden his horse very hard for the first 10 miles, before he had to give her a rest. He had no food, but he did find a nice stream where she could take water and rest for a while. He sat on a rock and removed the broken arrow from his leg. He was lucky they hit the fleshy part of his thigh. It hurt, but he cleaned the wound and tied a bandana tightly to stop the bleeding.

Cassidy was smart enough to head north and was nearly to South Tucson, where he and Q had laid low before the attempted theft. He knew the area and could get some grain, water, and rest for his horse before heading out again. The real question for him was, what next?

He had to get some help and knew the place to go was back to Sadie's to talk to Rosie. He knew it was a gamble. Her niece had double-crossed Quince and him when she left to hook up with Carmelita and her husband Gideon. But Rosie was a larcenous soul and he believed money was a greater motivator than blood. Mollie could have the gold in México, if there was any. It was a fool's errand. No one knew what happened to the treasure that Cortés stole from Montezuma. Treasure hunters had been trying to find that cache for centuries. Most thought it

156

was lost near *México City*, but there were reports that it had been hidden everywhere from Arizona to Utah to Kansas and all points in between. Even though they had a highfalutin historian from New York City, he doubted very much anything would come of this lost cause.

He would get some help from Rosie, but manipulate her by giving her information on a fictitious destination, and throw her niece, the rest of the ragtag treasure hunters, and most importantly, the cops, off his trail. The more he thought about it, the better he liked it.

---

Gideon, Carmelita, and Lena stepped into the sheriff's office. The sheriff was in, which was unusual at this time of the day, but lucky for them. Lena craned her neck, looking for the deputy, who appeared to be elsewhere.

The sheriff didn't know them or their connection to the church and cross, although the deputy had briefed him on the events. Still he had questions and was somewhat skeptical.

Gideon and Carmelita spent some time explaining how they had brought the cross with them after leaving Cananea just after the turmoil at the Cananea mines. They explained that the turmoil was widely credited as the event that sparked the Méxican revolution four years earlier. Once they arrived they had donated the cross to the church in memory of Carmelita's parents and all that had happened at Cananea.

"Just so I understand," the sheriff recapped, "this Colonel Greene, who wasn't a colonel at all, gave you a cross of gold filled with precious jewels, because he *liked* you?"

Carmelita slowly nodded her head. She had never really thought of it like that and it did seem odd, even with all she knew.

"You two then came to Arizona, got married, and donated this valuable cross to the church, specifically to *San Xavier del Bac.*"

Again, Carmelita nodded.

"Now you claim this Cassidy, a cripple who just escaped from the prison in Florence with my prisoner, Quince Thibodeaux, and is now on the run, may be your father because he raped your mother?"

Carmelita nodded again. The way the sheriff recounted the story made it sound completely ludicrous. She began to wonder if maybe she had it all wrong.

"Look, Sherriff," Gideon interjected, "Father Mendoza at the church can confirm the story. We're just trying to find out what you know about Cassidy. The man is a menace. We want to be sure Carmelita isn't at risk."

Carmelita never tired of marveling at how Gideon seem to subconsciously choose words that highlighted his sibilance.

"OK. You're right. The deputy did tell me some of this and the rest I got from the Padre, but I had to check it out. You have to admit, it's quite a story."

Now it was Gideon's turn to nod his head.

"Ok, here's what we know. Thibodeaux has dummied up. He plays the dumb card and plays up his Cajun accent to make it seem he doesn't know better. But this guy went to college. He's no dummy. Claims that prior to the escape, when Cassidy fell at the prison, he reached out to try and prevent the guard from hitting his head on the bars. The guard, of course, says otherwise and that it was not only intentional, but intentionally brutal.

"He says that once Cassidy opened his prison door, he had no choice but to do what he was told. After all, as he claimed, who would believe a person on death row whose door was opened by a fellow inmate?

"He further claims that Cassidy held this against him the entire time and forced him to do what he wanted or he'd turn him in. Claims he even made him wear a woman's dress."

Gideon turned his face away from the sheriff to hide the expression on his face after that comment. Carmelita only turned red and fumed inside at the sickness of the man she thought might be her father.

"At any rate, Thibodeaux is going back to death row. He doesn't seem to know the whereabouts of Cassidy and he would definitely try to kill him if he were to see him again. I'm afraid there's not much we can do now but continue to search. He'll show up soon. He's crippled, has little money, no friends, and every law enforcement agency in the territory is looking for him, as well as the tribes."

"As well as me," Carmelita spat out angrily.

# <u>Chapter Nineteen</u>

## *Dilemma*

Mollie walked into the office of Verde Transportation late in the afternoon, just as the sun was beginning to settle. Gideon had clearly been prescient when he sold his stagecoaches noticing that the interest in automobiles was not a passing trend.

"Hello, Luisa."

Luisa looked up from her work and her heart skipped a beat. She had never felt this way before with anyone and wondered why this woman affected her so. She had known for years she preferred women to men and had experimented many times when she was younger, but the relationships never lasted.

This woman was different somehow, she made her feel young and alive, even though she had only met her once and had hardly spoken to her.

"Hello, Mollie. It's so nice to see you again. Gideon and Carmelita aren't here. Is there anything I can do for you?"

"Actually, it's you I've come to see. I'm heading into town to visit with my aunt and wondered if you would like to join me."

"I would love to, but as I said, Gideon and Carmelita aren't here, so I have to stay to manage the business. It looks like I'll be handling that for an extended period now that they have both decided to go to México with you and Sofie. Perhaps another time?"

She cursed herself. She couldn't believe she actually batted her eyes.

"Yes, that would be great, Luisa."

"Please, call me Malu"

"Alright, Malu. Another time."

Mollie turned on her heel and left the office to head downtown to meet with her Aunt Rosie.

---

Cassidy waited until dark to approach Sadie's. When he arrived in South Tucson, he swapped horses with a man who had been in the saloon all day. The man just didn't know it, and Cassidy wondered if he'd even notice when he came out to ride home. He stole some clothes off a line and pulled his hat down very low to hide his hair. He couldn't do much about his gait so he tried to stay on the horse as much as possible. He was able to get some water and grain for the animal, but he was almost out of money. He needed cash and a place to rest. He was hoping Rosie could help. He still found it odd that her place was called Sadie's, although the name she went by was Rosie, just as he was sure that wasn't her real name either, no matter what Mollie said.

"People sure can be twisted," he reminded himself again, ironically.

An hour after the sun went down and the night sky twinkled with the light of a thousand stars, he approached the rear door of the establishment. Fortunately, it was a new moon and while the stars shone brilliantly, the moon didn't cast any light.

He entered through a back room which served as Rosie's office. The lights were on but the office was empty, so he assumed Rosie was somewhere nearby and decided to wait. Keeping a low profile was most important now and he didn't need any witnesses to his whereabouts.

He was just beginning to nod to sleep when the door opened loudly and jerked him awake.

"Well, well. Cassidy. What are you doing here, you miserable snake?"

He looked up to see Mollie standing over him, drawing her gun.

"Mollie. I'm, I'm glad to see you," he stammered. "They captured Q. I tried to help, but he was stopped by the tribe before I could reach him. I was driving the buckboard and circled back to get him when…"

"Shut your trap, you conniving, lying, little shit. I don't believe anything you say. No. I take that back. Whatever you say, I believe exactly the opposite. So, in this case, you specifically didn't try to help Q. I already heard he's heading back to solitary and the row. The difference between you and Q is that Q didn't give me up. No one else except Aunt Rosie knows I got involved with you and your slimy schemes, so I have no reason not to shut you up permanently."

"Listen, Mollie. You misunderstand me. I really did try to help Q, but I know you won't believe me. But believe this – this wild goose chase you're about to go on with Gideon and the rest is just that – a wild goose chase. If you'll work with me, we can get that cross and it'll be enough to make us both rich. Why else would I show up here at your Aunt's place? México is a mess right now. They've been fighting a revolution for years, and the north and south don't even agree. Getting across the border is tougher than ever. Carmelita might be alright, but you and Gideon are gringos through and through. You'll never survive if you're caught."

"Save it, Cassidy. I'm not stealing a cross from a church. It was a bad idea from the start. I'll take my chances with the treasure, which is up for whoever finds it. I have my reasons, which you'll never understand."

She reached down and took his Bowie knife out of the sheath on his boot. She tied his hands to the chair he was sitting on with a length of cloth that was on the desk.

"I'm going to get the sheriff. If you even think about escaping, I'll hunt you down and shoot your dick off. I'm letting Rosie know you're in here, so don't try anything."

It was a bluff, because Rosie wasn't in the building, which was why Mollie had checked the office in the first place, and she didn't really expect anyone else to pay any attention if they heard noises. Sadie's was full of rooms with strange noises. She had to find her Aunt and figure out what to do with Cassidy. She knew he would give her up in a heartbeat about the scheme to steal the cross from the mission, so she couldn't turn him over to the authorities. She hoped her Aunt would know what to do.

The moment she left, Cassidy started rocking the rickety chair Mollie had tied him to. The fabric of the cloth wasn't that strong, but he couldn't break it. He had to see if he could break the chair instead. After several rocking motions, the chair tilted to his left side and he fell to the floor with a loud crash. The chair didn't break completely, but the arm was loose and after a time, he was able to break it free. He slid the fabric off the arm and stood up and broke the other arm of the chair and removed that as well. He bolted out the same door Mollie had and disappeared into the shadows to find a way to cut the fabric and then go find his friend Desi. He knew he hadn't gone back to the mission yet. He only hoped he hadn't left town.

Mollie went back to Sadie's feeling dejected. She hadn't been able to find Rosie, and was fearful of what to do with Cassidy. She was thinking she would have to kill him and bury the body. She just couldn't afford for the sheriff to get involved and knew Cassidy wouldn't voluntarily leave Tucson without that cross. She cursed herself for ever getting involved with him

She opened the door to find her aunt sitting at her desk, holding her lockbox in her hand. The chair Cassidy was sitting in was broken on the floor, the arms removed, and there was no sign of him.

The lockbox was where Rosie kept her cash from the take each evening until the bank opened in the morning. It was well hidden in a secret drawer in her desk, but if someone were to hunt hard enough, they would be able to find it. She always said she needed to install a floor safe.

Mollies' heart jumped into her throat when she realized that Rosie was holding the cash box.

"Mollie! Someone must have broken in. I don't know why the chair is broken, but thank goodness the cash is still intact."

Mollie breathed a sigh of relief.

"I can explain, Auntie."

Mollie recounted what had happened with Cassidy to her Aunt. She trusted her. Besides, Rosie had more friends in Tucson than the mayor. In fact, the mayor *was* one of her friends. She would know how to deal with this.

"Well, I'm glad he absconded quickly. As long as my money is here, we're OK. Don't worry about it Mollie. He's an escaped murderer from death row in a federal prison. No one will believe anything he has to say. I'm your alibi. Besides, didn't you tell me the padre at the mission is your friend? You'll be fine. Let's just hope they catch him fast and put him back where he belongs. Come on, let's go talk to the sheriff. We have to report this anyway."

While Mollie and her Aunt Rosie went off to find the sheriff, Cassidy was skulking through the shadows through the back alleys of town, looking for the Lone Stallion, the place where he had met up with Desi just a few nights ago, but for what seemed like years ago.

It was a wild shot that he would be there, but he had no other leads. Someone there would know of his whereabouts, he was sure.

He entered through the kitchen, which was a poor excuse of a place for preparing what passed for meals in a joint like this, and peeked through the door to the bar. It was getting late and the kitchen had long been closed.

He spied Desi, sitting at the exact same table he had been in the last time he saw him, talking to a young woman who looked to Cassidy to be the exact same one who had slapped his face the last time he was there.

Cassidy couldn't risk showing his face. Too often there were lawmen in saloons like these. He dug a penny out of his pocket and flipped it off his thumb to try and catch Desi's attention. He was lucky. The first penny bounced off the wooden table and clinked off Desi's glass.

Desi looked around to see where it came from, and his eye caught Cassidy peeking out of the kitchen door.

"Wait, here, Nell. I have to see a man about a horse," he winked at her as he jumped to his feet quickly and moved towards the kitchen door.

"Cassidy, you son of a bitch! What the hell are you doing here?" Desi was fuming and looked like he was about to punch Cassidy in the face. "You know there's a bounty out on you?"

Cassidy hadn't thought about that, but it made perfect sense. Q wouldn't be able to take advantage of that, but Desi could as could Mollie or anyone else who saw him.

"A bounty? Is it posted? How much?"

Desi shook his head at Cassidy's' arrogance.

"A hundred dollars, double the usual amount, and I can use the money. Let's go, I'm turning you in." He went to grab Cassidy by the collar, but Cassidy used his characteristic quickness to avoid Desi's grasp. "Wait, wait, Desi. Give me a minute to explain. I have a way to make ten times that amount, just hear me out."

Desi looked at Cassidy. Every instinct he had told him to ignore this man and turn him in for the quick cash. But he wasn't sure what implication Cassidy would cast on him if he did go to the authorities, so he decided to hear him out.

Cassidy was stalling for time, frantically trying to think of a way to keep Desi from calling the sheriff.

"Listen, Desi. The cross is worth at least a hundred times that amount, even from a bad fence. Let's stick to our original plan and we can split the take. Tell you what, to make it even sweeter for you, I'll even split Q's portion with you. What do you say?"

Desi couldn't believe the audacity of Cassidy. He nearly exploded.

"Split Q's portion?" he said in the loudest voice he dared. "Are you crazy? I don't even need you. If I wanted to take the cross, I could do it myself. But I'm not going to risk it. Q has already been captured, so they'll be doubly cautious. Besides, stealing from a church is the worst kind of sin. Let's go."

Cassidy leaped up to avoid Desi's reach and at the same time slashed his face above his eyes with a kitchen knife. The blood began to pour down Desi's face, making it almost impossible to see.

"Sorry, chump. No one's taking me in. Thanks for the heads up on the bounty, though."

Cassidy ran out the back, but now he had a new dilemma. Almost out of money, he had no one left to turn to. He had to fend for himself and decide how he could get as far away from Tucson as possible. Cassidy was alone, broke, tired, and extremely dangerous.

# **Chapter Twenty**

## *Border Crossing*

The day before they were to leave for *Mexcaltitán*, Gideon, Carmelita, Sofie, and Mollie stopped by the mission to say *adiós* to Padre Mendoza. They had received a message in response to their note to Francisco de Torres who agreed to meet them at the border on Wednesday.

Gideon was especially excited, because his Sears and Roebuck replica watch had arrived that day. He immediately attached it to his fob, which he had continued to wear on his waistcoat, and must have opened it dozens of times since.

"Padre, thanks for your help in all this. I promise to try and get word to you if anything develops, but I don't know if there will be any way to do that. In the meantime, please stay in touch with Luisa and make sure she's safe while we're gone."

"Of course, my son. God be with you on your journey. I did tell you about the man who offered to travel with you, si? His name was Desi."

"Yes, but I don't think we'll need any help since Francisco has agreed to escort us."

"It's just as well. He never showed up."

"Keep your eye out for Cassidy, Padre. By the way, do you even know what he looks like?"

"No, I can't say that I do, although I have heard so much about him."

"Well, he's short, with bright red hair. You can't miss that. He's also bent over a bit from a knife wound he suffered. But I can't imagine he'll show up again. He has to be long gone by now."

"Thanks, Gideon. Carmelita, Sofie, Mollie – you take care of each other and be safe. Godspeed and I hope you find what you're after."

Today, April 22, 1914, was a Tuesday, and they were all excited and couldn't wait to leave the next morning to travel the sixty-six miles to Nogales. Mollie had never ridden a train before, and Sofie was excited to be going to the border and crossing during the revolution.

Sofie's vision was that the battles would be very much like what she had read of the American Revolution – battles done on foot and horses with swords and rifles. Maybe not muskets, but her New York view of México was that it was still the Wild West and antiquated in terms of its ability to wage conflict. The only thing that really concerned her was that the enemy the revolutionaries were fighting were not an ocean away, but rather in charge of the government with all the resources at its disposal.

She thought that while several countries had had to fight a revolutionary war on its own ground, the U.S. experience had been different, with the government an ocean away. She supposed this would perhaps be more like the War between the States rather than the Revolutionary War.

Still, she found it exciting and was eager to get there, as dangerous as it was.

Gideon told them all to pack lightly. The rails would be fine for moving their luggage, but once they crossed the border, they didn't know what they would find. They needed to travel light and be ready for anything.

They each planned to bring something special; Sofie packed an erudite tome on the Aztecs, Carmelita a silver St. Christopher medal which had belonged to her mother, and Gideon would hand carry the ersatz cross made from the mold of the amulet of Cananea.

Carmelita took hold of her mother's St. Christopher medal and held it in her left hand as they prepared for the ride to the train station. Her thoughts turned to her return to México and all the old emotions it stirred in her. In spite to the excitement of the adventure, she was more than a little afraid. She wondered what had happened to Cassidy and if she would ever learn the truth about him.

Mollie also brought a special item, but one that posed a dilemma. She wanted to be sure she had her weapon with her. Taking the gun to Nogales on the Arizona side of the border was not a problem, but crossing put her in violation of international law. She would have to see what could be done about that. Carmelita had assured her that Francisco would be helpful and could be trusted – and he was on the side of the revolutionaries. Still, she wouldn't go if she couldn't be armed.

Luisa had volunteered to drive them to the train station and promised to be diligent in managing the affairs of the business while they were gone.

In her heart she was surprised at how worried she was to see Mollie go, but knew she had to keep this feeling to herself for now.

Just that morning she learned that U.S. President Woodrow Wilson had sent troops to the port of Veracruz on the Gulf of México since the diplomatic relationship between the two countries broke down after the Tampico affair. Although this incident was occurring on the opposite coast of México, it had widespread impact and would certainly make the border crossing very difficult. She mentioned this to Gideon.

"The Church is sanctioning this trip. We'll be protected because of that alone," Gideon stated optimistically.

"Veracruz is more than thirteen hundred miles away. Clear across the country. I don't expect it will have any direct impact on our trip. Plus, we have Francisco's help and he has close ties to Villa. Villa and Zapata have created their own alliance. I'm sure we'll have safe passage. But we still need to be very careful."

Francisco had promised to meet them at the border crossing and ensure them safe passage to a place on the Méxican side of Nogales. He and a couple of his men would then escort them part of the way to their final destination.

Although border tensions were high, it was still possible to cross in both directions with the proper authorizations. Padre Mendoza had helped with that on the U.S. side and Francisco was able to assure passage on the Méxican side. It was still dangerous, but much less so than trying to make an illegal crossing which was the original thought.

Timing was not especially good for Americans to be going into México. Earlier that month, there had been the skirmish which led to the Tampico affair. Although far away on the Gulf coast, it nevertheless created an atmosphere of tension along all of the border crossings.

The journey to Mexcaltitán was expected to take several days, maybe as much as a couple of weeks. The plan was to take the rail line from Nogales to Guaymas, a line that had been built by the Sonora Railway Company and completed in 1882 as part of the Méxican government's desire to increase trade to the United States. The rail was eventually sold to the Southern Pacific Railroad of México.

The Méxican Revolution created havoc on the lines however, and they could not be relied upon to operate on time, or sometimes, at all. Even with consistent service, which was now virtually nonexistent, the Sonora rail line was less than half the distance to their final destination on the Riviera Nayarit and Mexcaltitán.

Carmelita had long known there were trains from Cananea to the border at Naco and back – Colonel Greene himself had built some of the lines to ensure safe passage of his copper to America.

Even with the internal revolution in México and the border troubles between the U.S and México, commerce still ruled and the trains continued to operate, albeit sporadically. Fortunately for them, the revolutionaries, native tribes, and military all virtually ignored the passing of civilians on this route when it was in operation.

The challenge now was in determining how to get from *Guaymas* to *Mexcaltitán* overland.

Carmelita was sure Francisco had a plan. He had assured her in his note that he could get them safe passage to their destination, although he indicated he could not go further than the end of the rail line in *Guaymas*.

The two premier generals of the Méxican Revolution, Villa and Zapata, were fairly well aligned. Pancho Villa led the revolution in the north against the current administration of Huerta and railed against the U.S., often crossing the border and committing crimes on U.S. soil.

Emiliano Zapata had control of the south, and while also fighting the military leadership of Huerta, his was a revolution of the people and agrarian reform.

Although both revolutionaries were working in concert, there was still a clear demarcation between their two territories, and Francisco felt he would actually be putting the travelers in jeopardy if he continued on past *Guaymas*, encroaching on Zapata's boundaries. Of course, his primary concern was Carmelita, who always held a special place in his heart.

Early the next morning, Luisa climbed into the driver's seat of the taxi while Mollie got in on the passenger's side. Carmelita, Sofie, and Gideon, sat in the back. Padre Mendoza had decided to come by to see them off anyway although they had said goodbye to him the day before at the mission. With a tip of his hat out the window, Gideon bid the Padre farewell and they started the journey to search for the lost treasure of *Cortés*.

The roads in South Tucson had long been established, but each year in late spring, when the air warmed, monsoons would sweep through the area wreaking havoc. Deep gullies would form on any remaining dirt roads or paths where wagons and horses had passed. They would fill with water causing many wagons to lose a wheel and horses to break a leg. Although a potential disaster for homes, farms, cattle, and horses, it was beneficial in bringing life to the flora and fauna of the area. The Tohono O'odham would harvest the fruit which grew on the huge saguaro cactus which dotted the land like seeds on a strawberry, and prickly pears would bear their fruit which was sweet and rich, but well protected by the spines of the cactus.

When the rains passed and the sun heated the land, the water would evaporate quickly, creating steam which rose off the road like spirits being lifted into the sky. As the three in the back sat talking about the journey and their excitement and apprehension at the prospect of their undertaking, Mollie turned to Luisa.

"So tell me, Malu, how long have you known Carmelita and Gideon?"

"Only a couple of years now. I was introduced to them by a man I knew. Jorge. Carmelita worked for him at the Iguana Café. I had waitressed there when I was younger, but then got lucky and found a job in an office. It was because of my office experience that they decided to take me on to help with the taxi business. It's different, but a lot of fun, and as the business has grown, they've given me more responsibility and money. What about you? Have you know them long?"

"Uh, no, actually. I met them at the mission only recently. I was there helping the padre and he introduced us."

Mollie realized she should stay away from talking about personal things. She didn't want Luisa to know too much about her past.

"So, Malu. What do you like to do when you're not working?"

"My favorite thing is to go to the movies. Have you seen *The Perils of Pauline?*"

"No. I don't go to movies. I never saw the point."

"Oh, well, it just came out last month. I heard it was the first of a serial. It follows the escapades of a clever woman who always outsmarts a man who tries to steal her money. You'd like it, I think."

"Well, I do like to see a woman outsmart a man. Maybe we should go sometime, although I don't know when we'll be near a movie theater again."

They travelled on in silence, taking in the sites of late spring and enjoying the vegetation which was blooming everywhere at this time of year. The saguaro cactus were enormous, some standing over forty feet tall. The flowers were still in bloom, although Luisa knew they would close once the sun was high and not come out again until evening when the sun sunk low and the air cooled.

It was a bumpy ride, but Mollie knew these bumps were nothing compared to what would come next.

"What am I thinking," she thought silently, "heading into México in the throes of a revolution, looking for a lost treasure over two centuries old with an escaped convicted murderer on our tail. What could be more fun?"

They rode the rest of the way not saying a lot. Mollie asked Luisa about her home in México and if she still had family there, which she said she didn't. Luisa seemed to be lost in thought and the rest of the trip to the station was uneventful.

Once they arrived in Nogales, Luisa dropped Carmelita and Gideon off at the *Cantina de la Frontera,* known to the Americans as the Border Café. The café had been there since before the border was split nearly sixty-six years earlier.

Gideon was surprised at the number of cars here. He had suspected that horses and carriages were primarily still used near the border and in México, but there were many more cars than horses. He could see to the other side of the border from where he was standing and the same seemed true there.

They slowly walked through the wooden doors which led to a small room with a dozen tables and a standup bar against the wall to their left. The tables were half full as it was just after noon, and the room was lit only by natural light.

Still on the U.S. side of the border, most of the patrons appeared to be native to the area based on the color of their skin and dark features, and there were no women at all. Gideon stood out like the North Star on a cloudless night, and although Carmelita was obviously native, she stood out for different reasons.

Two men were at the bar and stared at them as Gideon and Carmelita approached the bartender. One of them looked vaguely familiar to Carmelita.

"You two looking for Francisco?" one of the men asked.

Gideon nodded, but didn't offer anything more.

"Wait here."

The man left out the back door and was gone no more than two minutes when he came back.

"The lady has to come with me. Alone."

Gideon looked at Carmelita and his face turned ashen.

"There's no way that I'm going to let her go with you alone. I'm going too."

"My orders from de Torres is for him to talk to the lady alone first. Take it or leave it."

174

"I'll be fine Gideon. I'll talk to Francisco and come right back. If I'm not back in ten minutes, go get the sheriff."

Reluctantly he agreed. He felt a little bit better since they had mentioned Francisco's name first. He gestured to the other man who had stayed behind at the bar. "O.K., but this one stays with me until she's back."

He nodded and stepped aside for Carmelita to exit towards the back as he had just done.

She exited the rear door of the café into the bright sunlight and immediately she saw Francisco sitting on a stack of old crates. She hadn't seen him in four years, yet he hadn't changed that much. He was quite tall and still ramrod straight with the black eye patch that made him look so intimidating. He was, as always, dressed all in black, although now he was wearing a cape over his shoulders, giving him a greater air of menace than usual. As Carmelita approached, he stood up and went to her quickly. He took off his black vaquero hat and bent down to kiss Carmelita's hand. She noticed quite a bit of grey sprinkled through his hair and drooping moustache, and lines etched in his forehead and around his mouth.

"Carmelita, welcome. It is so good to see you again."

"*Gracias*, Francisco. I can't thank you enough for offering to help us in our quest. I thought of you when I read of Colonel's Greene's passing. It was so sad."

"*Sì*, the Colonel was a great man. Very misunderstood, but he created great wealth for a lot of people. He gave many of us good jobs and improved conditions in Cananea, although still people complained. He will be missed."

"*Sì.*" Carmelita paused for a second to gather her thoughts. "Francisco, I'm sure you have lots of questions about our journey, but I only have one. How do you plan to get us to *Mexcaltitán* at the end of the rail line in Guaymas?"

"Ah, a very good question, Carmelita. Do you want me to tell you now, or wait 'til we meet with the others?"

"Tell me now, *por favor*. Not all the details. That we can save, but I need to know before we cross the border."

"Well, it's very simple, Carmelita. You know that *Mexcaltitán* is a man-made island, *sì?"*

"*Sì*. Francisco. We have all learned a lot from a woman who is travelling with us from New York. Sofie. She knows more about the history of my country than I do."

"And probably much more than I do. But I do know the geography. And you know that *Guaymas* is located near the coast, *¿Es correcto?*"

"*Sì*." Carmelita was trying to figure out what Francisco was trying to say, when it finally hit her just as the words came out of his mouth.

"That makes it easy, then. We will go by boat." The corners of his mouth turned up slightly, which was as close to a smile as Carmelita had ever seen on him.

Carmelita was struck by the sheer simplicity and cleverness of the plan. The majority of the distance to *Mexcaltitán* would occur from the end of the rail line to the island. She had been very worried about the risk with the revolution. Both *Guaymas* and *Mexcaltitán* were on the water. Travelling by sea was the best way to get there anyway, it had just never dawned on her, and she was willing to bet none of the others had thought of it either.

"Better yet, I have arranged for your return by boat as well, to *Bahía de Kino*, less than seventy miles from *Hermosillo*. From there, you can take the train back to Nogales. Of course, we may want to change your plans if you find the treasure. You won't want to take a train and try to cross the border illegally with treasure. Have you thought about that at all? What the plan is if you do find the treasure?"

Carmelita had no idea. The romance of searching for treasure had them all excited and they really believed it was possible. But she didn't think anyone really gave much thought of how to remove it if it was there. Who would it really belong to anyway? Could they lay claim to it if they found it, or did it belong to the tribes or the government? That could be a nightmare, since the government was under siege and there was even some confusion as to who was in charge. The regime of Huerta was the result of a military coup he led to oust and assassinate President Madero. If word leaked that Americans, even a soon-to-be naturalized American of Méxican heritage, had come back over the border to stake a claim on the Aztecs gold fortune which *Cortés* had long ago stolen from them, she could not imagine how any of them would survive.

She was sure that Sofie knew all this, and maybe Gideon too. It was time to introduce them all to Francisco.

"Francisco, I must introduce you to my husband, Gideon, and the others we will be traveling with. Please, come back with me to the cantina so we can discuss our plan."

"Carmelita, I took a chance coming across the border this time. I have to get back. The border is being watched, although all of us who work along this border have known each other for years. It is possible to manage these things, but they must be done carefully. You have the note from your government and the Church?"

"*Sí, aquí.*

"*Bueno.* Go to the customs gate and present it to the officer. Check his name tag. It must be Eduardo. He will be sure you pass through with no problem. If you have any items you don't want confiscated, make sure to place them in your luggage. *¿Comprende?"*

"*Sí, gracias."*

"I will be just across the border, you will see me from the gate as you cross. *Adiós*."

Carmelita returned and told Gideon and the others what had to be done. Mollie packed her gun in the saddlebags she had brought – she had no other luggage to use. It was a risk, but she would refuse to go if she wasn't armed. After all, that was perhaps the most important part of the reason she was asked to join them.

They walked to the gate with great trepidation and Carmelita handed the required forms to the officer, whose name tag read "Eduardo." He took the forms, gave them a cursory glance, and motioned them all forward. In less than a minute, they were on the Méxican side at Nogales.

Francisco was there waiting for them as they picked up their bags, and Carmelita introduced them all to Francisco.

"That was so ridiculously easy." Gideon said as he shook Francisco's hand. "I expected a very difficult time of it and thought we would be seeing armed forces all along the border."

Sofie nodded her agreement as did Mollie and Carmelita.

"The border crossings can sometimes be difficult, but if a person wants to smuggle goods or cross illegally, they rarely attempt it at a border crossing. Most of the *Federales* and U.S. officers patrol the border at out of the way spots. It's part of the reason we were able to get you across so easily. Remember, the current border is only two generations old. Sixty-one years ago the Gadsden Purchase changed the border, but many, many people do not honor where the lines are drawn."

They walked towards the train station, which was located only half a mile from the border crossing.

"That's only ten city blocks." Sofie commented when she asked about it. Sofie may be the most important person to have on the trip due to her knowledge of the native culture and ancient language, but she was of the most concern to Gideon because of her city background. He didn't know how she would fare in the desert. But once he saw how fast she walked the streets in Nogales, he put his fears aside.

They boarded the train without further incident and settled in for the long journey to *Hermosillo* and on to *Guaymas*.

---

The noise of the freight train clicking over the tracks from Tucson to Nogales in the middle of the night was loud but not disruptive. The only ones to hear the activity were the coyotes, diamondback rattlesnakes, mule deer, roadrunners, great horned owls, and other creatures of the desert.

Cassidy had been traveling through the night on the same line of tracks that Carmelita and Gideon had ridden. He relished in his new role as a hobo and was pleased that circumstances had brought him back to the rails.

Cassidy had initially been brought to Cananea by Colonel Greene as an overseer to the "gandy dancers" a term used to describe railroad workers who laid and maintained tracks for the railroad. Cassidy was known to be the most brutal of bosses. He was particularly savage with the Chinese workers. He knew the railroads well, so after his altercation with Desi, he made a decision to lie low and ride the rails.

He had jumped into a sliding door boxcar a split second before it was about to leave the yard in Tucson. He had just settled down into the rhythm of the movement of the train, when he realized he was not alone.

"Who's there?" he called out into the darkness. He squeezed his eyes shut to acclimate them and when he reopened them seconds later, he was staring at a man with a rail dog in his hands raised to shoulder level. The rail dog was another name for rail tongs which were used by installers or maintenance workers to lift the heavy metal rails from the ground to avoid injury to the hands.

It could be a formidable weapon.

"Who are ya? What are ya doin here?"

The man holding the raildog was wearing denim bib overalls which were stained and had a strap missing that was replaced with rope. His beard was short and ragged and he had a floppy hat with a dirty white feather sticking straight up out of the band on the left hand side.

Cassidy knew this was a seasoned hobo who had probably been riding the rails for a very long time. Hobos were a misunderstood class of people. Unlike bums, who didn't work and just looked to take advantage of handouts, or tramps, who worked at odd jobs but didn't travel, hobos, loved the rails and traveled from town to town looking for work.

They weren't lazy. Quite the contrary, they wanted to work and had their own code and a unique language, which Cassidy understood. He had hired many a hobo in his time supervising the workers on the rail lines after his forced relocation from Ireland. He did his best to ingratiate himself to this man and exaggerated his Irish accent.

"Evenin', mate. Oi'm Lord Declan Rails. Sorry, mate. Didn't know this car was taken."

The hobo lowered the weapon and sat down next to Cassidy. They talked during the short ride from Tucson to Nogales, and the Hobo, who referred to himself as Mex Dust-up Angel, told Cassidy that he had picked up a job at ASU as a janitor.

"I hobo the rail back to Nogales for the weekends. It's easy to jump out as the car slows going into the freight yard. I walk into México away from the crossings. It's easy, really. The guards all know that many of us work in the U.S. They don't bother us. We bring money home for our families and we do work the U.S. folks don't want to do. Sure, there's a revolution going on, but that's part of the whole point. Everyone on the border looks the other way. You just have to make sure you don't get caught by the railroad bulls."

They spoke until the train began to slow. Cassidy had told his new friend of his work on the rails in México for the copper mines. Dust-up, as Cassidy now referred to him, was fascinated. Cassidy knew quite a bit about railroads and how they worked, and Dust-up knew how to ride, eat, drink, and sleep without getting caught.

As the freight slowed approaching the Nogales freight yard, Cassidy asked his new friend if he might be able to help him get a job the University. He once again fell into a pot of crap and came up smelling like a rose. He now saw a new way to accomplish his goals. He could bide his time working at the University as a virtually invisible worker, and go back to México on weekends to enjoy his earnings while waiting to get word of Carmelita and her cronies return. He was suddenly very content with this vision of a new version of his life.

Cassidy said goodbye to his new friend and made plans to meet him on Sunday night to catch the ride back to Tucson. He slipped out of the car he was riding and disappeared under the cloak of a moonless sky.

Ambos Nogales ("both Nogales") was the name used for the joint communities of Nogales, Sonora, México and Nogales, Arizona. U.S.A. It was a town split in two by the man-made borders created by the Gadsden Purchase. The governments of the U.S. and México decreed that no buildings should reside within sixty feet of the border, creating an imaginary "fence" between the two communities.

Telephone lines dotted the area in the middle of this space, highlighting the illusion of a fence. There were two border crossings between the two sister towns; one at Morley

Avenue and another further west on Grand Avenue, which was the one that all residents on both sides were required to use. The practical reality was that anyone could cross at any point if they didn't get caught, and it was commonplace to do so. The communities had been split for a little over half a century, and yet many still had families on both sides of the border.

Cassidy's original plan had been to stay in Ambos Nogales, moving back and forth from the Arizona side to the Sonora side to await the return of the treasure hunters. He figured he would be able to avoid authorities on both sides of the border by his movements, then find a job to give him enough money for food, booze, and sex, and give him plenty of time to devise a plan for when they returned. Now, he felt he had the means to find a job and a way to stay in México when he wasn't working. A perfect piece of luck once again.

He made the decision to stay in Ambos Nogales, befriend Dust-up, get a job at ASU, and plot his ambush of the returning treasure hunters.

The single biggest problem he had with this plan was keeping track of the treasure hunters' movements. He thought he knew how to solve that problem, and planned to visit the taxi office while they were gone to put his plan into place.

# Chapter Twenty One

## *Hermosillo*

Francisco and Gideon spent most of the time on the ride from Nogales to *Hermosillo* in deep discussion about the treasure, ownership, and how Francisco would be compensated once the treasure was uncovered.

Once that was settled, they discussed how to get any treasure they found back from *Mexcaltitán*. When Gideon was satisfied with Francisco's proposal, they discussed what would happen if a treasure *wasn't* found, a prospect neither one of them wanted to consider. The risk, cost, and aggravation would simply not be worth it if they came up empty.

"There is one piece of business I would still like to discuss with you, Gideon."

Gideon tensed at the ominous tone in Francisco's voice. He pulled his watch from his pocket, flipped it open, and stared at it for several seconds.

He and Francisco seemed to be getting along well, and Francisco would obviously do almost anything for Carmelita, but he knew that didn't automatically extend to him. He knew Francisco was headstrong and redoubtable. He did not want to have to worry about their relationship and wondered what was on his mind. He didn't have to wait long.

"Thom MacMurrough, or maybe you know him as Declan Cassidy."

Gideon froze. He never expected this to come up in México with Francisco. He waited.

"What do you know of him and what occurred in Cananea?"

Gideon took a long beat and studied Francisco closely. He was a daunting figure who never seemed to smile, with the ubiquitous eyepatch which hid his left eye and gave him the look of a pirate. He knew from Carmelita's accounts that Francisco hated Cassidy, but wasn't sure how to respond. He decided the truth was best.

"Carmelita told me that Cassidy, who I guess was using the alias, Thom MacMurrough, was a loathsome man who ran construction of the rail lines for Colonel Greene. She said he was hated by all and had a reputation of being a womanizer and abuser, of both women he paid for and the workers he managed. Carmelita said he had to pay for it because no self-respecting woman would go near him."

"Did she tell you about her mother?"

Gideon hesitated. Carmelita had only spoken to him one time about her mother's problems with Cassidy, but he was certain Francisco knew the entire story.

"She only mentioned it once, but yes, she did tell me that Cassidy had raped her mother. He made the claim that he was her true father, but Carmelita would never believe it, and her mother denounced the notion on her deathbed. Still, she wants to be sure. She wants to look him in the eye, and says when she does she will know the truth. I asked her about that. She never really had the chance to look into his eyes, although she came close a couple of times. Her passion is to find him, find out the truth, and make sure he's punished for good. If she wasn't the person she is, I think she would kill him herself. I'm certain she wishes she could find the resolve to do it."

"Yes, Gideon. Carmelita and I share the same wish. The difference is, I will carry out the threat. For Carmelita, her mother Edelmida, her father Manuel, and all of the people Cassidy has hurt. He truly is an evil man."

Gideon's version of events was correct, but truncated. Carmelita never really told him all of the detail of Cassidy's background and the evil her family endured.

Cassidy was in the U.S. illegally. He had emigrated from Ireland after murdering a British Policeman during the dry run of a planned theft of ammunition from an armory in Dublin. He had been affiliated with the Green Brigade, a ragtag radical group sympathetic to the Irish Republican Army, who helped him emigrate. Their alternative had been to kill him, thereby eliminating him as a liability to protect their interest in disrupting the British, but it was felt discovery of his death would bring undue scrutiny of the radical group.

As he was awaiting trial for a robbery he committed, the murder he committed of a Méxican worker at the mines in Cananea came to light. In the vigilante atmosphere of Tucson at the time, jurisdiction of the crime was not even a consideration, and Cassidy was tried for the murder as well.

Cassidy was still officially a citizen of Ireland and the worker he had murdered was Méxican, killed on Méxican soil. But México was in the midst of a revolution, so extradition was unlikely, if not impossible. Arizona, had only been admitted to the Union two years earlier, and was still dealing with many issues that were being resolved on both sides of the border, regardless of jurisdiction. There was increasing talk of U.S. involvement in a potential war in Europe, and the state was simultaneously dealing with border wars spilling over from the Méxican Revolution.

Tensions were high all throughout the region and several skirmishes between U.S. and Méxican forces were erupting on a daily basis. Justice was meted out largely by local authorities and the Tucson authorities took it upon themselves to avenge Cassidy's violent and murderous actions. Cassidy had created so much turmoil that Albert Bacon Fall, who previously worked for Colonel Greene at the Cananea mines and who was now the Senator from New Mexico and longtime nemesis of Cassidy, testified remotely via a notarized accounting of the murder leading to his conviction.

Cassidy's tenure at the Cananea Copper Mines had been fraught with tension. He was hated by the men he managed, took part in all types of illegal activities, raped many women, and killed at least two men. It was a wonder he stayed on as long as he did, but he was successful at laying a tremendous amount of track for the railroads in a surprisingly short time. Francisco hated him with a passion and wanted him dead. Perhaps even more than Carmelita did.

At one point Carmelita got up from her seat next to Sofie and across from Mollie to see what Francisco and her husband were discussing. But when she approached she could tell instinctively that she should leave them alone.

She went back to her seat and looked out the window at the cacti which bloomed in the desert sun while Sofie read about the Aztecs and Mollie napped.

They arrived without incident in Hermosillo and all left the train to stretch their legs and get some fresh air. The next train would be leaving soon for the final leg to Guaymas.

Gideon and Francisco were walking together into the cantina for a drink when Francisco stopped suddenly at the newsstand. All of the newspapers were in Spanish, and although Gideon had acquired fairly good spoken skills after living in Tucson with Carmelita, he still did not read it very well.

Carmelita had come up behind them to speak with Gideon to find out what he and Francisco had discussed on the train, but before she could ask, she saw the headlines of the papers on the newsstand and sucked in a sharp, deep breath.

"¡Dios mío!"

Gideon turned around. She never took the Lord's name in vain. He looked to her, confused.

"What is it, Lita?"

Carmelita and Francisco each grabbed a copy of a newspaper and began to read.

Carmelita interpreted for Gideon.

"There are riots in *México City* at the American Embassy."

"Why? What happened? Gideon inquired.

"An incident occurred earlier this week in Vera Cruz. It seems a German freighter, Ypiranga, tried to dock with machine guns, rifles, and munitions for Huerta's army. *Los Estados Unidos* has an embargo of arms on México."

Carmelita was slipping back and forth between English and Spanish, but Gideon was able to follow her.

"There is also an article quoting Pancho Villa as saying the Americans are his friends and he is sure they don't want war. Villa has always hated Huerta and will do what he can to fuel the fire. He calls Huerta a drunk, because, as you know, Villa is a teetotaler."

She had to be careful what she said about Villa, because Francisco was fighting with him. Her personal feelings were that Villa was a two-faced egotistical pig.

Francisco chimed in, "*Sí,* there is much conflict and the Americans are being drawn into it. There is another story in this paper that three people have died and another twenty-five injured near the rail lines between Vera Cruz and *México City.* These are all related to the embargo, but the fact that injury and death is occurring near rail lines tells me there is more violence to come. Even though we are across the continent, over a thousand miles away, it shows the disposition of the Méxican people. I believe Americans are more at risk than ever. We need to be very careful, Gideon. Make sure the woman are well protected. I will get you to Guaymas but then I will have to bid you *adios.*"

The trip to this point had gone smoothly, much more so than any of them had hoped. They had seen no demonstrations of violence or even any real dissension. But the headlines on all of the papers were filled with stories of the revolution, animosity towards America and its' people, and the impending war in Europe. It seemed to Carmelita that the whole world was on the brink of disaster. She shared this observation with Gideon, who agreed.

"Lita, we must talk to Sofie and Mollie about what's happening here. We've only travelled a third of the way. It's still early enough for them to go back. Let's at least give them the option."

Gideon and Carmelita sought out Sofie and Mollie, who were enjoying a cool drink in the train stations' cantina. They explained the danger of the situation in terse detail.

Sofie and Mollie looked at each other and both shrugged their shoulders.

Sofie said, "This is what we've just been discussing. Mollie and I are well aware of what's going on. Mollie has seen it for years, living in Tucson near the border. This is nothing compared to what they're talking about in Europe. I think the U.S. will get sucked into that war and forget all about México. The internal fighting may continue, but what threat can we possibly pose? Besides, we'll be travelling the west coast of México, as far away from the turmoil as we can get."

Mollie nodded her agreement and they all headed back to the train to settle in for the next leg of the journey. None of them could have foreseen what was to come.

---

The University of Arizona opened its doors in 1891. That year, although thirty-two students applied, only five were admitted. The rest went to a school the University had set up for preparatory classes. It took seventeen years until the number of students at the University outnumbered those in the prep school. The challenge faced was the lack of secondary education in the Arizona territory. Consequently, it took years before the number of students at the University level surpassed those at the prep school.

Cassidy approached the entrance to "Old Main," the original building that had housed the entire University for years, with trepidation. He walked up the steps slowly and looked around. The University was set in a fairly remote location, but he was still unsure of his safety since his escape. He could feel the energy which emanated throughout the campus from the students. He hadn't felt this much enthusiasm in years and was sure he would love to work at the University in spite of the menial labor he would have to perform.

"Hell," he thought, "it's a damn site better than working in the prison. No complaints from me."

His new hobo pal, Dust-up, had recommended him for a position at the school. He was fairly certain to get the job, because most of those who applied were illegals. Many were from México looking for a way to change the choice their ancestors made after the Gadsden Purchase, but almost as many were from the Orient, and had to find new work now that many of the railroads were complete. Their other option was to try and find work on the rail lines in México, but the revolution was a major concern and money was uncertain, not to mention the risk to life and limb.

As he climbed the steps to submit his application and speak to Dust-up's boss, he looked around at the campus and vowed to make it work this time. He knew he could only stay a short while – until Carmelita and her crew returned with their treasure, but he also wanted to make sure he kept his nose clean and kept a low profile while he waited. He had never been able to accomplish that before, and he was determined to make it a certainty this time.

The total student population of the school now was 308 students and 40 faculty members. A small school by University standards, but thriving for the new State of Arizona. The University was expanding at a very fast clip, growing from the original building "Old Main" to 18 buildings with over 22,000 volumes in its libraries spread over the forty acres that was bequeathed to Tucson from the Morrill Land Grant Act. Not bad for a town that initially didn't want the University at all.

On this day, as Cassidy walked down the hall, he knew that Tucson was not only proud of its University, but many citizens felt they had won the jackpot. They had a burgeoning sports program and the citizens of Tucson regularly attended sporting events at the school.

Cassidy wouldn't admit it to himself, but his biggest challenge would be the attraction he always felt for young women. The University was diverse, and although the number of female to male students was small, it was still co-ed and the sporting events brought even more girls out to the campus.

In spite of his age and infirmities, Cassidy still felt a stirring in his groins whenever a young lass was nearby.

Cassidy was hired for a janitorial position with little fuss, primarily based on the recommendation of his friend, Dust-up (he didn't even know Dust-ups' real name, but the woman in charge of hiring had Cassidy's name on a list).

He came as close as he could to skipping down the stairs as he left the building. He now had a job, a place to stay during the work week, and he was off to catch a ride on the rails to find a place to stay on weekends over the border. His short-term plan was to establish himself at the school and then find Verde Transportation. He planned to work see if he could ingratiate himself to the dispatcher to monitor the return of the treasure hunters. For Cassidy right now, he was on top of the world.

---

The four treasure hunters got back on the train for the last leg of their land travel. They sat facing each other, the women on one bench seat facing the direction of travel, and Gideon and Francisco on the seat facing opposite.

On the ride, Sofie peppered Francisco with questions of the revolution. She understood the history of México as well as anyone, and was acquainted with the events which lead to the revolt, but wanted to know more about the characters which were written about so widely in the papers in New York. Villa and Zapata were larger than life figures and stories appeared about them in the Times, Herald, Tribune, and other papers every day.

As they once again approached their destination, the port city of *Guaymas,* without incident, Francisco explained to Sofie that the major battles were in the larger cities which held strategic importance.

"With the exception of *Hermosillo,* which we just left, the route we are taking goes through lands belonging to native tribes. I don't expect we will see anything of consequence until we reach the port in *Guaymas.* That may be a different story. Last year, when Huerta claimed the office of the President after Madero was assassinated, General Alvaro Obregon of the rebel forces dropped bombs from an airplane on five ships at the port. It was the world's first ever aerial bombing of a naval target."

Sofie spoke up excitedly, "I remember reading about that. Even though aerial bombs had been used before, it was the first time ever for an aerial attack on a ship at port. *Guaymas* has had a long history of conflict. Didn't the French try to take over the port at one time?"

"The French, the English, the Germans, and now the rebel forces are trying to take it over from the corrupt *Federales*. You are correct Sofie, *Guaymas* has had a long history of conflict. We will have to be diligent when we arrive. A boat will be waiting for you when we arrive and we will have to get from the train to the boat and out of the port as quickly as possible. This is the most dangerous part of the trip."

They all looked at each other with concern. This was first they had heard about the problems in *Guaymas*. They knew the trip was risky, but to this point, it all seemed so easy. They had been lulled into a false sense of security. Carmelita was the only one besides Francisco who had witnessed the kind of terror that could be generated in México. She was fearful that now the risk would become all too real.

# Chapter Twenty Two

## *Guaymas*

The train station at *Guaymas* was packed with people. Trains arrived and left with hundreds of passengers. Military presence was ubiquitous with soldiers roaming the platforms, checking identification, and searching luggage.

"Francisco, what is happening here? I didn't expect it to be so crowded and confusing. I thought this was a sleepy port town. Why is it so crazy and busy?" Carmelita asked.

"I'm sorry, Carmelita, I should have warned you. Since *Guaymas* is less than three hundred miles from the Arizona border, it is a hotbed of import and export activity for the Arizona territory. It is also, as I told Sofie on the way here, a contested port. Both the sitting government and the revolutionaries want to control activity in and out. Right now, the *Federales* are in control, but the potential for battle is always close at hand. There is danger everywhere – from the pirates who roam the seas to the thieves who steal goods all along the port, to the government itself, as well as the opposition. It is a very dangerous place. We must get to the port and your boat as quickly as possible There is no telling what might happen here."

Carmelita, Gideon, Sofie, and Mollie gathered their belongings and prepared to make haste to get to the boat. The train platform was several miles inland and they would have to arrange for transportation. Francisco explained that there were no taxis in *Guaymas*. They would take a street trolley drawn by a burro. It was slow and painfully intermittent service, often interrupted and irregular.

As they were about to disembark the train and step onto the platform, Mollie strapped on her holster. She prepared to place her weapon in its place, when she heard Francisco shout.

"Mollie! What are you thinking?"

Mollie was confused. It appeared to her that all of the people on the platform had guns in holsters.

"What's the problem, Francisco? Everyone here seems to have a gun. "

He stroked his beard and closed his good eye as if in prayer.

"Mollie." He took a deep breath. "First, you are a woman. In México, you shouldn't have a gun at all. Second, you are obviously American. Most of the people here do not need more than that as an excuse to kill you. That is one thing that both the *Federales* and revolutionaries agree on. Most Méxicans believe that the U.S. stole their most valuable land. There is no love for Americans. Only their money. You show a gun and you make yourself a target. Take it off or find your own way."

Mollie looked at Sofie, who she thought might be an ally, but all of them just stared at her and she instinctively knew that Francisco was right. She reluctantly agreed and removed her holster and stowed the gun.

"I'll trust you are going to protect us, Francisco."

He turned away and went to find a tram.

Francisco was an imposing figure and he carried himself in such a way that all others around him gave him wide berth. He quickly found a driver and herded the treasure hunters rapidly towards the trolley.

Amid all the confusion, they didn't notice as two Méxicans stood watching them with interest. The two looked like they hadn't shaved for days, and both wore stained sombreros, white shirts that looked like they hadn't been washed since they last shaved, and huarache sandals that were worn and filthy. Both were shorter than Mollie and Carmelita, and both had drooping moustaches. The only discernable difference between them was that one had long stringy hair midway down his back, while the other was nearly bald. They both carried standard Colt SSA (single action army) guns tucked securely in their belts.

They watched the *Americanos* and exchanged glances before while eyeing Carmelita.

She had always been a beautiful woman, and men lusted after her. These two *hombres* had been without a woman for a very long time. There were few women in the port city to speak of and those that were there were paid for sex and long past their prime.

Gideon was stashing the bags in the back of the tram as Francisco gave the driver their destination and Mollie and Sofie climbed up onto the plain wooden seat in the back row of the two row trolley.

Carmelita had stopped on the platform to gather the folds of her loose fitting summer dress, and was about to climb into the tram when the two who had been watching approached her quickly.

They each grabbed one of her arms and pulled her quickly away back towards the platform. Just as the one with the long hair reached around to cover her mouth with his filthy hand, she yelled out at the top of her lungs "Gideon!"

Both Gideon and Francisco heard the scream and quickly turned to see Carmelita being dragged away.

Francisco ran towards her, just slightly ahead of Gideon.

"Gideon. Stay here. Watch and be ready, but let me handle these *pendejos*. I don't want to give others here any reason to attack an American."

Gideon did not like standing by, but he knew Francisco was right and he had no real choice. His involvement could only lead to a much bigger altercation.

Francisco drew a long knife, ran quickly, and yelled out to the men.

"Let her be or the wrath of Kosterlitzky will be brought down upon you."

Kosterlitzky was a legendary figure throughout México. He was known by reputation as the Méxican Cossack and his exploits were legendary. He was feared by all. Francisco evoked his name, knowing it would cause the men to pause.

He was right. They took a look at Francisco, who was a force in his own right, and realized they had made a mistake. They had seen Gideon, Mollie, and Sofie with the Méxican woman and assumed she would be an easy target. They didn't count on the tall, imposing Méxican with the eye patch, who looked as much the image of a pirate as anyone, as being her protector.

They each let go of Carmelita's arm and turned to run. Their sandals proved to be inadequate for running and they nearly tripped over one another. The long haired *pistolero* dropped to his knees, pulled out his Colt, and squeezed off two rounds towards Francisco.

Francisco was surprised as he hadn't expected them to fire a shot. He dropped to the ground and pulled his own weapon. As he drew, he heard another shot ring out from behind him. He turned his head and saw Mollie standing with a smoking gun in her hand. The long haired gunman was on the ground screaming with pain and clutching his left side.

"Quick let's get out of here," she yelled to Francisco. Gideon and Mollie came up to him and saw he was cringing as he tried to stand. Blood spurted from his thigh.

"Go! You two have to get out of here. Now!"

Mollie spoke first. "We can't just leave you here, Francisco. You're hurt. We have to get you to a doctor."

Gideon concurred. "She's right, *amigo*. Carmelita will never forgive us if we leave you here."

Francisco turned his good eye towards them and Gideon saw in his face a look that would strike fear in even the most psychotic of men. He knew then why he was so feared yet respected.

"Listen to me. I am a soldier in Villa's army. I will be fine. Look around you. These are all *mí hermanos*. Get to the boat as I told you. You remember the name of the boat and *el Capitán*?"

"Yes. *Capitán Flores* of the *Camarón Barco*."

"*Sí*. Go there. Now. Tell my *pequeña flor* to write me at the copper mine when you are returning. *Buena suerte*."

Carmelita had run back to Sofie when the shooting started. Gideon and Mollie reluctantly turned back, then broke into a run towards the trolley. Carmelita issued stern orders for the driver to get them to the port immediately.

As they rounded a corner, she turned back to see Francisco who was being helped up as he raised his arm in salute. Carmelita waved frantically and blew him a kiss.

The driver of the tram did his best to encourage his donkey to move faster, but he met with only lukewarm results. The tram continued on its route and Mollie rode facing the rear with her gun at her side to be sure that no one was following.

The driver spoke only Spanish, so Carmelita asked him if he had witnessed the gunfight. He had, but told her it was a common occurrence and no one would really pay it any mind. He did tell her she was lucky. Most times when a *senorita* was abducted, she was raped and left to die on the streets. Hearing that made her think of Cassidy and her mother. God rest her soul.

The treasure hunters finally made it to the port area and the tram drove along the docks until they found the *Camarón Barco* at the end of a short pier. They all knew enough Spanish to know that the name meant Shrimp Boat. An unimaginative name, to be sure.

But humor eluded them when they saw the boat.

It was a working shrimp boat, with long trawlers on either side used to sweep the sea bottom for the crustaceans. Below decks was nothing more than engines and enough room to store the catch. The smell of shrimp permeated the air, and the boat itself looked like it hadn't been scrubbed since its last outing.

Carmelita called out in Spanish, "Are you *Capitán Flores?*"

"*Sí. ¿Estás Carmelita ?*

"*Sí.*"

He looked visibly relieved to see her. He nervously looked around several times as they all quickly boarded the ship. *El Capitán* wore a blue, peaked sailor's hat, which was at least one size too small and sat on the crown of his head over black, straggly hair. He had the stub of a fat cigar in his mouth, which was unlit and might have been permanently attached.

While Carmelita spoke to the captain about accommodations, the journey, and Francisco, Gideon paid the tram driver. Sofie unloaded their bags, and Mollie kept lookout with her gun ready.

Carmelita called them together and gave them the bad news.

"There are no other options for us. We must take this shrimp boat now, and he's got to leave right away. He says he's been waiting for us and it's dangerous for all of us here. It seems he is not legally allowed to work this area and other shrimpers take this very seriously. Francisco arranged everything, but we will have to help him with his catch to make it look real."

Mollie suddenly called out.

"Not sure if this is about us, but the *policía* are coming this way."

They all looked at each other and back towards the town and the oncoming authorities.

*Capitán Flores* called something out in unintelligible Spanish and two swarthy, sweating men came up the steps from the hold and gave their new shipmates the once over.

They both had oily, black hair worn long and one of them sported a sad looking goatee. He also had a lazy eye and Carmelita couldn't tell if he was looking at them or staring off into space.

He leered at Mollie, apparently fascinated by her blond hair and freckled face, and she stared him down as he bent over to release the ropes from their moorings.

Sofie and Carmelita looked at each other with worried frowns on their faces. None of them had expected other deckhands to be aboard.

"Let's go," Gideon called out tersely, and they all settled aboard the shrimp boat, holding their noses at the smell of the rotting crustaceans in the oppressive Méxican heat.

# <u>Chapter Twenty Three</u>

## *Serendipity*

Not long after the skirmish the treasure hunters had faced in Guaymas, Cassidy walked onto the University grounds arriving after a wild weekend across the border. He had settled into a rhythm in the past couple of weeks - staying with his new friend, Dust-up, after long days working at the U. They were both exhausted at the end of their work days, and would meet for a bite to eat with a little tequila or beer, and went to sleep so they would be fresh the next day. Cassidy knew he was on borrowed time, and right now he knew he had it too good. He was determined not to mess this up.

On Friday after work, they would head to the rail yard and find a freighter to ride to the border. Once there, they split up and each enjoyed a weekend of their choosing, riding the rails back to Tucson Sunday night, sometimes alone in separate cars or trains, and occaisionally, if they saw each other at the rail yard, hopping the same car and swapping stories.

Cassidy had reverted to his kinky, idiosyncratic ways, adopting the behavior he couldn't control before prison and apparently was not able to control now.

Once on the border at Nogales, he would seek out a bar and after a few drinks go out to find a willing *furcia* whom he would treat cruelly, stopping just short of physical torture. He would treat the sex as if it were rape, although at his age and with the deformity he had suffered at the hands of another *puta*, he certainly had to pay handsomely for his pleasure.

The last thing Cassidy wanted was to be noticed. He had to severely curtail his desires so word did not get out on the street about him. He had enough trouble maintaining any sense of anonymity due to his unique physical impairments.

Once back on campus in Tucson, he kept a very low profile and kept to his work.

Now that he had established himself, the time had come for him to implement his plan. He didn't know how long the treasure hunters would be in México, but he didn't want to miss their return.

Today was the day he had planned for. He went to work very early, 5 a.m. His normal work day was 8 a.m. to 5 p.m. and there was little room for flexibility. But today he specifically asked if he could come early and leave early for some business he had to attend to. Since there were no classes over the weekend, Monday was a day of cleaning up on the grounds and most of the work could be done at any time. Cassidy had been working hard and took on any task his manager asked of him, so he was given the time on this day to take care of business.

In this case, his business was to find out what was happening with the treasure hunters. He never thought about Carmelita in any way other than as an obstacle to his goal to steal the cross. Now, with the possibility of possessing the cross a near impossibility, his plan was to take any treasure she and the others might find on their journey. The idea that he might be her father never entered his mind. As for the rape he perpetrated on her mother, if he thought of it at all, and he never did, it would only be to remember that she deserved it and the harm she caused him by hiding the cross under his mattress and pinning the blame of the theft on him. When he did think of it, it incensed him and his only thought was of retribution on her daughter, Carmelita.

Cassidy had been trying to make friends at the university since the day he started. In spite of his larcenous heart, evil mind, and psychotic condition, he could use his Irish brogue to charm when he wanted to. One of his first targets and closest ally was the receptionist at the Old Main. Her name was Guadalupe and she was Méxican by birth. Guadalupe was short with long braided hair and a wide flat nose and dark, almost black, eyes. She had a perennial smile on her face and spoke flawless English with only the slightest trace of an accent. She was thirty-three years old and had never been married, but had borne a son the previous year. The father was a man she thought would marry her one day, but she was wrong and never saw him again after she told him she was pregnant. Guadalupe had crossed the border looking for work during a time of University expansion. The former receptionist, like many at the school at that time, wanted to move into one of the new buildings. That opened up opportunities for people like Guadalupe. She landed the positon in spite of her accent and had been there ever since. She studied for her U.S. citizenship and achieved that status only four years prior. She was a dedicated employee, staunch women's rights advocate and unabashedly loved her adopted country.

Cassidy spoke to her every day when he arrived at work and was always courteous and charming. He came to her with stories about life on the Méxican side of Nogales and gave her a synopsis of the sermon the priest said at mass on Sunday. He made it all up of course. He could never tell her what really transpired when he was gone on the weekends.

Cassidy finished his work at 2 pm and checked with his boss to remind him that he would be leaving early for an appointment. He went to his locker and changed into his best clothes, dark cotton slacks, black tie shoes, a blue long sleeve shirt buttoned to the collar with a light herringbone jacket purchased just for the occasion. He had also invested in a felt hat which gave him a rakish look with the added benefit of hiding his red hair.

He approached her on this Monday with a smile, walking as straight up as he could, barely using his cane.

"*Hola*, Guadalupe."

"Hello, Declan," she replied smiling broadly. She noticed the clothes, but resisted asking him about them.

Cassidy was using his given first name, but no one at the University knew his last name, except his boss. He had used a combination of his given name, Declan Cassidy, and the alias he adopted in the United States, Thom MacMurrough. On his application he used the name Declan MacMurrough. He had been imprisoned under his given name, so felt this would protect his real identity. Plus, he felt comfortable using the combination. Long accustomed answering to both first names, it worked well for him.

"Guadalupe, I have a favor to ask. I need to go into South Tucson on important business. Would you do me a favor and call a taxi for me? Verde Transportation."

"Of course, Declan. I'll do it right away."

Guadalupe picked up the phone and called the taxi company. They promised to have a cab over in ten minutes.

Cassidy chatted with Guadalupe while waiting for the cab. He learned when he first met her that she had never been married, but had a son who was only sixteen months old.

Cassidy had initially wondered why he wasn't attracted to her. He began to believe that he could almost smell when a woman had children. He was only interested in virgins. Young ones. It didn't matter to him what they looked like. He listened to her prattle on as he thought about his plan.

He knew that Mollie was going to México with Gideon and Carmelita, so they had to leave someone in charge of the business. That person would have to be kept abreast of the couple's whereabouts and when they would be returning. His plan was to go to the cab company and inquire as to the treasure hunters return. As Guadalupe was telling Cassidy about how her son was in the first phase of "finding his voice," he interrupted her.

"Guadalupe, you must tell me more about your boy, but my taxi is here and I have to get to my appointment. I don't want to be late. Thanks for your help and I'll see you tomorrow so you can tell me more."

Guadalupe smiled and Cassidy walked out of the administration building and into the waiting taxi.

---

Luisa had just finished addressing the next shift of drivers as the night manager took over. This had been a particularly long day, but she couldn't complain because business was booming. Gideon and Carmelita would be very pleased when they came back and saw the increase. She needed to talk to Gideon, and soon, because she felt they could justify adding another taxi - maybe two.

She was looking forward to going home, preparing a glass of *xocolatl* and soaking her feet in a tub of cool water.

Luisa packed up her desk and rinsed out the lunch bowl she brought with her each day so she could eat at her desk. Just as she was about to walk out the door, a short man with a felt hat and a cane appeared at the door.

"Can I help you?" Luisa asked curiously. It was very rare for customers to come to the taxi office.

"I'm hoping you can," Cassidy said in his best Irish brogue.

"My name is Declan and I am visiting from the old country to see my niece. I heard from her mother that she comes here often. Perhaps you know her. Mollie McGuire?"

Luisa's heart skipped a beat. She had thought about Mollie every day since they had all left for México to find the treasure, but always tried to put the thought out of her mind. Now, here was a stranger asking about her.

"Your niece?" Luisa managed to ask.

"Yes, I'm her mother's brother. I'm here teaching at the University for a short time and had the occasion to get away. I wanted to see if I could see little Mollie. I haven't seen her since she was an infant. Is she here?"

Cassidy smiled and cocked his head like a young man. He began to feel stirrings for this attractive young lady, but there was something different about her that he couldn't quite figure out. No matter, he was here on business and couldn't let his feelings get in the way of his mission.

"No, I'm sorry. She's away for a few weeks. How long will you be here in Tucson?"

"Not that long, I'm afraid. Do you have any idea when she'll be back? Is there any way to get in touch with her?"

"I don't have a way to get in touch with her, but she's with my boss and he checks in when he can. They're in México, and I am not sure when they'll return. I can mention to my boss that you came by to see Mollie the next time he sends a telegram if you like."

"No, no, please. Don't do that. I want this to be a surprise. I'll tell you what, can you call me to let me know when they'll be returning? I can surprise her when they arrive."

"Of course. She will be happy to see you, I'm sure. How can I get in touch with you?"

Cassidy gave her the telephone number at the Old Main that Guadalupe inevitably answers and said, "My assistant's name is Guadalupe. As soon as you know their schedule and when they'll be arriving, please call. I'm often out of town and want to be sure to be there when she arrives. But remember, I want this to be a surprise."

"Oh, of course. Don't worry. I can keep a secret." She winked at Cassidy, and that riled him but he kept his cool.

"What is your name, ma'am?"

"Mi nombre es Luisa."

"Gracias, Luisa. I do come back this way from time to time, so I'll stop in to see if you've heard from them."

Cassidy reiterated his desire for secrecy. He wanted to be certain she didn't say anything about him in advance of their reuturn. The bait had been set now he just had to wait to spring his trap.

# Chapter Twenty Four

## *Riveria Nayarit*

The shrimp boat baked in the hot sun creating a stench of burned diesel and spoiling crustaceans. Gideon and Mollie helped *Capitán Flores* as they dragged the sea bottom for shrimp. Once the hold was full, they would put into the next closest port to sell their catch. The work was hard and Gideon had developed oozing blisters on both hands. Carmelita and Sofie cooked and cleaned. They eventually became accustomed to the smell, and Mollie became particularly good at unraveling the netting when it fouled.

On the second day at sea, the deckhand with the paltry goatee, who went by the name of Paco, approached Mollie.

*"¿Senorita, quieres un poco de tequila ?"*

Mollie stopped what she was doing with the nets and stood up straight. She didn't know if this man spoke English or not, but really did not care.

"Listen, asshole. I'm not interested in you or any other man. Stay away from me and the others or I'll take a knife to your heart."

The man didn't understand English, but he didn't have to. He could tell her intent from the look in her eyes and the force of her words. He thought about standing up to her and causing a scene, but he was outnumbered. *Capitán Flores* would not be happy if his passengers, who doubled as deckhands, were upset. He decided to laugh it off and wait for another day.

He shrugged, smiled, took a flask from his hip pocket and took a short pull. He wiped his mouth with the back of his hand, replaced the flask in his pocket, smiled at Mollie, and walked away. Mollie returned to her nets, but she decided she would start wearing her knife on her hip since she couldn't wear her gun.

Back in Tucson, she would wear her gun on her right hip and the knife on her left, with the knife-edge pointing out, so when she removed the weapon, she could slash quickly, grabbing the handle with her right hand and slashing out in one quick movement.

In spite of the heat and the malodorous scents on the *Camarón Barco,* it was a modern ship boasting a powerful diesel engine and a new otter trawl which vastly improved the ease of the catch.

*Capitán Flores* stayed close to shore, scooping shrimp at low tide and bringing the catch to small ports along the way, helping fund the cost of gas, food, and water.

Travel was slow and tedious due to the near constant trawling and the time it took to sell the catch. The Sea of Cortés sounded romantic and calm, but it was an angry sea and could be treacherous at times. They had to stay close to shore without getting too close to the huge waves and swells that had scuttled many a boat.

The evening before they were to arrive at the port in *Riviera Nayarit,* Mollie and Sofie were on the starboard side of the ship away from the others, who were enjoying the sunset on the port side. The sun burned like scarlet flames cutting through the clouds as they stood at the rail discussing a plan for their return if they actually ever did find the treasure.

As a librarian and historian, Sofie had a better than passing understanding of the area, and she spent much of her time studying the maps. She had taken maps with her from New York and quickly realized many of the charts were inaccurate. She spent quite a bit of time making changes to them and began to fancy herself as an amateur cartographer. She and *Capitán*

*Flores* would spend hours charting the maps and he would teach her how to read the waters.

Sofie had given quite a bit of thought to their mission and fully expected they would find the treasure and would need a solid plan for their return.

But either way, she knew they had to figure a way to get back. Getting into México during the revolution was difficult, but getting out would be much more challenging. Mollie seemed to recognize this, but Gideon and Carmelita seemed oblivious. She knew they believed they could rely on Francisco to help, but during a revolution, she thought it possible he might be otherwise engaged.

Although they all believed finding the treasure was more than possible, no real plans had been made for returning to the U.S. It was as though they were standing in an open field with a metal rod in their hands extending towards the sky during a storm. The potential of being hit was all too real, but until it did, you didn't really think it could happen to you.

Sofie put away her charts and turned to Mollie, "I'm going to go watch the sunset with the others. Are you coming?"

"Go ahead. I'll catch up in a few minutes. I need a little alone time. We haven't had any time to ourselves since we left Tucson."

Sofie walked around the wheelhouse to view a spectacular sunset. Gideon and Carmelita were staring out into the water as the sun slowly sank into the ocean. It was quiet, cool, and peaceful and they all knew they were now getting close to the *Riviera Nayarit* and *Mexcaltitán*.

"Gideon," Sofie whispered. "I've been thinking quite a bit about our return. I've spent a lot of time with *el Capitán* charting our course and correcting the maps. We need to give some thought to what we will do when we find the treasure."

"Sofie!" Carmelita stood up quickly, "We all agreed not to say anything about that while we are on this ship. If any of the crew overhears we could put ourselves in extreme danger!"

"I'm sorry, Carmelita. I'm just worried, that's all. The crew is below decks so I thought it would be a good time to talk. I'm sorry."

Carmelita looked around, but didn't see anyone in the dusky light. They all sat back down and maintained their silence as the sun continued its fiery plunge into the horizon.

Mollie came back just as the sun finally dipped into the ocean leaving behind a spectacular reddish/purple glow.

They sat in silence until they heard the watch bell indicating it was time for them to get to sleep. They had a long day ahead. As they got up to head below deck, they didn't notice Paco skulking behind the winch, smiling to himself.

Mollie woke before dawn from a sound and dreamless sleep. The others were beginning to stir, but she wanted to get above deck before the dawn to see the sun rise. Mollie didn't think of herself as having a poetic soul but she loved the idea of seeing the sun set and being up first to see it rise. She went above deck just as she heard the ships bell sound.

The others would be up soon, she knew, so she sat quietly and watched as the sun peeked up out of the blue horizon.

Carmelita, Gideon, and Sofie were stirring when they heard the sound of the watch bell. Carmelita thought she was hearing things when the pleasant peeling of the sound was shattered by an agonizing scream. It sounded like a wounded whale, but was the heartfelt scream of a man in excruciating pain.

Gideon ran up the ladder and around the wheelhouse, arriving first on the scene with the others close behind. He saw Mollie's back and her body was heaving like a bellows pumping a hearth. He thought she must have been hurt, when she turned around and he saw the deckhand, Paco, lying face down with the hilt of Mollie's knife protruding from the top of his hand. Blood was pooling all around him as he writhed half naked on the floor, clawing at the knife blade, which had passed all the way through his hand.

Mollie had a grin on her face and walked quickly aft.

*Capitán Flores* came out of the wheelhouse and pulled the knife quickly out of his man's hand. Sofie grabbed a cloth and soaked it with water to try and stop the bleeding.

"What the hell happened?" Flores yelled out to Mollie's back.

Mollie spun quickly around, her face contorted in anger.

"I'll tell you what happened!" she screamed.

Spittle was flying from her mouth as she roared.

"This asshole came topside while you were all still asleep, came up behind me and grabbed my tits. Then he grabbed my right hand to force me to stroke his naked penis. He's goddamned lucky he had my right hand or I would have cut off his dick."

They looked down at Paco and for the first time noticed his pants were around his ankles, which is why he couldn't stand.

"Paco – is this true?" Flores ordered his deckhand to speak.

Paco couldn't get a word out, he just shook his head as he cried out again and again. Flores noticed the other deckhand standing at the top of the stairs to the hold.

"Alejandro, hitch up his pants and take him below. Get out the first aid kit and patch him up. Give him enough tequila to curb the pain."

Carmelita and Sofie went over to Mollie in an attempt to calm her down and walked her around to the port side of the boat as the sun was rising in a blaze of crimson.

Flores turned to Gideon. "Gideon, I'm sorry for this trouble. Paco is not right in the head and he can do the stupidest things sometimes. It is very surprising though, because he almost never speaks. He is able, but he is very slow and rarely opens his mouth. I hope Mollie will be all right."

"She's tough. You can see that by how quickly she reacted. You can't scare Mollie. But I suggest you keep Paco below decks until you drop us off."

"Don't worry about that. He will be severely disciplined. I'm going to break out some of my *reserva tequila* to help us get through this."

Flores was true to his word, and the tequila flowed. Mollie drank more than her share and was laughing about the incident by lunchtime. They all enjoyed what they hoped was their last shrimp meal for a while, and took a siesta before their final approach to the island.

Unfortunately for Paco, although the tequila helped a bit, he was in horrific pain and would have to be dropped off at port to recover. Flores wasn't sure his hand would be useful at all in the future. Mollie's knife had ripped through several tendons and muscles.

"Tough shit," she said when she heard about his injuries. "serves the asshole right."

# Chapter Twenty Five

## *Mexcaltitán*

"Gideon, we have a problem,"

Sofie was bent over her charts, as she had been most of the trip, peering through her *pince-nez* glasses, which had somehow survived the trip thus far. She had swapped out the elegant satin band she used to keep them around her neck, with a sturdier, heavy, linked chain.

*Capitán Flores* was preparing to disembark his passengers. The deal he had made with Francisco de Torres was to take them along the eastern shore of the Sea of *Cortés* (known to many as the Gulf of California) and bring them to the entry of *Laguna Grande de Mexcaltitán*. At that point, he would provide them with a small wooden rowboat, which they could use to navigate the rest of the way to the island.

"What is it, Sofie?"

"There is no way this boat will be able to navigate from the Gulf to the lake. The water is too shallow. *Capitán Flores* and I have been studying these charts for days. They are far from accurate, but never conservative. These charts say the water is too shallow and we have to trust that. We have to find another way in to the lake from the Gulf."

Gideon peered over the charts. He was originally from Tennessee and had lived in Arizona for many years, so charts of bodies of water were a complete mystery to him.

He and Sofie went off to find *Capitán Flores*. Carmelita and Mollie prepared some food and drink for what they thought would be a short ride in the rowboat to complete the trip.

The two found *Capitán Flores* below deck, and although it was early in the day, he had clearly already been drinking his beloved tequila. He looked awful. His beard was rough, his eyes bloodshot and watery, and he smelled as though he hadn't bathed in days. He wore a filthy cap tilted back on his head and his dark hair, which was thin and scraggly, was pasted across his greasy scalp and wet with sweat.

"Captain. Sofie doesn't think we can get to the lake in this boat. Do we have an alternate plan?"

The Captain looked at them with his eyes unfocused.

He spoke to them in a slightly slurred voice, in almost a whisper.

"Mis amigos, I tell you. This trip has been a disaster. I have great respect for Señor de Torres, and he did promise me a box of wonderful cigars when I get back, but this has been the trip from hell."

He paused and took another small sip of his drink.

"What is that? Sofie asked. "It doesn't smell like tequila."

"Ah, you have a very good nose, señorita. What I am drinking is mescal. I think of it as the father of tequila. In fact, tequila is a form of mescal, but I find the smoky flavor so much more appealing. Tequila is wonderful and very easy to drink, but when I want a rich, bold taste, I always open the mescal."

"Thanks for the lesson on alcohol Captain," Gideon said with obvious disdain, "but we have a problem. Sofie?"

"Capitán Flores, the charts are unmistakable. It shows that we cannot navigate the estuary leading to Laguna Grande de Mexcaltitán. The waters are too shallow. The ship has too much bottom."

Capitán Flores looked at Sofie with a sideways glance and smiled. But his gaze held dead eyes, with no hint of humor. His voice rose as he responded.

"For a city lady, you seem to have some knowledge of the sea. But let me tell you something."

He stopped to take a final sip of his mescal and slammed down the empty glass, breathing heavily through his nose.

"The chart datum is tidal datum, that is, measured at the lowest astronomical tide. You are right that it is shallow, and we will have to play the tides, but we can make this trip. For me, I want to get you off my boat and get back to what I do, which is catch and sell shrimp. This trip has been a nightmare for me and my crew. I will never take gringos again, no matter what *Francisco* says. There is a reason working ships don't allow women. Now, get out of my cabin. I'll let you know when the tide is right. Good luck when I drop you off at the dock."

Gideon and Sofie went back above deck and found Carmelita and Mollie all packed up and ready to go.

"I can't wait to get off this damn ship." Mollie said as she placed her Stetson back on her head. "What did the Captain have to say?"

Gideon looked at Sofie and nodded to her as she recounted their conversation.

The Captain was right. They waited a few hours for the tide to rise and he was able to navigate quickly through the shallow channel to their destination. They passed through mangrove swamps and fought the tide of the river spilling out to the sea.

Silence fell like a shroud over the ship as the captain expertly navigated the shallow channel towards their destination.

Gideon sat back and observed his fellow treasure hunters objectively.

Mollie nervously paced about, itching to get back on land and take up the task of finding the hidden treasure. Her Stetson sat on her head at a cocky angle with just a wisp of her strawberry blonde hair peeking out.

Her denim outfit highlighted her feminine form, but her attitude was anything but soft.

She tapped her boots to the rhythm of the engine and her kinetic energy almost willed the boat to move more quickly.

Now, however, she had her holster and gun strapped to her leg, ready to draw at the slightest provocation.

Sofie sat on an upturned bucket at the rail, her *pince-nez* glasses precariously perched on the end of her nose as she studied the charts as if daring the captain to take a wrong turn.

Gideon wondered how she inevitably managed to look so cool in her ubiquitous black outfit. Her dark hair coiffed with a perfect bun atop her head.

He turned his attention to Carmelita, his lovely and loving wife. She was dressed in another of what seemed to be an endless inventory of long, traditional Méxican dresses. Her regal presence commanding the need to find the lost treasure of *Cortés.*

Gideon marveled at her quiet strength and knew that none of them would be on this dangerous and fantastic journey if not for her. He watched as the Captain approached the end of this phase of their journey in stony silence. His crew below deck not daring to show their faces.

Gideon reflected. He was proud, honored, and pleased to be teamed with the strongest, most determined posse he could ever imagine. He realized then that this was all about guts, drive, and determination.

When they reached the dock, they disembarked quickly, without a word passing between the passengers and the crew as the Captain pulled up to a short wooden dock.

Mollie had barely waited until the boat was within distance before jumping onto the dock with her bag.

As they were about to push off, Paco came out of the hold. He needed to find a doctor so he could have his hand tended. His arm was in a makeshift sling keeping the wound above his heart.

Within minutes after landing, the Captain pushed off and was out of sight.

"Well, not sure how we'll get back," Gideon said as they made their way towards the town, "but it has to be easier than that."

Little did he know that his words couldn't be farther from the truth.

# Chapter Twenty Six

## *Resolve*

The Captain had set them off at a dock, but not on the island of *Mexcaltitán,* rather at a dock on the peninsula with deeper waters, although the island was easily within their sight.

They took a small shuttle boat over to the southwestern point of the island, which became their orientation point during the time they spent there. It was hard for Gideon to imagine that there was so much activity in this small, out of the way place. Sofie had said that the shrimp fishing on *Mexcaltitán* was among the best in the world. It appeared a lot of the traffic was related to the buying and selling of shrimp.

Carmelita sat in the bow of the shuttle with a young man with straight black hair cut short on the sides, with long bangs in front that fell across his eyes. He ran the boat back and forth as often as visitors arrived.

He had a perennial smile on his face, and the two conversed rapidly in Spanish as Gideon and Mollie scanned the island looking for obvious signs of treasure. Sofie sat on the boat's only other seat, leafing through her pages in search of something that would indicate the site of the treasure.

They finally came to rest on a narrow stretch of beach with three wooden planks tied together with coarse rope. The treasure hunters stepped off the boat as Gideon handed the young man some coins in thanks for the ride.

"So, Lita, did you learn anything from the *hombre joven?*"

"*Sí*, Gideon. I learned much from him."

Mollie and Sofie crowded close to Carmelita as she spoke.

"It seems we are not the first to come here to look for treasure. The boy said they get visitors regularly who believe this is the birthplace of the Aztecs. They come for the history. But he said many also believe that when the Aztecs migrated to *Tenochtitlan*, which we now know is *México City*, they must have left some of their treasure behind. Partially because they couldn't know if their journey would be successful, and partially because it didn't makes sense to carry all of their valuables in one trip. Even though the migration took years, maybe decades, the common belief is that the Aztecs left some things behind and just never came back for them."

Mollie jumped in. "Well, what about the lost *Cortés* treasure. Did he say anything about *Cortés* visiting the island and hiding treasure?"

Carmelita frowned. "I asked about that. He said people who come here come mostly to see the birthplace of the Mexica people. *Cortés* never came to *Mexcaltitán* – but it is documented that he spent a brief amount of time in *Riviera Nayarit*, and we all know that is the area where *Mexcaltitán* is located."

She paused and took up the folds of her dress to keep it safe from the mud on the banks of the island.

"Lita, you're keeping us in suspense on purpose. You know what we all want to know. Is there really a treasure here and has anyone found it?"

Carmelita paused and frowned again.

"No, Gideon. No one has found any treasure here. When I mentioned it in passing so as not to create too much interest, the young man laughed.

"He said to me, '*Señorita*, this island is underwater during the rainy season. If there was treasure here, everyone would know. It would float to the top!' "

Gideon looked back and forth between Carmelita and Sofie. Mollie swore loudly and stomped off.

"Did we come all this way for nothing?"

They continued to walk towards the town in silence. Sofie was lost in thought and mumbling.

"Let's find a place to sit and get some food to help me think," she said loud enough for even Mollie to hear as she continued to stomp away from the rest.

"Good idea, Sofie," Carmelita agreed, "as long as it serves something other than shrimp."

They found a small cantina, which did serve many shrimp dishes, but also fresh grilled fish, dishes with beans and cheese, and even some chicken. They all sat at a small table and enjoyed the food, which was the most delicious they had since leaving Tucson.

Sofie had her charts, books, and journal open on a table next to where they ate their food. She would take a mouthful and go to the other table to review her information while chewing slowly. They sipped water and sat in silence, each thinking that this may have been an expensive and dangerously ill-advised adventure.

As they finished their meal and thought about finding a place to stay the night, Sofie jumped up suddenly and knocked over her glass, spilling water all over the remnants of her food. The pressure of the events of the past few weeks had seemingly built to the boiling point in her, causing the aberrant response.

"Wait!" Her glasses fell off her nose as she picked up one of her charts. "We're letting ourselves get down over the words of one twelve year old boy. We've come too far. Let's review what we know before we subject ourselves to defeat."

Carmelita and Mollie were both stunned by Sofie's sudden outburst. She rarely spoke and had never raised her voice in their presence. They listened intently as Sofie carried on.

"We know that a cross – the amulet of Cananea - was given to a priest, Padre Pachero, when he left Spain to come to the new world and spread the word of God to the natives in New Spain, correct?"

They all nodded in silence.

"We know from the *corridos* of the Papago that the priest passed the cross on to a native girl as he died from the bite of a scorpion, right?"

Again, they nodded their assent.

Sofie paused, took a long sip of water from a fresh glass and continued the soliloquy. As her excitement grew, her bohemian laced New York accent became increasingly pronounced.

"We learned that the Papago, who had been converted, followed Padre Pachero's instructions and had given the cross to the church they built to serve as the altar crucifix. Then, decades later, the cross was sold to an unnamed benefactor to fund reconstruction of the church. He then bequeathed it to a church in New York City, St. Peter's. It remained there for decades, until an entrepreneur, William Cornell Greene, known to all as Colonel Greene, boldly asked the pastor of the church if he could use the valuable cross as collateral for a loan to fund his search for lost mines in México. He struck a bargain - if the trip were successful, he would pay back the loan and buy the cross for an exorbitant amount. If not, he would still have to pay the loan, and come back to New York continuing his work as a stockbroker, while the Church retained ownership of the cross. It was an enormous gamble for both men. Colonel Greene did not find lost gold mines, but he bought a copper mine, which became hugely successful. He then bought the cross and brought it back to México."

She halted and looked up to see the three of her colleagues were all staring at her with eyes wide open. She continued.

"The cross was stolen by an unknown intruder, which we now know was Carmelita's mother, Edelmida. She hid it in the room of her tormentor, Thom MacMurrough, also known as Declan Cassidy. We know that Cassidy had brutally raped Carmelita's mother and she had done this to take her revenge." She looked over at Carmelita who had her head down and her eyes closed.

"I'm sorry Carmelita. We have to go through all the detail."

Carmelita just shook her head gently and muttered, "Go on."

"It turns out Cassidy had been set up by Carmelita's mother as repayment for the horrific rape she suffered. Do I have everything right so far?"

Carmelita nodded slowly.

"The cross went missing in the confusion surrounding the arrest and never came to light until many years later when Carmelita was a young woman. We now know that our friend, Francisco deTorres, who was then head of security for Colonel Greene, had hidden the cross on the Colonels property. He said it was to protect the artifact, which Colonel Greene believed to be a good luck piece. Francisco claimed it had still been his good luck piece, even while hidden away.

"Regardless of the motivation, once it had been returned to Colonel Greene, he gave the cross to Carmelita as remuneration for all the suffering she and her family had suffered at the hand of MacMurrough/Cassidy. Carmelita then turned around and gave it back to the Church. In this case, to *Mission San Xavier del Bac,* the White Dove of the Desert. The very church that was built on the foundation of the church that received the cross from Padre Pachero as an altar piece, centuries earlier."

The others had never really thought about all of this as one continuous story before and now could hardly imagine the incredible string of events. Even Carmelita, who knew this story as only one who lived it every day can, was fascinated.

"We also know that Cassidy broke out of prison and tried to steal the cross again - at least twice - almost succeeding once."

Mollie turned bright red, but no one seemed to notice. She squirmed uncomfortably in her seat while Sofie continued.

"Now we come to what brought us here today. We recently learned that the Náhuatl word for Aztlán is inscribed on the cross, which we believe was commissioned by *Cortés*. We also believe that the cross was part of the treasure *Cortés* received from Montezuma and the Aztecs. Have I stated everything correctly to this point?"

They all nodded, thinking about all they had uncovered.

Gideon spoke up. "Sofie, you may have mentioned this when we were in New York and I may have missed it so forgive me for asking, but remind me why *Cortés* would have the word Aztlán embossed on the cross? He hid it, so he would know where to look, right?"

"That's a good question, Gideon. I had given that quite a bit of thought before deciding to go to Tucson to see you. We don't have a lot of details about *Cortés,* but we do know some of the high points. You may remember I told you about *Doña Marina* known today despairingly by her Aztec name, *La Malinche?"*

"I don't," Mollie commented.

"*Cortés* first came to México and landed on the southeast Gulf coast in Veracruz. There he met a woman called Doña Marina. She became his confidant, interpreter, lover, and mother of his child.

"When *Cortés* got to *Tenochtitlan*, Montezuma and *Cortés* met and exchanged gifts. The way some tell it, Montezuma mistook *Cortés* for an Aztec god, but many believe that was really revisionist history.

"Either way, *Cortés* was impressed by the riches the Aztecs had - gold and jewels that Montezuma had amassed from all his tribes throughout the Aztec kingdom.

"Remember when I told you about the massacre in the great temple? When *Cortés* learned that he was to be relieved of his duties for insubordination by the governor of New Spain, and he left for the coast in Veracruz to confront the expedition? Instead, he convinced them to join him when he described all the riches the Aztecs had amassed. They then agreed to return and steal the treasure.

"Meanwhile, things had changed for the worse and his lieutenant, Pedro de Alvarado, had ordered the slaughter of Aztec nobles and priests, infuriating the tribe. *Cortés* convinced Montezuma to address his people in an attempt to quell them, but during the address, he was struck by a rock and killed. No one knows if the blow came from the hand of an Aztec warrior who had become tired of his alliance with *Cortés,* or from the Spanish who now feared for their lives.

"Either way, with Montezuma dead and *Cortés* under siege, he made the decision to leave the city under the cover of night. The Aztecs had already destroyed all of the bridges leading from the city in anticipation of this tactic.

"As you know, *Tenochtitlan,* which is now México City, was founded on an island in a large lake, just as this one is, the assumed birthplace of the Aztecs. *Cortés* had a temporary bridge built, and as they tried to escape with the treasure the Aztecs attacked him.

"The resulting debacle killed hundreds of both Spanish and Aztecs. It was reported that the devastation truly effected

*Cortés.* It is widely believed that he had much of his treasure with him and he agonized because it was lost forever in the bottom of the lake during the battle.

"That is the part of the story that is the most challenged. Many believe, myself included, that *Cortés* was too smart, some say too cruel, to keep all the treasure in one place then try to leave with it intact at the last minute. I, for one, believe he had been sending it away for months to different locations by teams of a dozen or so conquistadors at a time. The only question for me has been – where did he send it?"

Sofie paused to take another sip of water.

"Excuse me, Sofie," Mollie interrupted uncharacteristically politely, "we weren't there in New York, so can you give us a little more background?"

Gideon took up the story.

"When I met Sofie in New York, she had been researching this for years. It turns out the cross was the clue she needed. We now believe *Cortés* had at least some of the treasure distributed in multiple trips. We know for a fact that some of the treasure was sent to Spain to King Charles V. Sofie believes, and I agree, some was sent back to the place where the Aztecs originated, *Aztlán. Cortés* sense of irony made him believe no one would ever think to look there."

Sofie continued, "So, the only part that is conjecture is *where Cortés* believed Aztlán was located. This is where all of my research and knowledge comes into play. I can tell you that I am absolutely convinced that *Cortés* believed that Aztlán is *Mexcaltitán,* no matter what a twelve year old boy says. So, to answer your question, I believe he had the word *Aztlán* inscribed on the cross as a clue to where that part of the treasure was hidden, perhaps for future generations. There was no guarantee that he would ever get back to retrieve it. He wanted to leave clues in that event. Even a scoundrel like *Cortés* wouldn't want such a treasure to be lost forever. I also believe that it was Doña Marina who told him the location of *Aztlán* and suggested he inscribe the cross in Náhuatl glyphics to keep the location secret from other Spaniards. It was never designed to be easy to find.

"Now, are we going to go look for this treasure after coming all this way, or are we going to go down in defeat?"

Gideon stood up suddenly. He pulled out his pocket watch and, taking a quick glance, once again chose words that accented his sibilance.

"Sofie's right. She's the expert. We have to trust ourselves and shore up our resolve."

Mollie, ever the cynical one, piped up. "So, what's the plan?"

Carmelita said, "All of this started with the church. I say we find a church in *Mexcaltitán.*"

# Chapter Twenty Seven

## *San Pedro y San Pablo*

*Mexcaltitán,* a small island developed by the Aztecs, covers less than one square mile in area. It features a central plaza with two main thoroughfares running north to south and two running east to west, like overlapping crosses. The entire island, which can be traversed in only a few hours, has one church, the church of *San Pedro y San Pablo*.

During the summer rainy season, the streets flood and boats are used as the primary means of transportation.

Gideon, Carmelita, Sofie, and Mollie, now sated and relaxed, walked towards the central plaza to find the padre of *San Pedro y San Pablo*. They walked side by side down the middle of the street. The sidewalks were unusually high. They were purpose built to accommodate the floods that occurred during the rainy season, turning the streets into canals which earned the island the nickname as the "Méxican Venice." The rest of the year they doubled as a place to dry shrimp that was caught each day by the natives. Shrimp was the primary crop in *Mexcaltitán* and often dried for export.

The church was easy to find. Set on a slight hill, it is easily the tallest building on the island. A humble structure, it is composed of white adobe with a bell tower above the vestibule. Sitting above the bell tower is a widow's walk which offers a spectacular view of the island and the surrounding waters. Above that sits a small bell gable, giving the whole image one of a large, multi-tiered wedding cake.

Sofie and Mollie followed Gideon and Carmelita onto the church grounds. Just as they approached the front doors, a priest emerged. He was quite old, with thin, white hair and a pronounced stoop when he walked. He shuffled over to them with measured steps.

"*Hola amigos. Soy el padre Gómez.*"

Gideon slowed, realizing he would not be much use explaining the reason for their visit to the priest.

Carmelita stepped forward and extended her hand. She spoke rapidly in Spanish to the priest who nodded sagely. They conversed for several minutes and both of them chuckled at one point. Finally, the priest nodded once again and shuffled over to Gideon to shake his hand.

"*Hola, Padre,*" was all Gideon could say. The priest smiled and looked back to Carmelita.

"*Padre Gómez* does not speak any English, but he is a learned man and understands why we're here."

Sofie and Mollie gingerly walked towards them to listen to the conversation.

"He understands about the treasure and says that there actually are corridos sung about pirates and treasure, but no one ever paid them any mind. They were always thought to be fantasy tales told by the ancients."

The three of them waited without speaking.

"The priest studied in Ciudad de México – México City. When I mentioned the treasure of Cortés, he immediately told me about the similarities between the two islands – the birthplace of México City, which as you know is *Tenochtitlan*, and here, the island of *Mexcaltitán*. It's remarkable how similar they are."

Sofie stepped forward.

"I'm embarrassed to say this, but I knew all about the islands similarities. I held it back, but for a very good reason. I just didn't want anyone to get too excited. The possibility is that the treasure exists. It may exist here, but if I told you all I know, I was afraid you would think it's not just possible, but assured. I couldn't risk being responsible for the letdown if we don't find it."

Gideon nodded his head with understanding. Carmelita put her arm around Sofie's shoulder.

"I understand, Sofie. We're all very excited about this. But you're right. Even though there is evidence that it exists and it is here on this island, it is just as possible this is a fool's errand. I think we all know that deep in our hearts."

Sofie spoke up. "Here. Let me show you some drawings and tell you what I know and you can draw your own conclusions.

Sofie rummaged through the worn leather briefcase that she had slung across her shoulders. It was old soft brown leather, and was stressed and cracked. She wore the buckled leather strap tight across her chest so it could not easily be taken from her.

"See, here." She laid out two documents on yellowed paper. Crude drawings of similar looking islands.

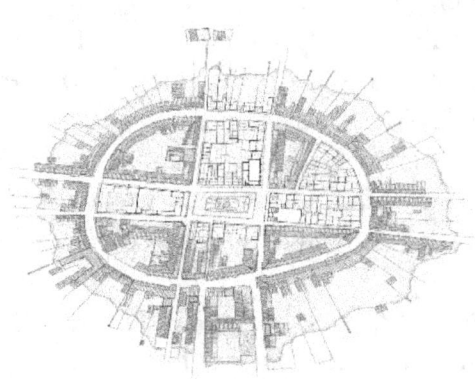

*Mexcaltitán*

"The first one is the island we stand on today, *Mexcaltitán*. You can see it's a very small island. It was laid out by the Aztecs in cruciform. That is, in the shape of a cross, as I mentioned once before. It was designed that way intentionally. You see that the church is in the center of the island, which sits on a lake or Laguna as the Spanish call it. *Laguna Grande de Mexcaltitán* to be specific. The lake we came through today."

Once again, as Sofie spoke, she became more excited and her speech more pronounced with her New York/Bohemian accent.

"There are two primary roads running north to south and east to west, approximating the sign of a cross. This appears to represent their orientation of the quadrants of the universe, which is consistent with Aztec religion."

"Sofie, are you saying the Aztecs had a cross, like that of followers of Christ, as part of their religion?" Gideon asked. His expression indicated bewilderment and skepticism at the same time.

"No, no. Not at all," Sofie responded.

"The Aztecs were certainly religious, but their view was totally different from those of European background. They worshipped multiple gods and goddesses, for one thing. No, the cross was more representative of their worldview of quadrants of the universe. Theirs was a complex society and their religion was a combination of beliefs and superstitions."

She continued. "This church was built in the 1800's and I am certain an Aztec temple once stood where the church stands today."

As Sofie explained all this, the priest stood silently by, watching without understanding the words, but still knowing what was being said. He could sense their excrement.

"The second drawing is *Tenochtitlan*. You can see the similarities between the two even in these crude drawings. This

230

is where the Aztecs migrated. There are many who postulate theories about their migration; when and why it occurred, as well as the manner. Some think it took decades to complete the migration.

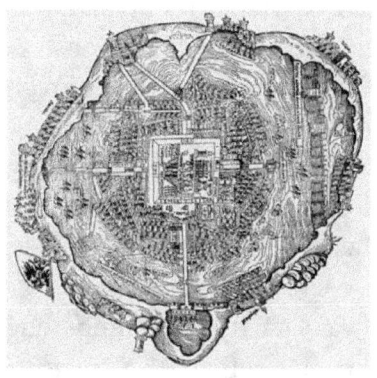

Tenochtitlan

"For our purposes, we don't really need to know all that. It's only important for us to know that *Cortés* believed that *Mexcaltitán* was the legendary, ancestral home of the Aztecs. Maybe *Doña Marina* informed him or perhaps Montezuma himself. Either way, it's seems likely that this is what he believed."

"So, Sofie," Carmelita piped in, "why would *Cortés* dispatch his soldiers to such a place? Had he ever been there? Wouldn't he have sent anything he had back to Spain?"

Mollie spoke up, in her usual impatient manner. "Look. Who cares what he thought or where Aztlán was located? What does all of this have to do with finding the treasure?"

"You're right, Mollie. It is not directly related to location. But let me tell you a little story.

"*Cortés* was a smart man. He may have been an egotistical, brutal soldier and explorer, but he studied law before taking to the sea. We have his own accounting of the events of *La Noche Triste,* and many believe that all the treasure was lost that night.

"However, it is well documented that the events leading to that tragic night occurred after he had left to confront *Pánfilo de Narváez* in Veracruz on the Gulf Coast.

"*Narváez* had been sent by the Governor of Cuba, *Diego Velázquez de Cuéllar* to dispatch *Cortés.*

"*Cortés* had initially been backed by the Governor, but he later changed his mind. *Cortés* decided to go to México anyway which is why Governor *Velázquez* sent *Narváez* to have him recalled.

"*Cortés* was vastly outnumbered when he got to Veracruz, but still he defeated *Narváez.* He convinced the remainder of the men to accompany him back to *Tenochtitlan.* I may be skeptical, but I have to assume they followed him in part because of the promise of riches. Certainly *Cortés* would have sent some items back for the Emperor when he got to Veracruz. As I told you all before we set off on this journey, unbeknownst to *Cortés,* his lieutenant, *Pedro de Alvarado*, initiated the massacre in the Great Temple, triggering the rebellion."

"Sofie," Mollie huffed, "you're driving me crazy. What does all of this have to do with the location of the treasure? By his own words, *Cortés* wrote that it was lost at the bottom of Lake *Texcoco.* Why are you so convinced the treasure is here?'

"Sorry, Mollie. The history is important for you to understand. Think about it. Why would he leave *Tenochtitlan* to fight and leave all the treasure behind? How did he win at Veracruz when he was outnumbered five to one? Why would he claim all the treasure was lost when he also wrote that he had sent gold and precious stones back to the King in Spain? We know that the Amulet of Cananea was part of his booty, and that *had* been sent back. Don't you think he was smart enough to send small increments of the treasure to other locations prior to the events of *La Noche Triste?*"

Mollie stood looking at Sofie with her mouth open. She, Gideon and Carmelita all looked around at each other as the truth dawned on them.

Slowly, she asked. "Okay, so assuming that's all true, and I believe you're right and it is, why do you think he would send it to a place he had never been, even if he did think it was Aztlán?"

"Like I said, *Cortés* was smart. He would try to hide it in a place neither the Aztecs nor the Spanish would think to look. He knew that eventually he had to go back to Spain and report what happened in México. After defeating the Governor's representative, he had to have a credible story of what happened to all the treasure. Like I said, he was smart. We now know that sixteen years later the Spanish "discovered" the Baja peninsula."

Carmelita, who was by far most familiar with México and its territories, spoke right up.

"Of course. It was *Cortés.* The body of water we came in on is named the *Sea of Cortés.* Are you saying he hid the treasure there and waited sixteen years to retrieve it?'

"Think about it. Most of the documentation on what happened at *Tenochtitlan* came from the letters *Cortés* wrote to Emperor Charles V, who was the ruler of the Spanish Empire, the Holy Roman Empire, as well as of the Habsburg Netherlands. Clearly, anything he wrote was to put himself in good light. But ask yourself this – is it likely that the Aztecs allowed their entire treasure to be dumped into the river on the Night of Sorrows, but that *Cortés* escaped, only to return years later to repress the natives yet again?

"Not only am I saying he hid the treasure, I am saying he sent small shipments of the treasure to various locations and used the wealth of the treasure he hid to self-fund his explorations of the Baja. I'm sure he sent items to the Emperor and occasionally used some of it to buy loyalty and influence. But he kept the bulk of the treasure for himself, and he hid the largest portion where only he could find it. He is widely credited with "discovering" the Baja peninsula. History tells us he went there to try and find a mythical "island of gold," part of the legend of Cibola. I believe he stopped here on the way. In his letters, he claimed to have never found Cibola.

"While we know for certain that he visited *Riviera Nayarit*, there is no record he ever came to Mexcaltitán. He died a wealthy, yet bitter man. So," she looked at each of them in turn, "what do *you* think happened?"

# Chapter Twenty Eight

## *Conflict*

Mollie was upset. She was back in her room, running a comb through her freshly washed hair. They were lucky to find an inn, *La Posada,* another unimaginative name. They had ample vacancy, so Mollie and Sofie each had their own room. The accommodations were small, yet spotless, and a far cry from the shrimp boat. It was absurdly inexpensive and included a full breakfast. They shared the shower and bath, and Mollie was first to take advantage of the shower. The water had a slightly salty tang to it, but it felt fresh and clean and she was able to wash the grit of the last several days off her body.

As she sat and slowly combed her hair dry, she thought about the last several days since they left Tucson. She got a slight tingle when she thought of Tucson, and her mind immediately envisioned Luisa. Malu.

Mollie realized she was lucky. She really didn't have any claim to the treasure – "if they find one," she thought ironically. She knew she was fortunate that none of the others ever questioned her about her relationship with Father Mendoza.

Her thoughts traveled back to Tucson. To Malu. Mollie always thought of herself as a tough, strong willed woman. A person who could stand with any man and never backed down from anything.

But for some reason, thinking of Malu, she questioned the legitimacy of what she had come here to do. Gideon, Carmelita, and Sofie were becoming more than friends since they had shared the challenges of this mission, with untold risks lying ahead. She was upset because she was so fearful that they might find out the truth about how she came to be in their company.

She decided to talk to Carmelita. She wanted to come clean and also wanted to see if they had been in touch with anyone back home. She wanted to know about Malu, or Luisa as they called her, and wanted to spend a bit of time with Carmelita, who she had come to admire. After all, she thought to herself, none of this would have been possible without her. She was clearly the power behind Gideon and a sweet and caring woman. She also wanted to check to see if there was any sign of Cassidy. Her hatred for the man intensified since getting to know Carmelita and hearing the stories of what she endured in Cananea. She vowed that when she got back to Tucson, she would take care of him once and for all. She dropped the hairbrush onto her table and got up quickly to seek out Carmelita.

---

"How will we know where to look, Sofie?"

"Well, we don't."

Gideon and Sofie were walking back towards the church in the center of *Mexcaltitán*.

"You saw the drawings, Gideon. You can see that the two islands that the Aztecs settled are very similar, just different in size.

"Both had a place of worship at its center. We know for certain that before *Cortés* left *Tenochtitlan,* he kept the treasure in the palace. The palace was huge – much, much larger than the church here in *Mexcaltitán.* It had its own aviary, gardens, salt and fresh water ponds, and even its own zoo. We have to explore every inch of the area where the church now stands and all of the surrounding area. I don't know what we're looking for, but we'll know it when we find it."

Gideon was growing skeptical, but he had come too far to give up now.

As they approached the church, Padre Gómez was out in front clipping sprigs of a magenta and deep purple vine he called bugambilia, which Sofie recognized as bougainvillea. The thorny and attractive plant had overgrown the white stucco walls surrounding the church.

He looked up in greeting as he continued to clip the brightly colored flowers, careful to avoid the waxy thorns.

"We should have had Carmelita come with us," Sofie commented, "the padre doesn't speak English."

Gideon continued undaunted. Gesturing with his hands, he asked in English if they could go to the courtyard behind the church. The Padre smiled, nodded, waved his hand, and continued his cutting. They didn't know if he understood them or not.

They came into a large courtyard with a much higher wall than the one in front, with bugambilia and cacti towering over it. To their far left, there were several wooden chairs and two small tables. To the far right, close to the surrounding wall, was a covered baptismal font. It appeared the area may have also been used to host baptisms and outdoor weddings.

In the center of the courtyard was an old well, which looked like it hadn't been used in decades, if not centuries. It was also covered in vines and was barely recognizable.

Sofie went towards the well, which was covered by a piece of wood, cut round, that looked like it had been there for years. She used the top as a table and removed the cross from a beautiful brown leather satchel that Mollie's Uncle Vern had crafted to carry the cross. The satchel featured a strong brass clasp and a long, wide leather strap which she wore across her chest just as she had with her old briefcase.

She withdrew the folded up drawing of Mexcaltitán and laid it out on top of the well, holding the edges flat with stones she picked up off the ground.

"Sofie? What's the plan? Now that we're here, how do we find the treasure? We're not even sure there *is* a treasure."

Sofie held the cross up so it overlapped the drawing of the map of the island. It was much larger than the drawing, so she moved the map onto the ground and held the cross high to align the dimensions. It didn't fit exactly, but then, the map was a drawing and not completely accurate.

The cross appeared to align itself best when the top of the cross was pointed west. Once she was satisfied, she said to Gideon.

"Come, take a look. What do you think?"

"I think it looks like the island is sort of like a cross and the cross sort of fits into the paths on the island. But other than that, I don't see it gives us any clues to a treasure."

Sofie was crestfallen. She felt this proved her theory. But Gideon was right. This didn't really prove anything.

"O.K. I know it's a long shot. But we're here. This island is small. The main branch of the New York City library where I work is the same length as this island although it's only half as wide. Still, it can easily be explored in a day. Everything I learned tells me that the treasure is buried here. After all that we've been through to get here, we can't give up now. I know we're all tired and eager to get home, but let's give it another day. O.K.?"

Gideon nodded his assent and they discussed a plan to explore the island. Sofie folded up her map, put away the cross, and they headed out through the church back to *La Posada* to talk with Carmelita and Mollie and tell them the plan.

As they walked back around the church and out into the front plaza, they nodded to Padre Gómez, who continued his pruning.

They paid no attention to a man sitting on the high curb nearby with a wide sombrero and a serape, which covered a sling that kept his hand above his heart.

---

Carmelita sat on the porch of the inn thinking about the events that got her here. She thought of her mother who became more of a hero in her eyes every day. The hardship she and her father had faced in raising her. Her sister, Rosita, now living a successful life in California, after graduating college there and finding the love of her life to whom she is now married. She hadn't seen her in eight years.

Her brother, Juan. He moved east to Houston, and enrolled in the Army. She knew he was doing well there, but worried about all the talk of the U.S. getting pulled into the turmoil happening in Europe. She hadn't seen him since they left México, either.

She thought of Gideon. How she met him and how quickly and deeply they fell in love.

She tried to stay focused on the positive thoughts of her family but no matter how she tried, the image of that sinister bastard, Thom MacMurrough, or Declan Cassidy, or whatever his name was today, would sneak back into her thoughts.

"Carmelita?" she heard a quiet voice nearby whisper.

"Can I talk to you a minute?"

Moving slowly in front of her was a young woman with strawberry blond hair who smelled as fresh as an ocean breeze. Her wavy hair was flowing and still damp. Carmelita hardly recognized her.

"Mollie?"

Mollie pulled up a chair and sat in front of Carmelita. She had on a white, cotton, Méxican peasant blouse, capping her typical jeans and boots. Still, the effect of the blouse was transforming and she appeared to be a completely different person. Her demeanor was soft and a dramatic change from her normal, blustery self.

"What is it Mollie?"

"I have something to tell you. I have to tell you the truth."

"Truth about what?"

"Please hear me out. I'm here under false pretenses."

Mollie spilled out everything in a rush. She told Carmelita of how she met Cassidy, how she finagled her way into the church and manipulated the priests' trusting ways to infer she knew him more than she did, and lastly how she had planned to betray all of them and take the treasure for herself.

"But Carmelita, I've changed. I've seen the way you and Gideon are when you're together. I've heard about the pain and suffering you and your family have been through. I see why it's important to you to find this treasure. Not for the possibility of wealth, but because it's important to the world. I hear Sofie talk about the historical significance and I see how important this is to her. A woman who has no business being in this part of the world, and yet she has been dogged throughout this ordeal, many times spurring the rest of us on when we feel there's no hope.

"I hope you can forgive me."

Carmelita looked at her and took a deep breath. Hearing about Cassidy and how he, yet again, caused conflict and pain, even in his absence, gave her pause. But she now saw Mollie as a young girl who had been abused by a stepfather and grew up tough because she had to. She didn't have to tell Carmelita all of this. Even if her feelings had changed, she could have kept it all to herself and just continued on. She gave her credit for her honesty.

Just as she was about to respond, Gideon and Sofie came into view and Gideon called out. Carmelita stood up and put her arm about Mollie.

"Thank you for telling me all this. Let's keep this between us, OK?" She winked at Mollie who smiled and gave her a hug.

"You two look happy. Did you find the treasure while we were gone?" Gideon looked at his wife and smiled.

"No. Just some girl talk. What about you two? You weren't gone long."

Sofie spoke up. "Look. I know we're all anxious about the treasure. We don't know if it even exists, and if it does - if it's here. But we've come a long way and gone through some tough things together. I have a plan."

She laid it out for them. They all felt a little better afterward and agreed they would give it another day - two at the most. If they didn't find the treasure, then they would give up and go home. In the meantime, Carmelita was tasked with finding transportation back to the States while Gideon, Sofie, and Mollie fine-tuned the plan.

That night, they spent a little extra on a nice meal and a drink apiece before turning in early. They each slept soundly knowing they would be going home soon.

The next morning, they all rose early. It was Tuesday, so there were no visitors to the island, the children were either in school or out fishing with their fathers, and the mother's home doing chores. Such was the life on this tiny island. But they had decided to wait until afternoon when the sun was high and they would be able to see all the nooks and crannies that the island held. They ate an early lunch together and waited until most of the islanders took their siesta.

The four treasure seekers walked to the church which was located on a slight hill at the center of town. They walked around back so as not to be observed by passersby. Carmelita and Mollie watched as Sofie went over to the old well and laid out the maps and cross. Gideon leaned on the edge, careful to avoid any of the thorny branches.

The plan Sofie devised was simple. Each of them would branch out from the church and walk towards the water in a different direction. Mollie offered to head west, from the direction they arrived; Carmelita would head north; Sofie, south; and Gideon would go east, which was the longest segment. It roughly mirrored the cross if it were laid west to east with the head to the west. Once they arrived at the water, they would each travel clockwise to the next cross street and head back towards the church, thereby double checking each other's work. During their journey they would explore as much of the area covered as they possibly could.

"Look for signs of ancient stones with any type of marking. The island floods during the rainy season. We don't know if *Cortés* knew that or not, but we have to assume he did. He would need to find a spot that would be relatively elevated and one which was less likely to be disturbed over time. Boulders or caves, anything that would be left alone and not inhabited."

Gideon jumped from the side of the well, took out his watch, glanced at it without really reading it, and continued. "Take as much time as you like. At the end of the day, we'll meet back here. If you find anything at all, see if you can locate one of us right away. It's not that big an island. Any questions?"

They put their hands in as a pact of unity and left one by one to see what they could find.

The man in the sombrero watched from across the square to see Mollie heading south. Once she was out of sight, he slowly got up and sauntered after her.

# Chapter Twenty Nine

## *Redemption*

Mollie was once again dressed as they all knew her; boots, Stetson with her hair tucked up underneath, jeans, and work shirt. She turned and walked towards the water's edge on the western side of the island.

The island was indeed very small. She figured it would take her no more than 15 minutes to get to the shore, but she decided to take her time and walk it slowly, exploring any little areas that looked promising. At the halfway point, Mollie turned back to look east and could still see Gideon bending down, looking at stone outcroppings. She turned back around and continued down the path. There didn't appear to be anything out of the ordinary, and she quickly reached lands' end.

She decided to sit at the water's edge for a bit. She would have liked to take off her boots and dangle her legs to cool off, but the water was murky, and she couldn't see what might be lurking beneath the surface. It moved at a steady pace and after a few minutes of watching the playfulness of the kingfishers and herons, she uncrossed her legs to head back to the road north.

She felt like someone was watching her, so she bent down as if to pick something up and looked around stealthily. She didn't see anything, but still felt uncomfortable. Gideon warned her against carrying her gun in the open, so she had to settle for a boot knife. Before she straightened up, she made sure it was easy to remove if she needed it quickly.

As Mollie turned to head north, Carmelita had already started her move to the east. Her quick walk north was uneventful. There was little in the way of anything more than houses and empty lots. At the water's edge, she saw a mangrove forest with storks and other wildlife but nothing remotely resembling a place to hide treasure. Carmelita didn't want to tell the others, but she did not believe that the treasure, if there was one at all, was located here on *Mexcaltitán*. She did believe that *Cortés* sent treasure away, but she thought it was very unlikely he would think to send it to what he believed was Aztlán. She looked as best she could anyway and hoped this segment of the journey would be over soon. She was tiring of lost treasure, the amulet, Cassidy, and anything to do with México. She had begun a new life in Tucson and wanted to get back to it. The only other thing she really wanted was to look Cassidy in the eyes once and for all and know he is not her father. Then she hoped to figure a way to get rid of him forever.

Gideon had a slightly longer walk than the rest, but the first half of it was quick. He examined every crevice he came upon. This side of the island was rocky and there were many very large rocks that could have been used as markers, but as he examined them it was obvious they weren't hiding places. Besides, he thought, the island floods in the rainy season and they had already agreed they had to operate under the assumption that *Cortés* was aware of that.

He arrived at the eastern shore and his view was different than what Mollie or Carmelita observed. Here, the movement of the water was swift. There was an incredible array of birds, and he saw many instances of them swooping for fish in the shallow undertow. But there was no place to hide treasure, so he turned and headed south. As he walked he thought about going home empty handed. Of course, he would be disappointed, but he had a thriving business to get back to. Another day was all he felt he could spare.

Sofie took a very long time to reach the southern shore. She was the most passionate about this search and believed with all her heart that this was the location of the lost treasure of *Cortés.*

The water at the southern shore was very calm. She also saw various types of birds in large concentrations, and was fascinated by the tangles of roots and mangroves, although it wasn't as dense a forest as Carmelita had observed.

She was really starting to feel the heat. Up to this point, she could hide in the shade wherever she went, but now, her ubiquitous black outfit was too much for the late spring sun and the heat of México.

Sofie examined every nook and cranny she encountered. She looked under rocks and walked right up to the water's edge and peered out trying to find any hint of a place to hide treasure. She took off her glasses and dunked her head under water, hoping to find an underwater cave. Eventually, she decided to head north to the western shore and took the same meticulous care examining that area to no avail.

She started down the path east, back to the church to see if the others had found anything. She hoped they had, but couldn't shake the feeling that she would have known if something had been found.

Sofie was the last to arrive back at the church. Gideon was at the edge of the water well again, this time sitting on top, bouncing one foot then the other off the worn stone walls. Mollie was leaning against the closest stone wall which circled the church, and Carmelita was sitting nearby on a patch of grass, her traditional cotton print dress spread out around her.

They all looked up expectantly as they heard Sofie approach, and when they saw her, immediately knew they had come up empty handed.

"So – nothing. I'm not surprised." Mollie spoke first.

None of them could hide their disappointment, but no one wanted to speak or even move.

Gideon finally jumped off the wall of the well.

"It's late. Let's go to the cantina and get something to eat and a well-deserved drink. Tomorrow we'll have to see about getting a boat back to the States."

They walked down the street towards the only proper cantina on the island. No one said a word and they all walked with their heads down and the feeling that they had wasted an enormous amount of time and taken far too many unnecessary risks.

They each ordered a drink, even Sofie, who rarely drank alcohol at all. Mollie fumed, and everyone could feel her anger. Carmelita nursed her *pulque* and water and watched as two musicians, one with a *vihuela* and one with a guitarrón, got ready to play. The classic mexican guitar and bass usually accompanied *corridos*, traditional ballads which were stories or poetry set to music. These were typically sad songs of oppression or the difficulties of daily life.

"Maybe we should leave," Carmelita suggested, knowing the music would be sad. She seemed to have forgotten that the others did not speak Spanish, and the words sung would be meaningless.

"No, we came all this way. Let's at least have a few drinks and drown our sorrow. We have a long way back and we might as well enjoy ourselves for the brief time we're here," Mollie said. "What do we have to look forward to when we go back? A revolution in México, border wars, and possibly a war in Europe. We don't have any idea what it will be like back in the States. *If* we can get back to the States."

They realized Mollie was right. They were here and should enjoy the time they had left.

The two musicians started playing and even if the words may have been sad, the music was lively and lightened the mood.

Mollie and Gideon shared a bottle of good *Añejo* sipping tequila, which they downed as shots for the first two each. Sofie and Carmelita, nursed their drinks and had barely sipped them After pouring a third drink for herself and Gideon, Mollie raised a glass.

"To treasure hunters near and far, may their luck be better than ours so far."

Gideon raised his glass, as his wife sat there thinking even *she* could come up with a better toast and rhyme than that, and English wasn't her first language.

She turned her attention to the music and listened to the plaintive song.

Sofie spoke to her, "Carmelita, can you tell me what this songs means? What are they saying?"

Carmelita was listing to the music and hadn't even thought about the lyrics. She began to interpret.

"It is a song about loss. They are saying that a very long time ago, strangers – all men - came to the island. The women here were afraid at first, but the strangers didn't even seem to notice them. They brought with them much baggage as if they would stay a long time. They slept on a small boat which was docked on the southwest side of the island.

"Every day they would go to the highest point of the island and work. They dug a well, but the well was dry. They told the natives that they couldn't dig deep enough, got discouraged, and left. The moral of the song seems to be that even though you may be surrounded by water, and the streets flood during the rains, that doesn't mean you can build a well for water to drink. Kind of an odd story and moral."

Sofie looked pensive. She turned her glass around as she thought about what Carmelita had said.

Mollie and Gideon were laughing and almost half the bottle of tequila was gone, when Sofie raised her head. She looked at Carmelita and the two of them opened their eyes wide at the same time and their mouths dropped open.

"The well!" they said in perfect unison.

"How could we not have thought of that?" Carmelita asked loudly.

The two musicians began to play another soft, sad corrido.

"Thought of what?" Gideon turned to look at Carmelita, his eyes glazed over.

"Gideon, you're already drunk!"

"Aw, leave him alone," Mollie slurred. "We've all been through a lot. Let's have some fun tonight and tomorrow we can start back home. I can't wait to see Malu again."

Gideon looked at Mollie and grinned. Sofie and Carmelita looked at each other and both shook their heads. They decided to keep this news to themselves for tonight. Tomorrow they could talk about their options.

The cantina was very small and there were not a lot of people to cover his presence, but that didn't stop Paco from trying to overhear. He sat just outside the doorway on the sidewalk with a sombrero on his head, tilted low to cover his face. He looked to be an islander who had had too much to drink and simply stopped on his way out of the cantina to sleep.

He couldn't hear much because of the music, but after Gideon and Mollie had a few drinks, they became loud. He thought they might all be leaving soon and he would have his chance with Mollie.

"Mollie, are you and my Luisa friends?" Gideon asked innocently. His whistle was acutely pronounced when he was drunk, and he was completely oblivious to anything other than heterosexual relationships.

"Friends? Yes, I guess we are. But I want to be much more than friends."

Gideon looked to Carmelita. His gaze was glassy, but he clearly didn't have a clue about what he was hearing.

"Gideon, I think Mollie is trying to say she likes to be with other women, not men, and she has a crush on Luisa."

Gideon looked at Mollie for several long seconds. He shook his head as if to clear it, took out his pocket watch slowly, opened it, glanced down, snapped the lid shut, opened it again, glanced down, shut it again, then said, "Ooohh."

Sofie burst out laughing, and so did Carmelita and Mollie.

They all sat there a bit longer. Carmelita got Mollie to open up and Sofie talked quite a bit about the women's movement in New York and how common it was for women to be with women, compared to what she had observed in Arizona.

"That may be true," Mollie countered, "but you'll have to meet my Aunt Rosie. She knows lots of women like you talk about. We talked about this when we first met, remember?"

Sofie thought about that and was about to respond, when Carmelita piped up, "OK. It's time to go home. You two have had too much to drink and we have a lot to do tomorrow. Let's go."

With that, she and Sofie stood up to leave. Gideon and Mollie finished the last of their drinks and stood up much more slowly.

As they left, Mollie almost tripped over Paco. He never moved and they all continued on their way to their rooms.

Paco lifted his sombrero and waited until they were out of sight, then slowly walked in the direction they headed. There weren't many places to stay, and he knew just where they were going.

# Chapter Thirty

## *Eureka*

Mollie woke up later than usual the following day. Oddly, she felt no effects from the tequila. She went downstairs and was greeted by Carmelita. She poured herself some coffee and sat down with her and Sofie, who looked as if they had been up for hours.

"Where's Gideon?"

Sofie snorted a laugh and Carmelita responded.

"He should be out of the bath by now. He couldn't get out of bed, so I had to encourage him. Poor baby. He's a puddle."

Just then Gideon came into the room looking like a wet mutt. His eyes were droopy, his hair wet, and his clothes disheveled and untucked.

"Coffeeeeee."

Carmelita poured him a cup and set down a steaming plate of menudo. Gideon turned his nose up at first, because he had finally been told the ingredients, but he had eaten it before and it really was delicious. It was also a great remedy for a hangover. Carmelita spoke up.

"Last night, while you two were getting drunk, Sofie and I came to a realization."

"We weren't getting drunk, at least not intentionally. We were just trying to blow off steam," Mollie complained.

"No matter. Sofie, you're the expert here. Do you want to tell them what we think?"

"Carmelita was explaining one of the *corridos* the musicians sang last night. The song talked about strangers digging a dry well at the highest point of the island, which we all know is where the church stands. We never thought to look at the well, but we now think that's where the treasure could be hidden."

Gideon and Mollie looked at each other and had the exact same expression on their faces that Carmelita and Sofie had the previous night.

"Of course!" Gideon's face got all its color back and he immediately began to look like his old self again.

"Let's go." Mollie got up and began to walk away.

"Hold on." Carmelita called out. "Come back here a minute."

Sofie spoke up. "We've been talking about this since last night. We can't just rush up there and start digging in the well. Think about it. We have to have a plan. What if we do find something? How will we get it off the island without arousing suspicion? We came up with an idea for a plan. Sit down and listen."

Outside the inn, Paco was once again sitting on the sidewalk with his sombrero down and his serape hiding his arm.

He still couldn't really hear anything, but he did hear excited voices. He knew something was up, but he just didn't know what. He decided then that he was going to seek out Mollie after dark. He didn't have the nerve to approach her last night, plus she was clearly not in a state of mind for him to do so.

Paco was a simpleton, but he wasn't really a bad man. He just didn't know better. He was the kind of man who would fall in love in an instant. When he first saw Mollie with her strawberry blonde hair and sparkling green eyes, he was mesmerized. He fell for her immediately, and every time he saw her he swelled with excitement. He was simple enough that he was convinced that if he could only spend a few minutes with her, she would fall for him too. His plan wasn't to hurt her, but to love her. The complexities of romance eluded him, and it was certain he couldn't fathom Mollie's sexual orientation.

The excited voices told him something was going on and he had to make his move before they all left the island.

He got up and went off to spend his day working on his approach.

The treasure hunters plotted their assignments and left to pack and prepare for their final endeavor to find the valuables they believed were left behind by *Cortés'* men.

They decided to make their attempt just after dusk, with each of them prepared to leave the inn heading in a different direction. They didn't want to run the risk of looking as if they had a common goal, although that qualified as paranoia since no one took any notice of their comings and goings at any rate.

During the afternoon, Carmelita took care of lining up a small boat to take them to the coast, where they were assured they would be able to get on a larger boat offering safe passage up the Sea of *Cortés*. At the end of their journey on the sea, they would arrive at *Puerto Peñasco,* which was only 54 miles from the Arizona border. They could then cross the border overland, through a nature reserve just outside the Tohono O'odham nation. Once on O'odham soil, it was an easy path into Tucson proper. She sent a telegram to the leader of the nation to let them know they were on the way and the path they would take. The O'odham did not treat trespassers kindly and it was not uncommon for people to try and penetrate the border through their land. Advance notice was mandatory in this case.

While Carmelita was making her arrangements, Gideon found a place to purchase a pick and shovel, plus candle stick lamps, rope, and a couple of duffle bags.

Sofie prepared the maps and counterfeit cross, and re-read all of her research to be sure she knew what she was looking for.

Mollie armed herself with her boot knife and wore a leather vest, despite the heat, to cover her gun. It didn't really conceal it, but made it much less obvious. They all agreed that given their endeavor, they needed to be protected and Mollie relished the task.

Padre Gómez lived in the rectory which was across the hard dirt street from the church. The front of the rectory faced the side street which ran south towards the water, so they had little fear of being noticed.

Sofie was to arrive at the church first, just after dark. In part, because she was, as always, dressed completely in black, giving her stealth that the others didn't possess. She also had the counterfeit cross and they were convinced – if this was the true site of the treasure – that the cross was somehow the key.

As the crescent moon rose Sofie walked purposefully yet surreptitiously towards the church and quickly rounded the entryway. She made her way quickly to the well. As she lifted her satchel over her head, the others came up behind her, much sooner than she expected. The reflection of the sun softly bouncing off the moon, affording them just enough light for their mission.

They all walked around the well examining it closely. Carmelita was the first to notice something odd. They had agreed not to speak unless absolutely necessary. Carmelita took a fistful of her long cotton dress and pulled aside several of the thorny vines. As she did, they all looked at what she uncovered. Sofie gasped a quick intake of breath and Mollie whispered, "holy shit!"

"Appropriate response for a churchyard," Sofie muttered.

Gideon lit up one of the candle lamps and set its wick very low. Sofie removed the cross from its wrappings and held it out to the well. She moved it slowly towards the stone wall and placed the cross against an impression which was old and worn, but still clear. The cross fit perfectly into the depression in the well.

The well itself was roughly three and a half feet high and looked to be about twelve feet in diameter. Large enough for at least two men with pick and shovel to work. They couldn't estimate the depth because they couldn't see inside very clearly, which may have been the most important piece of information for them right now.

"Mollie, tie the end of this rope to that cypress tree. I'll tie this end to the candle lantern and drop it into the well to see if we can gauge its depth."

Gideon and Mollie easily removed the wooden covering and Gideon slowly lowered the lantern into the well, counting by hand an arm's length at a time.

"OK. Looks to be a little over 30 feet deep." He let go of the rope, retrieved his pocket watch and clicked it open.

"We can't spend a lot of time. Sofie, can you whistle?"

"Well, no one whistles like you, Gideon, but I live in New York City, so I do a pretty decent job of it."

Gideon laughed quietly, He knew his speech pattern seemed funny to others.

"OK. You stand watch near the front of the church yard. If you see anyone approaching, whistle. Then get back here as fast as you can. Leave the cross and satchel here. We may need 'em. 'Lita, you stand at the back entrance. Keep an eye on Sofie, but stay close by. We may need your help. Mollie and I are going down into the well."

Surprisingly, Sofie and Carmelita left right away. Gideon asked Mollie for her knife in the unlikely event there was anything to deal with at the bottom of the well. He then took Sofie's satchel and placed it under the spot where the rope crested the stones on the well to reduce drag and to prevent fraying. He took the counterfeit cross and stuffed it in into his belt. He then took a bandana out of his pocket and wrapped it around his right hand. He clamped the knife firmly in his teeth, went over the wall, and quickly rappelled down into the depths of the well.

"Mollie, come on down. Bring the other lantern," he called up to her softly.

Mollie quickly descended.

"I've never been inside a well before," she commented, "but it's pretty much what I expected – dark, damp, and dirty. I don't see any treasure."

Gideon was exploring the walls which were black, covered with centuries of dirt. He shined the light up the walls, thinking that if he were hiding treasure, he would hide it at a certain depth and then keep digging to distract potential treasure hunters. They would almost certainly not look up to find it.

There didn't seem to be anything there, so he scraped away dirt and examined the wall nearly stone by stone.

"Mollie, bring your lantern over here," he whispered.

He scraped hard on a thick patch of dirt knee high. "I don't think this is dirt. I think it's pitch."

"Pitch?" Mollie asked.

"You know. Like tar. They use it to waterproof boats."

"Why would there be pitch in the well?" Mollie asked.

"Well, it would be a good insulator for holding water in the well without having it leak out through the rough stones."

He continued to examine the stones looking for something, anything, to give him a clue.

"It's odd. The pitch is concentrated in only one small area. Wonder why they didn't line it all?"

They looked at each other and both felt there must be something hidden beneath the tar-like substance.

Gideon used Mollie's knife to scrape away the black substance. As he did, he heard the sound of metal. He renewed his efforts and uncovered a metal plate.

"This looks like part of a firebox. They used these to cook on all types of vessels while at sea. Clearly, someone hid something behind this plate."

They tried to contain their excitement, but both began to scrape away the rest of the pitch. After several minutes they uncovered a metal door that measured about three feet high and two feet wide.

"There are no hinges visible, so they must be on the inside," Gideon observed.

"There's no handle either. How do we get it open?"

Gideon raised the lantern and kept scraping. As he did, a large hunk of pitch came away revealing a horizontal slot in the metal. Mollie watched as Gideon took the cross by the short end and tried to push the longer end of the cross into the slot, as he would a key. It went in an inch or two and stopped, He tried to twist it, but nothing happened. He removed the cross, frustrated. Mollie's Uncle Vern had crafted it meticulously, even replicating jewels of the same dimensions as the original. One of these was at the base of the cross. He thought it might be inhibiting it from going all the way in, and thought about removing it. He mentioned this to Mollie.

"Let me give it a try," she said.

As she grabbed at the cross, it came out of Gideon's hand and fell to the ground.

Mollie picked it up quickly and entered it into the slot. She pushed a bit harder and it went further in. She turned the cross to the left, and heard a click.

"It takes a woman's touch," she crowed.

Gideon removed the cross. Mollie had inserted in upside down so the jewel was on the bottom, not facing up. A clever two step key entry. He thought that most people wouldn't think of inserting a key upside down, although Mollie clearly did so unintentionally.

"Nice job, Mollie," was all he said.

Gideon began to push on the metal door, when he heard Carmelita call down to them.

"Gideon, someone's coming. Sofie's been whistling, but I didn't know if you could hear her down there."

She was right. They hadn't heard a thing.

Gideon pushed without regard for the noise he might make. The metal sheet gave way and opened to a small alcove.

It was too small a space for either of them to enter, unless they knelt down on the ground and belly crawled, but Gideon was able to push the lantern through and poke his head inside. He reached in, grabbed onto something and extracted a heavy wooden chest. It was of a size that barely fit through the opening. The chest had a strong metal lock, but the lock was broken. He pulled it out of its hasp and lifted the hinge.

Gideon and Mollie could hardly contain their excitement. After all this time, it looked as if they had finally found a portion of the lost treasure of Cortés. One that had been missing for centuries and that no one until this moment had been able to find.

The sound of a man's voice echoed down the well.

"*Hola. ¿Qué estás haciendo?*"

"Gideon, **Padre** Gómez wants to know what you are doing?"

Gideon and Mollie looked at each other in a panic. They had come so far and felt so close to finally finding the treasure.

"What should we do? Should we put it back and come another day?" Mollie whispered.

Gideon grabbed the top of the chest and quickly pushed it up. He had to look inside. He wasn't going to come this far only to be disappointed.

They heard Carmelita's voice again.

"The Padre wants to know if you found the treasure chest?"

Gideon was suddenly conflicted. If he knew about the chest, then why leave the treasure behind?

He lifted the lid and he and Mollie looked down into an empty chest with a sole item lying flat on the bottom. Gideon lifted it out. It was a piece of soft chamois. On it were what they now recognized as several Náhuatl symbols.

He took the chamois, closed the lid, and pushed it back into the recess. He closed the door and replaced the broken hasp and latch.

"Gideon, Padre Gómez says to come on up. He has a story to tell you."

Mollie clambered back up the rope followed by Gideon, both feeling as if they had been punched in the stomach. They were confused and angry.

As they got to the top, the priest helped them out of the well. Sofie and Carmelita stood there smiling.

The priest began to speak and Carmelita interpreted.

"Padre Gómez wants to know if any of us have been inside his church - the church of *San Pedro y San Pablo*?"

They all shook their heads. Gideon looked at Sofie.

"No, of course not. But this is no time to pray. What's going on here? What about the treasure?"

Sofie spoke up. "Gideon, we should have thought to at least look inside the church. We've been everywhere else on the island, but we missed two of the most obvious and important things – the well and the church itself."

Gideon handed the chamois to Sofie.

258

"This looks like it's been revitalized recently. When I say recently, I mean within the last hundred years or so," she commented.

Carmelita said, "The padre wants us to follow him to the church."

She and the priest spoke rapidly as they led the others into the sacristy at the back of the church.

They all stopped as Carmelita and the priest continued their dialog. The priest did most of the talking, with Carmelita asking a question here and there. This went on for quite a while as Sofie studied the chamois and Gideon and Mollie tried to process what had just happened.

Finally, the priest stopped speaking and Carmelita addressed her colleagues.

"Padre Gómez wants us all to know he appreciates what we have been through and how hard we worked to find the treasure of Moctezuma."

"Moctezuma? You mean Montezuma, right?" Mollie asked.

"Well. Montezuma is the more popular pronunciation for Anglos, but natives, particularly those of Aztec or Mexica descent, use the more correct pronunciation of Moctezuma. It's a common misunderstanding."

"But I thought it was *Cortés'* treasure?"

"It *was* gifted to *Cortés* by Moctezuma by most accounts, but many of the Méxican people believe this was a horrible injustice. Although stories indicate Moctezuma had a vision which he believed *Cortés* fulfilled, many people think *Cortés* tricked the Aztecs out of their treasure. So, they still think of it as Moctezuma's treasure, or by extension, the Aztecs treasure. It is not unlike the sentiment today that the U.S. stole Méxican land after the Treaty of Guadalupe Hidalgo.

"At any rate, Padre Gómez says he wishes we had taken him into our confidences."

Gideon finally spoke, "Lita, what's going on?"

"Padre Gómez first learned about the treasure over fifty years ago when he came to the parish. Sofie's theory is correct. The padre confirmed that *Cortés* buried some of his treasure here, long before the church was built. "

"So, where is it?" Mollie chimed in.

Carmelita ignored the question and continued.

"Padre Gómez says that the true story of *Cortés* has been pieced together by the missionaries who passed down the pieces over time. He told me the old well has been here for centuries. It was built on the highest site of the island, long before the church was built. An Aztec temple was said to have previously stood on the same ground. We know that *Cortés* came through *Riviera Nayarit* on his way to what is now Baja California Sur. Apparently he passed through very quickly. He was very eager to get to his destination and did not stay long. It's said he had been told that there was a magnificent and mystical island called *Ciguatan* in the Náhuatl language, or the Realm of Women. It was said to be a place populated only by women."

Mollie interrupted, "That's biologically impossible, but if he found it, let me know where it is. I'll be the first one there."

Sofie laughed out loud.

Carmelita smiled and continued. "It was also said to be filled with gold, pearls, rubies, and other precious items and it was rumored that *Ciguatan* and Cibola might be one in the same. This would be the most important discovery in the history of the world. Keep in mind, virtually every explorer who left Europe to come to this continent, came to find Cibola. The added possibility that there was also a land populated only with women was too much for *Cortés.* "

"No surprise. Men have always thought only with their dicks." Mollie commented wryly.

Carmelita was appalled. "Mollie! We're in church!"

"Sorry, but it's true."

"Anyway, it's believed he never came to *Mexcaltitán* in his haste to find that mythical place, so left the treasure where it was buried by his men years earlier. Padre Gómez has never told anyone any of what he knows about the treasure. But when he saw you two in the bottom of the well, he knew that you had found the hidden vault."

"So, where's the treasure?" Mollie asked again.

"Follow me."

# Chapter Thirty One

## *Legend*

Paco waited in the shadows of a building across the street from the church as the treasure hunters spoke to the priest. He had trailed Mollie when she left her room on her way to join the others.

He didn't understand what they were up to, but he knew if he could help Mollie in any way, she would reward him with her gratitude. He could hardly contain his excitement at the prospect of seeing her again. He knew he had committed a horrible act and was ashamed, but felt he could make it up to her and get back in her good graces. Although he had followed her the entire time they were on the island, he didn't really have the nerve to approach her. In his simple mind, he felt he could prove himself worthy and show her the man he truly was.

---

Carmelita and Padre Gómez led the others through the sacristy into the main section of the church and out to the altar. Once inside the church, the amazement showed on their faces without exception. Even Mollie, who rarely showed any emotion, was awestruck. Sofie, in particular, as historian for St. Peter's, instantly recognized what she was seeing.

The church was small, and made primarily of adobe brick. There were perhaps forty pews; twenty rows per side with a break half way through for passage. On the walls were the fourteen Stations of the Cross, carved into the walls in relief. The stations had been painted over in striking tones, conveying a heartfelt rendering of Jesus' pain and suffering. As they approached the center of the altar, Carmelita bowed her head, knelt, and made a small sign of the cross with her thumb on her head, on her lips, and over her heart. She knew the sign of the cross was a sign of redemption and she fervently hoped she would be able to redeem the memories of her parents, who died so tragically and needlessly.

Gideon, Sofie, and Mollie were standing by looking up in awe with their mouths, literally, hanging open. For such a humble building, the amount of gold and jewels on the crucifix above the altar and statues throughout the nave and in the transepts, was stunning.

Mollie commented dryly, "I think we've found the treasure."

Padre Gómez offered a blessing and made some comments to Carmelita.

"The padre would like me to explain. According to information passed down through the centuries by the missionaries, *Cortés'* men did bury much of the gold and jewels here in *Mexcaltitán* that were given to him by Moctezuma. They built the well and spread the word that it was dry, and even if it ever did contain water, it would be salt water and brackish and not potable. *Cortés'* men had been smuggling the precious items out of Moctezuma's palace in small batches on his orders and burying each parcel in different locations outside the city. He gave these orders when he left *Tenochtitlan* to battle *Pánfilo de Narváez*, the Spaniard sent by the governor to recall *Cortés*.

"Once *Cortés* realized he had lost favor with his royal sponsors, he decided to spread the treasure to various locations and on his return to reclaim the wealth for his own selfish purposes. He sent some items back to Spain to prove the value of his efforts, and gave items to loyal followers, including the gold cross we now know as the Amulet of Cananea that was given to Onorio Pachero."

"'Lita – how could this have been kept secret for so long? This treasure has been the subject of hundreds of searches over the centuries. How has no one learned of this?"

"I asked that of the padre. Although the gold and jewels left here seem like a lot to us now, it's believed it's only a small amount of the total treasure *Cortés* and his men removed. It wasn't worth the effort for *Cortés* to return for it and he was eager to find *Ciguatan*."

"See? I told you men only think with their dicks," Mollie repeated.

This time, Carmelita ignored her.

"Plus, think of it. What better place to hide valuables? Churches have always been filled with gold ornaments. It's nothing out of the ordinary. See the Stations of the Cross on the walls? Beneath the colorful paint the relief is done in solid gold. No one would know. Many of the paintings you see have gold frames. Real gold! No one would know. The stones are so large, they seem fake. And the missionaries and priests have always maintained the illusion. The entire island and parish is poor. There is really no need for wealth here. It is a simple life and one that has been in existence for centuries. The people eat what they catch and grow, and love the simple life. No one wants that to change."

"Wait a minute," Mollie chimed in, "the gold Montezuma or Moctezuma, or whatever his name was, gave to *Cortés* weren't Catholic Mass pieces. They must have been pagan or Aztec icons. How can this gold be the lost treasure of *Cortés?*"

Carmelita relayed the question to Padre Gómez and they discussed for several minutes.

"The gold wasn't discovered in the well until the middle of the 1700's, nearly two hundred years after it was hidden. While no mission was built on *Mexcaltitán*, there was a church constructed in the central plaza. The priests at the time had explored the well and found the treasure as they were contemplating this site for a new church to be built. So, they faced a dilemma. Who did the treasure belong to? They knew of the rumors of *Cortés* burying treasure, but he was long dead and the Aztecs were essentially an extinct tribe. It did not belong to the State of México and certainly not to Spain in their opinion, so they had to decide what to do. Eventually, they decided it belonged to God and his people.

"But rather than try to sell the precious items, which would have brought too much attention, not to mention taxes and dispute over ownership, they decided to melt it all down and create items of worship. So, they made chalices, bells, ablution cups, patens, monstrances, crucifixes, and other items to honor the lord."

"So, how did they manage to keep this a secret? And, really, why tell *us*?" asked Mollie, ever the skeptical one.

"Keeping the secret was actually easy. No one knew about the treasure but the priests. They melted the gold and took it and the jewels and had it all made into items for the church. No one knew the source of the precious materials. The Catholic Church was well funded during the time of the building of the missions. Just look at the White Dove of the Desert."

They all nodded in understanding. They had all experienced the wealth of gold and precious items in churches throughout the world.

"As to why tell us? Well, that's simple. We are the only ones to have found the hiding place for the treasure. But as Padre Gómez says, if we were to tell anyone, what good would it do? The treasure is gone, used for the good of the church and its people.

"He can't stop us if we want to steal from the Church, but he has faith and doesn't believe that's our intent. However, he says we can all feel good about the fact that we found something that has been missing for nearly four hundred years."

Mollie, recognizing her new found altruism, nodded her head in agreement. She had truly come full circle.

Padre Gómez spoke to Carmelita again. It was clear to the others he was asking many questions and she was clearly disagreeing with what it was he was saying. After much back and forth, she shook her head yes and the priest went to the altar.

He went to the tabernacle and removed the chalice. He then went to the sacristy and returned with serval other items of gold vessels used to perform the Mass. He placed them on the altar and motioned to Gideon and the others.

"He wants us to take these items and –bequeath? - Sofie is that the right word?"

Sofie nodded.

"Bequeath them to *San Xavier del Bac.* He says if we have larceny in our hearts, he cannot stop that, but he has faith we will get these items safely to the Church."

"Poetic, isn't it? Right back where we started," Sofie commented.

# Chapter Thirty Two

## *Return*

The following morning, the four packed up all of the items that the priest had given them into the old wooden chest which they found in the well. Although old, it had been protected from the elements and was heavy and strong, with hinges and locks far superior to what was being made today.

Gideon had asked the padre to make inquiries on the status of the ongoing Méxican revolutionary fighting and U.S. involvement, as well as the war in Europe. He learned that the incident they faced in Guaymas was minor compared to what was happening now. There had been a tremendous backlash on all things American since the incident at Veracruz when President Wilson sent in troops to fight Huerta.

"It looks like we'll have a tougher time on the return than on the trip here." Gideon commented. "The good news is that most of our trip will be on water."

He had no idea what the fates had in mind.

They bid goodbye to the padre and made it quickly to the waters' edge on the southwestern side of the island, where they had arrived just days before. They had expected to be shuttled over to a larger boat just as they had when they arrived.

When they got to the dock, they saw a large wooden motorboat waiting. Unusual for this area of México. They figured the boat was large enough to accommodate all of them, and it did appear to have room for sleeping quarters below deck.

Carmelita had a strange feeling as she boarded just after Gideon. She smelled the cigar before she heard the voice and a shiver went up her spine.

"*Hola, mis amigos.*"

*Capitán Flores* came around the wheelhouse with his ubiquitous cigar stub hanging out of his mouth.

"I know. You never expected to see me again. Honestly, I never wanted to see you again either, but I have heard from Francisco de Torres, and he told me in very strong terms that I was solely responsible for your safe return. So, here we are."

Mollie came on board and immediately pulled her gun. She was fully armed now that they were on their way back and the political climate so unstable.

"What the hell is this?" she growled.

Carmelita quickly explained.

"Tell *el Capitán* I'm, not putting up with any shit. Let's go."

*Flores* had a new deckhand. The same young man who had brought them over in the skiff when they got to the island.

"I will do my best to get you to land quickly. We will not be catching and selling shrimp this time.

"Just a straight shot up the coast to *Puerto Peñasco*. My new deckhand has not experienced such travel before, so it may take more time than we all want. In spite of his issues, Paco was my best sailor. But since he's not here, any help you can all provide will make the trip go quicker. It is usually calm this time of year, but it's always possible we'll face rough seas ahead. We will need to move quickly but be careful at the same time. I could really use a good, experienced deckhand."

Carmelita spoke to her travel companions and assured them Francisco would not tolerate any problems and that they would be safe. The sooner they got back the better, they all agreed. Mollie and the others reluctantly got on board. They quickly stowed and secured all of their belongings.

As they were about to shove off, they heard a shout.

Paco came walking quickly up the ramp to the boat. His hand was bandaged, but no longer in a sling.

"What the hell is *he* doing here?" Mollie demanded.

*Capitán Flores* came off the boat and spoke rapidly with Paco. Carmelita caught the gist.

"Paco is saying he is sorry and will be on his best behavior. He has to get back home and he can still work even though his hand is bandaged. I think *Flores* is going to let him stay."

"Over my dead body." Mollie seethed.

*Capitán Flores* addressed them. "Your journey back is going to be much more difficult than the journey here. The sentiment in México right now is extremely anti-American. We will have to find a place to buy gas just past the halfway mark. I know a port small enough to allow us to approach without attracting suspicion, but it is not large enough to allow one of you to get word to the States to have someone meet you on arrival. There is no telegraph office. You will have to wait until we are at *Puerto Peñasco.*

"This trip will be very difficult. We need all hands. I cannot show up at port with only one inexperienced deckhand, and you cannot show your faces. The only one of you who might possibly be able to disembark and send a message is Carmelita."

"This is bullshit," Mollie fumed.

"No, he's right," Gideon spoke up.

Carmelita nodded in agreement. Sofie chimed in, "Mollie, now is not the time for being petty. We have to get back over the border as quickly as possible. There's too much at stake. You're fully armed. Let's work together to get back home as fast as we can. We have to work together."

Mollie resisted initially but then reluctantly agreed. Paco came on board and nodded to Mollie. He bowed his head and mumbled an apology in Spanish, which Carmelita interpreted for her benefit. Mollie turned her back on him and skulked away.

They immediately turned the boat south to take the river back out to the Sea of *Cortés*.

This time, the journey was much smoother. Since Flores had secured a motorboat and they did not have to catch and sell shrimp, the time went by much more quickly. Paco was valuable in helping the Captain navigate, with Sofie double checking her charts the whole way. Paco and the Captain took turns at the helm and thanks to a very fortunate waxing gibbous moon, they were able to navigate straight through the night.

The following day, they stopped at a small shore town to take on additional food and water, but there was no gas since it had been rationed due to the revolution, nor a place to send a message home.

They came into range of *Puerto Peñasco* after another day and night. By the end of the second full day, they had to make a decision to push on to the port, or settle outside in the bay and wait for daylight. Although they all wanted to dock, the decision was not so clear cut. If they attempted to push on, they may not be able to navigate the port in the waning light. It was almost certain the Captain would not be able to take on gas for the return trip until morning in either case. Plus, it was unlikely they could get word back to the States given the late hour. So, if they decided to make port, they would be waiting until morning to disembark anyway.

The Captain made a decision to make port. He figured they would have just enough light, and then he and his crew could go to town and get some proper food. He promised to bring food and drink back for his passengers. Despite Mollie's protests, the others reluctantly agreed. Carmelita tried to make a case for her to disembark as well and pick up food rather than waiting for the Captain and his crew, but Gideon vetoed the idea. They all knew the crew would eat and drink to excess before returning and could only hope they wouldn't forget about them.

Gideon pointed out that it was better for them to stay together and keep below decks than to take unnecessary risks.

Captain and crew made good time and were able to find a place to dock the boat away from the main section. It had a place to refuel which they would take care of in the morning. Gideon, Carmelita, Mollie, and Sofie sat below decks with the few left-over scraps of food and drink and discussed their plans, while the Captain and crew left to find more substantial sustenance.

"Mollie, you have to admit, this has been a very smooth return so far," Sofie commented.

"You're right, but we're not in the States yet. I'll be very happy when we're finally back."

"I have to find a place to contact Luisa first thing in the morning and get in touch with the O'odham," Carmelita commented. Mollie felt her heart skip a beat at the mention of Luisa's name.

"Lita, I'm a little concerned about you going alone," Gideon commented. "Maybe the young man can go with you. It will be like an insurance policy to make sure the Captain doesn't try to pull anything."

"I'll be fine. *El Capitán* wants to leave as much as we do. That's all the insurance I need. Sofie, can you help me rough up one of my old dresses and find something to cover my head? I don't want to draw any attention."

Sofie offered one of her black hats and a scarf and Mollie offered her a pair of jeans. They would be too short for Carmelita, but that would only add to the illusion she is poor.

Now that the plan was in place, they settled down for what they expected would be a long wait for the crew to return with some real food.

Sofie was checking her maps for the most efficient route back to the O'odham nation.

"By my calculations, it's about 65 miles from the port to the border, through the desert, and over mountains. We can't walk that. The only way is by wagon. Anyone have any ideas? We can't wait until someone gets here from Tucson."

"Tomorrow when I go to town to send a message to Luisa, I'll ask about passage to the States. I'll say my family was separated and I need to get back to my relatives quickly, and see if there are any options."

While they all agreed that was probably the best plan given their situation, they still felt very unsafe as three obvious American citizens, stranded 65 miles on the wrong side of the border. Particularly with Flores and Paco in town and out of their sight. Mollie was vocal about the possibility of being sold out.

As they contemplated their fate and waited impatiently for morning, they were surprised to hear laughter and people boarding the boat.

"*Hola, mis amigos,*" *Capitán Flores* called out. "Anyone still on board?"

Gideon poked his head up. He took out his watch, flipped it open and looked at the time. Flores, Paco, and the deckhand were boarding the ship. They appeared to be sober and in good spirits.

"Captain. I'm surprised to see you."

"I am sure you are, *amigo*. We are not going to have a replay of what occurred on the last trip. We had some food and a couple of tequilas, and came right back to the boat. I will see your wife off to the telegraph office first thing in the morning. When she gets back, you will meet her on the dock and we will be off, successfully fulfilling my obligation to de Torres. Look. I even you brought you all some hot food. No charge."

He held up a greasy bag filled with homemade tamales. They shared the tamales, which were actually quite good and filled up their bellies.

The three shipmates went to the captains' quarters where it was assumed they partook in the captains' special reserve tequila. The four travelers waited a while to digest their food, but didn't hear a sound for the rest of the night. The next morning, Carmelita woke first, and as she was rinsing her face, her other fellow travelers awoke.

There was no sight or sound from the crew, so Gideon knocked on the Captains door. Again, he was surprised, because the captain answered immediately and was freshly shaved and ready to go.

Carmelita made enough coffee for everyone and they all sat and drank it in silence. She promised to bring back more food for the next leg of their journey. The crew sat separately from the travelers and no words were spoken between the two. Paco covertly cast glances at Mollie without being noticed.

The captain called out to Carmelita that it was time to go.

"Carmelita," Mollie whispered, "I was thinking about our situation all night. This whole adventure has revolved around the Church. Different churches, but one religion. Perhaps you can find the church in town and see if the pastor will be able to help us. We can always offer to share one of the mass vessels. What do you think?"

Carmelita was more surprised that it was Mollie, a self-confessed pagan, who came up with this idea than she was of the idea itself.

"That's an excellent idea, Mollie. I will stop by the church on my way back from the telegraph office."

Again, things went flawlessly. Carmelita sent her telegram and informed Flores she needed to stop at the church near the port. The priest was in the nave collecting hymnals. She quickly explained their dilemma to him and offered one of the vessels for the church. She explained it had been given to her to bring to *San Xavier del Bac* from a church near *Puerta Vallarta*.

She mentioned that she had to get back across the border and was sure the priest in Tucson wouldn't mind. He politely refused the gift, but after hearing Carmelita's explanation of events, agreed to take them in the church wagon to the border of the O'odham nation.

Carmelita exited the church and she was thrilled. Things were working out for them after all. She stopped by a roadside stand along the way and picked up a few items for her fellow travelers.

At the boat, Gideon, Mollie, and Sofie were packed and ready to bolt as soon as Carmelita arrived back. Surprisingly, Paco had helped arrange all of their belongings, and had them lined up out on the dock ready to go. Mollie and Gideon kept the heavy wooden chest with the church vessels between them. They refused any help with this valuable piece of luggage.

The dock was bustling at this time of day as all the working boats that had caught their limit offloaded their catch. The crews were tired, but ready to spend all the money they had made that day.

Gideon and the others looked up when they heard Carmelita shout.

She was waving her kerchief from the shotgun seat of a vintage prairie schooner led by two sturdy horses. Gideon smiled when he saw the wagon, which could have been the same one he had with his parents when they first came west to Arizona. The schooner came to a stop at the end of the dock by the boat, with the back end at the ramp, ready to load up.

Carmelita climbed down with a huge smile on her face. She spoke in a rush.

"Gideon. The Padre has agreed to take us all to the border. It was Mollie's idea to ask him. We can all sit in the back of the wagon, so no one will see us. He says no one will stop a priest. Hurry."

Paco began to load the wagon as Carmelita hustled her fellow travelers into the berth.

"Here. I bought some clothes to help us blend in."

She handed a sombrero and serape to Gideon and Mollie.

"Put these on. Keep the hats low. No one will suspect you are American. Sofie, you can blend in better because of your coloring, so I got you a rebozzo. You can wrap it around your body and over your head. You can pass for Méxican, if you hide your glasses."

They dressed quickly and were ready to go. Gideon and Mollie picked up the wooden chest which contained their precious items and they all lined up to climb in the back of the wagon. The priest was speaking with Flores as they boarded.

"*Buena suerte, amigos,*" Flores called out. Carmelita thanked him in Spanish and told him she would have good things to say to Francisco. She climbed into the back after a last minute instruction from the Padre, followed by Sofie. Mollie and Gideon loaded the chest onto the back of the wagon and pushed it forward.

Mollie was about to climb in, when Paco appeared out of nowhere. He extended his hand to help her with a shy smile on his face. She turned to slap his hand away and slipped on the step. She began to fall and tried desperately to get a grip on the canvas top of the wagon. Her grip missed and she sprawled in a somersault onto the ground. Her sombrero toppled away and her strawberry blond hair cascaded out around her.

The bustle along the entire dock ground to a halt and not a sound could be heard.

Gideon was right behind her when this occurred.

"Quick! Mollie! Get up. Get in the wagon."

She scrambled up and jumped into the schooner with Gideon on her heels. The padre whipped the horse with his reins to drive quickly away from the area.

Paco bent down, picked up the sombrero and ran to the wagon to give it back to Mollie. He shouted something in Spanish. Carmelita said to Mollie, "He says you will need your disguise."

He ran with all his might and tossed the hat towards the wagon. Gideon reached with his hand outstretched and barely grabbed onto it in mid-air.

Just then a worker on the docks pointed and shouted "¡*Americanos*!"

Several of the angry workers ran towards the wagon in chase. Paco stood up tall and held his arms as wide as he could to prevent them from advancing. One of the men took his fishing knife and slashed at Paco's good arm. Blood spurted from the cut and Paco went down in a heap.

Mollie saw what happened and couldn't contain herself. She had hated Paco, but he tried to save her and her companions and she had to stop the assault.

She reached for her gun, took aim, and shot the fisherman straight through the heart.

The Méxicans immediately stopped their chase to help their fallen friend as the Padre whipped the horses to move as fast as they could travel.

The journey back to America turned out not to be as smooth as they thought.

# Chapter Thirty Three

## *Opportunity*

Luisa was beyond excited. She got up early and took an extra-long, steaming hot shower. She shampooed her hair three times and carefully braided it the way it had been done when she first met Mollie.

It had been two days since she received the telegraph from Carmelita and she expected that the travelers would be back sometime today. Of course, she couldn't wait to see Mollie, but she was also excited to see Gideon. Business was booming and she needed to talk to him about expansion and her suggestion for buying new cars. The new gas models were considerably quicker than the old electric ones and could travel much further on gas than on batteries, which had to be charged too often.

Luisa had taken some initiative and used her own money to purchase a used French-made Darracq gas powered taxi which her dealer had acquired from New York. Gideon loved the New York cabs and she knew he would be pleased with the purchase once he returned. She had to finance the car in order to afford it, and she needed Gideon to be able to use it in his fleet to ever hope to get her money back. She negotiated a great price with the dealer as the car had been used as a demo model, and also because there had been some trouble with the engine. She felt confident her mechanic would be able to fix it, and he had been working on it all week.

Luisa nicknamed the car Rick O'Shea. It was her idea of a joke, since the car backfired every time it was started. Her mechanic just called it Rick.

The growth of the University and the crowds coming to town for sporting events, coupled with constant western expansion, had been a boon to business. Luisa knew Gideon would be pleased with her work. She had devised a new system for tracking hours and had hired extra drivers so there would always be drivers available, day or night. She had encouraged tipping with a sign in the taxis' windows and it had also proved to be a great incentive to recruit new drivers.

The business was growing as much as possible without adding any other new vehicles.

She had forgotten all about her promise to get in touch with Cassidy.

---

Cassidy, meanwhile, was getting anxious. It had been too long since he visited Verde Transportation. He was certain he had convinced the manager there – what was her name again? Right, Luisa. He thought he had convinced her to let him know when she heard Mollie and the rest were returning. Tempted to go back several times, he didn't want to appear too eager. But now, too much time had passed. He couldn't miss their return, assuming they were even coming back. Who knew what they had to face in México? It was possible that Luisa became too excited if she heard they had actually found any treasure. Or maybe she just forgot. He finally decided he had to go back to the taxi office and see if there was any word.

He got dressed in the same outfit he had worn the last time. He thought that a visiting professor wouldn't have many clothes anyway. He was circumspect as he approached the taxi office. He didn't take a cab this time, instead getting a lift from a co-worker who dropped him off a few blocks from his destination.

He approached from behind the building and took a deep breath as he gingerly peeked around the corner. He had to make sure the treasure hunters hadn't returned yet. He didn't notice anything unusual, so he boldly walked towards the front door. Just as he was about to go in, the door flew open. Luisa came out breathless and nearly bumped into him.

"*Perdón*, I'm sorry. Oh, it's you."

"*Está bien.*"

"I'm sorry I didn't call you. I just forgot. I have to drive to the florist to pick up flowers. I just received a call. They have crossed the border and should be here any time now. You can wait if you like, but I've got to go. Bye."

Luisa quickly got into one of the company's electric cabs and didn't look back. Cassidy was so surprised, he didn't have the time, or even the presence of mind, to ask if they had found the treasure, or when they would arrive. It seemed obvious she expected them very soon.

His first thought was that he had to leave quickly. At least he knew they were back. But the element of surprise was gone. If they showed up when Luisa was there, she would tell them he was waiting for them. As he thought about this, he realized he had another, much bigger, problem. He had used the name Declan when he asked Luisa to call him about the group's return. He had to so that when she called the University and spoke to Guadalupe, he would be sure to get the message. His plan was to surprise them upon their return. It hadn't dawned on him at the time that it could work against him. In this area of the country, no one was named Declan. They would never think it just a coincidence. He had to think fast.

He walked back around the corner of the building so he would not be observed if they returned. He slammed his fist against the wall and cursed his luck. He took off his hat and ran his fingers through his hair, almost tearing it out with frustration. He had to think. This had messed up all his plans and created a number of complex situations. He thought through his choices.

He had to operate under the assumption they found something. If they didn't, it really wouldn't matter, and he could just leave. But now there was no way to know in advance if they had found treasure or not.

He certainly didn't want to warn them, so he had to figure a way to get Luisa out of the way in the event she got back before they did. But if they got back first, he had to devise a way to quickly and safely relieve them of any treasure they found. He realized he had to figure that part out in any case.

First things first. He pulled his new felt hat down low. It ruined the beautiful crease that the store had custom crafted for him, but helped to hide his face and hair. He pulled up the collar on his herringbone jacket to further hide his identity. If he did run into the treasure hunters, he did not want them to recognize him. His small frame and stooped posture due to the knife wound made him obvious enough.

He spotted a bicycle across the street leaning on one of the few horse rails left in town. He sauntered across, hopped on the bike, and started off in the direction Luisa headed. He quickly found a flower shop just a few blocks away. He looked inside and saw Luisa paying for a beautiful bunch of flowers. He jumped off the bike and fixed his hat the best he could. As she walked out, he acted as if he had just run the whole way. Breathlessly, he spoke to her in a rushed cadence.

"Luisa – I'm so glad I found you. I was waiting in your office and the phone rang. I thought I would do you a favor and take a message for you. A man said there had been a terrible accident and that one of the women travelling with Mollie was seriously hurt."

Luisa was alarmed. "Is Mollie OK? Did you speak with her?"

"There wasn't time to speak to her but the man I spoke with told me Mollie and Carmelita were fine. He said they're at

O'odham nation. He said you should get there right away to pick up the other travelers. I hurried down here to get you."

Cassidy had picked the reservation as the travelers' crossing spot, thinking it was more remote and in a different direction than the normal crossing point at Nogales. He thought, incorrectly it turns out, that he was sending Luisa on a wild goose chase. He failed to realize Luisa would not have to go all the way to the Méxican border to check on the story. The border of the nation was actually much closer to Tucson than Nogales. She could check the story right when she got to the Tucson/reservation border.

"Thank you so much. I'll head over there right now. Would you take these back to the office for me, please? I'm sorry, but what did you say your name was again? I remember it was unique and I have it written down, but I'm afraid I've forgotten it."

He gave her his best smile. "I guess it is unique for this part of the world, but it's quite common at home. My name is Quince. I hope everything turns out alright. Please don't mention you've seen me. I still want this to be a surprise. I'll get in touch with Mollie another day."

"I won't. I'll keep it a secret, Quince. *Gracias.*"

"*De nada.*"

Now that he had Luisa occupied, he rode the bike back towards the taxi office. On the way, he fantasized about the treasure and his plans for revenge.

---

Gideon reflected that he had been wrong about the trip back. Once they were out of the port area and moving quickly through the desert sage, they all relaxed, feeling closer to home and the end of their journey. He took out his pocket watch and checked the time without really seeing it. The remainder of the trip had gone smoothly and they met up with the Papago without incident.

The trip back to Tucson was hot and dusty but they hardly noticed. They were all in need of a good meal and a long shower, and agreed to go directly to the office where they could store the valuables. Although they would be passing close by the church, they decided to go the following day after food, showers, and some much needed rest.

---

Cassidy returned to the taxi office. The first thing he did was look for the note where Luisa had written down his name and number. He found it tacked to a cork board and ripped it off, tore it into tiny pieces, and buried it under a pile of trash in the bin.

The office was attached to a longer building next door that was used as a repair station for the taxis. A narrow door separated the back office from the front of the garage. He was impressed with the operation, which seemed to be thriving.

He expected them back at any moment, so he quickly left the office and went across the street to a small cafe. There he could observe any activity without being seen.

He didn't even have time to order coffee when a horse drawn wagon pulled up and Carmelita leapt out of the back followed by Mollie and another woman he didn't recognize. They each carried a carpetbag which appeared to be full of clothes.

Last out of the wagon came Carmelita's husband. The driver hopped down from the drivers' box and helped him remove an old, apparently heavy wooden chest from the back of the wagon.

Gideon and Mollie each grabbed a handle and seemed to struggle as they carried it to the office. Once inside, Cassidy couldn't see them, but he had noticed that Mollie was well armed.

His pulse raced at the sight of them. He knew instinctively what the chest contained. He watched as they went into the office and the wagon pulled away.

Minutes later, they all came out and started across the street towards the café. He hadn't expected them to come out so soon and was caught by surprise. He quickly rose and ran to the back.

"Hey, can I help you?" The waitress behind the counter called.

"Uh, no. Sorry. Where's the wash room?"

She pointed to a sign just above his head. He went inside. There was a window which was too high to reach, but was large enough for him to crawl out if he could. He located the wastebasket, turned it over, and stood on top of it to reach up to the window. He threw his hat out ahead of him. He needed to keep it to preserve his disguise. He then gripped the sill and climbed up. As his feet took purchase and pushed him forward, he was able to eventually force his torso out of the window. Gravity took over and he tumbled out of the opening head first and dropped to the ground. It was a bit of a fall and hurt pretty badly, but he'd felt far worse.

He sat up and took a few seconds to clear his head. This was it. He knew he had to go for the goods right now, or he may never get the chance again. He knew instinctively that it would be very difficult to move a chest that heavy, particularly since his upper body was not very strong, but he wasn't really thinking clearly about how to move any items he uncovered, just that he had to get them, whatever they may be. He was long past any rational thinking.

He slammed the hat on his head, pushing it down to cover his identifiable red hair. Cautiously, he passed behind several storefronts before carefully crossing the street. He was certain they would not be able to see him due to the angle he took.

He went to the back of the taxi office and found the door locked. He looked around for something to smash the window giving him access, when he noticed the adjacent building. He entered through the back door which stood wide open. As he walked in he saw a taxi with its trunk open, but no one around. He walked the length of the building and found a door that led to the back room of the office. It was unlocked and he entered without being seen.

Cassidy was beyond excited. He couldn't believe his luck. He would finally get his vindication and get rich in the process. Right in front of him, lying on the floor, was the chest he had just seen them remove from the wagon. He bent down to open it and what he saw made his heart skip a beat.

# Chapter Thirty Four

## *Retribution*

Luisa arrived at the entry point of the O'odham nation. She knew many of the tribe, and always suspected she had a touch of their native blood in her. After centuries of native Méxican tribes mixing with the blood of the Spanish conquerors and others, it was nearly impossible to identify a person's true heritage any longer.

"*Hola, mi amigo.*" She called out to Carlos as she exited the taxi in a rush. It was rare that any of the tribe had traditional O'odham names anymore. Many were Spanish and most were now anglicized. It wasn't unusual to address a Tohono O'odham native on the reservation as Charlie or Jim.

"*Hola*, Luisa. It's been a long time. What brings you here?"

"I had a message that Carmelita and the others had a problem and one of the travelers was injured. I was told to come here quickly to help. Where are they?"

"Carmelita? She's not here. They all came a while ago, but Miguel took all of them back to town. To your office. No one was injured. What's this about?"

"That's what I want to know. Thanks, Carlos."

Luisa jumped back into the taxi and quickly headed back to town. She was confused and baffled as to where Mollie's Uncle got his information, but she was determined to find out.

---

Cassidy was surprised the chest wasn't locked. He lifted the lid slowly, not sure what he would find. He was surprised to see that all the items contained in the chest were religious ornaments. He hadn't expected that, but then, he wasn't sure what he expected. Surprised, but beyond pleased that they all appeared to be solid gold. He sat back on his heels and took in the glistening images before him, trying to assess their worth.

Cassidy knew he had to move quickly. He didn't expect the others would be in the café long and he also had to wonder when Luisa would be back.

He grabbed the handle of the chest and heaved on it with all his might. It didn't budge. Looking at all the gold items in the chest, he knew it would be too heavy for one person to lift. Especially for him. Cassidy was small in stature to begin with, and after his injuries, he never had the sinewy strength he could rely on in his youth. He cursed his bad luck and handicap. He punched himself in the thigh. How could he have been so stupid! he thought to himself. He had a plan, but the plan didn't pan out. He improvised and thought everything was going his way. But now he had a fortune in gold at his disposal with no way to move it. He felt like a complete fool.

"Think," he scolded himself. "There's no time left to waste." He thought through a variety of choices in seconds. Should he take what he could carry and be happy? Should he try to hide what he couldn't remove to recover later? Should he use a tool as a weapon and force someone to help him? He was panicking and knew he had to move fast, but found himself frozen to the spot.

He heard a metallic noise which shook him from his immobilized state. It had come from the garage, and he realized then that there might be something there that could help him. He ran to the garage where he identified several tools which he thought he could use, but not by himself.

"If only Quince were here. He could probably carry the damn chest by himself, the big ox."

It never dawned on Cassidy that it was his own fault Quince wasn't there.

He found a dolly that looked like it would be used to move heavy auto parts, maybe engines. He grabbed the long removable handle, as well as a crowbar he found lying next to it, and wheeled them next door to the office. He couldn't lift even one end of the chest, so he leveraged the crowbar over the handle of the dolly to get lift. He then wedged one end of the dolly underneath and when he removed the handle, it levered upward. He moved the crowbar to the center of the chest and was able to lift it enough to move the dolly further under it. He did the same at the other end and was able to lever the chest almost completely onto the dolly. He reattached the handle and moved the chest easily through the doorway into the garage. Now he had to figure out how to get the chest into the trunk of the cab.

He was perspiring heavily and his back ached from all the effort. Since the stabbing years ago at the hand of a scorned woman, he had a difficult time with any physical labor. The task was really not that difficult, but he was a slight man to begin with and his infirmities only made it that much more demanding.

Cassidy was tired, hurting from the effort, sweating profusely, and breathing heavily through his mouth. He wasn't thinking clearly but knew he had to hurry. This was it. He had dreamed of owning the Amulet for decades, but this was so much more.

He finally realized he could never move the chest to the trunk of the taxi. Instead, he opened it up and starting tossing items from the chest into the trunk, not caring if he damaged any of the items. He planned to melt it all down anyway. The gold religious ornaments made a loud racket as they clanged into the trunk of the taxi. He suddenly realized he hadn't checked to see if the engine would start. He stopped what he was doing, and checked the dash. The cab had an electric starter. He had had never driven an automobile before, but he had seen others drive them. However, this one was different and had a shift mechanism. He put the gear in neutral, set the parking brake, and pushed the starter button. The taxi jumped to life. As he was about to go back to the trunk, the engine let out with an incredibly loud bang. The engine had backfired, then smoothed down to a low roar. He left it running as he went back to the chest to continue moving the gold ornaments into the trunk.

He picked up a chalice and just then the engine cut out.

"Shit," he mumbled to himself, "If it's not one thing, it's another."

---

Gideon, Carmelita, Mollie, and Sofie were enjoying their first substantial meal in weeks. The café served breakfast all day and they took full advantage. Gideon and Mollie had eggs over easy, thick slices of crispy mesquite smoked bacon, chunky slices of sourdough toast slathered with butter, and pan fried potatoes. Carmelita and Sofie settled for poached eggs, stewed tomatoes, and dry toast. They all had hot cups of strong black coffee and fresh squeezed juice.

They were sated and happy and talked animatedly about their trip. Even with all the challenges, they now looked back at it as a thrilling adventure rather than a risky endeavor. Time was a great equalizer when it came to looking back on things that ultimately work out.

Suddenly, they heard a loud bang coming from the direction of the taxi office. Gideon was leaning back in his booth next to Carmelita, but sat straight up when he heard the noise.

"What the hell was that?"

Mollie was out of her seat in a shot and started for the door.

"Stay here," Gideon said to Carmelita and Sofie. "No need for all of us to go. I don't want you to get hurt."

Luisa was less than half a block away when she heard the loud bang. She knew right away it was her taxi, Rick. Her mechanic had been working on it almost nonstop and was making progress, but still the persistent backfiring occurred. She would know that sound anywhere. She smiled thinking he was still trying to fine tune the car, and hoped he would get a breakthrough before Gideon arrived.

As she turned the corner to enter the garage, she saw Mollie and Gideon running across from the café towards the garage. Her heart leapt when she saw Mollie and she nearly lost control of the car. She braked suddenly and jumped out.

"Mollie!"

Mollie didn't hear her, as she and Gideon ran to the entrance of the garage. Luisa followed behind excited to see Mollie but also eager to tell Gideon about her purchase. She had no idea what she about to witness.

Mollie entered first, followed by Gideon, then Luisa.

Cassidy was bent over the chest, taking one of the last remaining pieces of treasure and tossing it into the back of a taxi that Gideon had never seen before.

The taxi was noisy and he didn't hear them as they approached. Mollie drew her gun and yelled out, "Cassidy!"

He turned suddenly, surprised by the interruption. His mouth turned up into a cruel smile when he saw the three of them standing there. Mollie with her gun in her hand and her finger tapping nervously on the trigger. He was soaking wet and looked like a madman, his red hair disheveled and his face contorted.

"Well, look what we have here. A reunion. Too bad I can't stay to enjoy it."

"Put the gold back, Cassidy. You're not going anywhere." Mollie said and lifted the gun to make her point.

Gideon whispered, "Mollie. Don't shoot him. We need to get the authorities. He'll go to jail for life."

She moved closer to Gideon to make sure Cassidy couldn't hear.

"Sorry, Gideon. This time it's personal. It doesn't seem the law can hold him. We need to end this now and forever."

Cassidy watched the two of them whispering. His instincts, which had never failed him, told him they were in conflict. He inched closer to the three of them.

Luisa came up behind and murmured "Don't Mollie. I love you. I don't want to see you in jail the rest of your life for murder."

Mollie turned to Luisa and smiled. She took her finger off the trigger for just a second, but that was enough, and Cassidy reacted. He still had the chalice in his hand and hurled it at Mollie, hitting her on the temple. She was temporarily stunned as he ran towards her to take the gun. Gideon stepped in between the two as Luisa moved towards Mollie. They were all tangled up in one pile of struggling humanity.

The car suddenly backfired again and startled them all into believing the gun had gone off. They all just looked at each other wondering who was shot.

It was instantly quiet. No one spoke, no one moved. They were all frozen.

Suddenly, a shot rang out and they all fell to a heap as one, blood oozing out across the cement floor.

# Chapter Thirty Five

## *Peace*

The church bells pealed at *San Xavier del Bac* as Padre Mendoza walked through the nave towards the altar. The White Dove of the Desert was completely full, with people standing in the doorways spilling into the plaza. Something he hadn't seen in quite some time.

It was the fifth Sunday of Easter, not a particularly special mass, although one he always liked. The gospel this day was John 14:1-12, and begins, "Do not let your hearts be troubled. You have faith in God; have faith also in me."

He always felt he was acting on His behalf when he read those lines, and today was no exception.

After he read the gospel Padre Mendoza gave a heartfelt sermon. He ended by leading the congregation in song as a mariachi band played. The band was comprised of a *bajo sexto* (big guitar), a *vihuela* (small guitar), two violins, and a trumpet.

The congregation clapped and sang along with the music as Mollie and Sofie brought the gifts up to the altar. Although the congregation didn't know it, the chalices holding the wine and the hosts, or sacramental bread, were pure gold. A gift from the ones carrying it and from those sitting in the front row.

Carmelita and Gideon sat watching and smiling from ear to ear. Gideon took out his watch. The one his father had given him, and snapped it open to check the time. This time he did pay attention. He wanted to remember this.

He turned to Carmelita and whistled out, "This is some ceremony."

Mollie and Luisa sat side by side. The congregation, indeed the town and the entire country, must never know about the relationship between Mollie and Luisa. They knew their love was real and would never be shaken, but society wasn't yet ready for their kind of love. They all prayed that perhaps one day a relationship such as theirs could be open and even embraced by others and the Church.

The priest concluded the mass, and the congregation all stayed to sing another song while clapping and dancing in the aisles and out into the street.

# **Epilogue**

Cassidy was pronounced dead when the police arrived. Just before they did, Carmelita bent down close to his body. She put her fingertips on his eyelids and lifted roughly, bending close and peering intently into his pupils.

Gideon reached out to stop her, but Sofie gently placed her hand on his arm and shook her head. Gideon moved away.

"This is not my father," Carmelita stated definitively.

"I should have known. Maybe I always did. This man was a liar, thief, murderer, rapist, and misogynistic scoundrel. He didn't have a decent bone in his body. I won't pray for his soul, but I will pray for his victims. My true father, Manuel, was a decent, kind, hardworking, faithful husband and dedicated parent. I like to think I have the best qualities of both he and my mother."

Mollie said, "Carmelita, I know evil. I've been around it all my life. Even I couldn't stomach Cassidy and his ways. I knew all along you couldn't be his child, but you had to know for yourself. You are the nicest, most generous person I have ever known. I'm proud to call you my friend."

Sofie spoke the thought that everyone except Carmelita had. "Mollie, what do you mean you couldn't stomach his ways. Did you *know* Cassidy?"

Mollie and Carmelita had discussed this and decided it was best to tell the truth. The potential that it could come out at some future time was too great, and Mollie had created a strong bond with her fellow treasure hunters.

"Yes, Sofie. I'm sorry. I wanted to tell you all but the timing was never right. I met Cassidy through my Aunt Rosie who runs a place called Sadie's. It's not a nice place. OK, frankly, it's a cathouse. Cassidy wanted to hire me to find out what you were doing and report back to him with all the details.

But I couldn't go through with it and told him it was no deal. He hounded me until I threatened to shoot him. I finally did."

Gideon asked, "What do you mean, you finally did? It was an accident. We were all part of it."

"It was no accident. I know my gun. I kept my hand on it the whole time and when the scuffle started, I turned the gun on him and pulled the trigger. You can turn me in if you like, but I'd do it again in a heartbeat."

"You're wrong, Mollie. I had my hand on the trigger and squeezed it too." Carmelita commented.

"So did I," Sofie chimed in.

"Me too," Gideon offered, "Well, I guess we're all to blame, so let's just let it go. The police ruled it accidental and that's good enough for me."

After Mass, they went to the café across from the taxi office for breakfast. Along the way, Carmelita stopped and sent Francisco deTorres a telegram about Cassidy's demise. She knew he would be ecstatic. She didn't really mention the treasure, since telegraph messages would be read by many people, but she did note that their efforts in México were not profitable. They weren't. The gold they brought back was all donated to the Church, so there was no profit. The less said the better. She concluded with her heartfelt thanks and best wishes for him and the future of her native country of México.

At breakfast, Sofie announced she would be leaving in the morning to go back to New York. She asked them all if it would be OK with them if she wrote a book outlining their adventures. They were all enthusiastic.

Mollie commented, "I can't wait to see how you describe me."

"But I am going to change the particulars. I don't want people trying to go back to find the treasure. It's too dangerous. The lost treasure of Cortés is better left unsolved."

"Luisa, you have done a fantastic job with the business." Gideon whistled out. "Lita and I want to invest in the new taxis you mentioned. We'll all go to the bank in the morning and see about a loan for the business. Mollie, Lita and I have discussed it and we would like to know if you would be willing to come and work with us. I can't think of a better person to manage taxi drivers."

Mollie was thrilled. She wanted to stay close to Luisa but didn't know what she was going do next. She had changed for the better and wanted to keep it that way. She eagerly accepted.

Carmelita spoke next. "Gideon, what do you say we accompany Sofie to New York? Sofie, do you mind?"

She nodded enthusiastically

"We can talk with your friend Pauli and meet Anna and Stach and learn about changes in the taxi business for us to use in Tucson. Maybe Gideon will even get his watch back. What do you say?"

"Luisa, do you think you can run the business for  a few weeks with Mollie's help?" Gideon asked.

Luisa nodded, Mollie smiled and Gideon paid the bill. Then they left to get a jump start on their new lives.

## *Author's notes*

The historical components of this story are all true based on extensive research on the history of México and the greater Tucson area.

Colonel Greene was one of the most prominent millionaires of the early 20th century. His biography includes an upbringing in Chappaqua, NY, selling shares of his company "on the curb" on Wall Street, killing a man at the OK Corral, and building and losing several companies and a great fortune. His son was the first child ever born at the Waldorf=Astoria in NYC.

Several important events which were referred to in the book occurred after the completion date of this story.

On November 4, 1914, Frances Lillian Willard "Fannie" Munds was elected as Arizona's first woman State Senator.

On January 1, 1915, Arizona was the first State in the union to enact prohibition – 4 years before the federal regulation.

Victoriano Huerta resigned as President of México in July of 1914.

World War 1 began in Europe on July 28, 1914.

Albert Bacon Fall, who worked closely with Colonel Greene at the copper mines in Cananea, was nominated by President Warren G. Harding and ratified by the Senate as Secretary of the Interior, He served March 5, 1921 until March 4, 1923. He was implicated in the Teapot Dome Scandal for bribery and was the first Cabinet member in U.S. history to go to prison. Fall had his own fascinating story and had also served as a U.S. Senator (New Mexico), and successfully defended Jesse Wayne Brazel, the man who confessed to killing Sheriff Pat Garrett.

I encourage all to read about this important time and place in history.

The Lost Treasure of Cortés